Dearly Remembered

Dearly Remembered

Rachael Rawlings

Printed in the United States of America

ISBN: 1942212038
ISBN-13: 978-1-942212-03-4

Hydra Publications
1310 Meadowridge Trail
Goshen, KY 40026

www.hydrapublications.com

Chapter 1

A hot splash of panic hit my system half a second before my heartbeat drove out the foreign sound. It was just too friggin' dark to see anything beyond my nose, and the streetlights out the windows were almost nonexistent. I was left in the dark, so dark that the shadows of furniture had melted into an inky stain against the white walls. I sat up in my bed and threw the covers back, swinging my bare legs over the side of the bed and grabbing the tennis racquet resting against the bed frame. My pounding heart had lessened slightly, and I strained to hear the sound, the sound that had driven me from my mundane dreams of home. Again I heard it. It wasn't the sigh of the door, the click of the knob as it turned. Not that. And it wasn't the footfalls of someone creeping outside my door. It was more terrifying than that. It was a whisper, softer than the breeze, begging and straining, wanting and beckoning me to do something and go somewhere that I had never been and never wished to be. I was pretty sure Death had come calling, and I was trying to face him off with sports equipment.

At the doorway I stopped my hand on the cool metal of the knob. I didn't want to open it. Out in the hall there was more dark, more silence, and more empty doorways. The house wasn't huge, but it was bigger than our own little downtown apartment had been, and most of the rooms were echo empty with warped wooden floors that would give beneath my feet, alerting anyone who cared that I was out and about with my racquet.

I turned the knob anyway, peeking first from the crack between the door and the frame, and when I saw nothing, looking out into the wider gloom. The hall spread out right and left, ending in a turning staircase at one end of the corridor. At the dead end, a window leaked spare light onto the floor, moonlight that seemed to suck the color from everything around me until my own skin looked like smooth grey stone. At the other end of that hall, at the head of the stairs, one door stood slightly ajar, my sister's room. I didn't worry that she might catch me in my black rose tee shirt and bare feet, and black painted toenails looking like drops of blood pooled on the wooden floor. She slept the heavy sleep of the exhausted and fulfilled, the sleep of someone thrown into adulthood with a brutal shove.

I finally forced myself to move, sliding the soles of my bare feet over the cool floors. The doors on either side of the hall were closed but for my sister's. Behind the heavy panels were the other bedrooms, two for my sister and me, two that sheltered dust bunnies and boogie men under the old bed frames and tattered linens, and one that my sister had made up into a makeshift office complete with cardboard desk. I wouldn't go in those. Whoever had come into my house wasn't some incorporeal spirit. He wasn't wafting through the heavy doors or seeping under the door jam. He was real, and he had real footfalls and real hands that would need to open those doors to hide inside. And that I would have heard. This antique house was eerily quiet at rest, but put a living body in it, and it squealed, squeaked, groaned, and protested as though inconvenienced by our presence. I would have heard any of the doors opening.

I was speeding up now. I raced down the steps, the racquet held in front of me, my hand skimming the wooden rail. All I could hear now were my own footsteps and the house responding to my weight. My breathing was unnaturally loud in my ears, and my heart was a more subtle thunder. At the bottom of the stairs I paused at the landing. To the right was the dining room, empty but for a towering stack of boxes still unpacked since the move and some forgotten pieces of furniture we hadn't decided what to do with yet. Behind that was the kitchen, the only slightly updated room in the place, with its eighties wallpaper and Formica countertops. To my left was the parlor, perfect for greeting gentlemen callers a hundred years ago, but now a little bit of wasted space until we could figure out what to do with the room. The living room behind that was generous for the age of the house, but the carpet we had thrown on the floor would hide any sounds of footsteps if the intruder went there. Could that be why it was silent now? Was he waiting in the gloom, still enough to cover his presence with silence?

I went toward the living room. The kitchen had a doorway to the backyard through a mudroom, and since the kitchen and living room shared a wall and a doorway, it was the easiest way out of the house besides the front door straight ahead of me. If he was still in the house, I could only hope that he was seeking an exit and was moving toward it. I slipped into the parlor, keeping my back to the wall and my eyes so wide that I felt blind. I followed the plaster wall, skimming my fingertips over the uneven surface that we still meant to paint, and moved toward the living room. A stingy glow of light came from the back where a neighbor had an outdoor light hung on the rear of his garage. It cast uneven shadows across the dark floors and lighter carpet. I stopped in the living room door and stood for a long moment in the silence.

"Give it up, little girl," the whisper moved in the darkness, so close but not. A brush of something on my arm, the distinct feeling of warmth of another human so close, and then gone. I spun like a dancer that I would never be, racquet held out with both hands, feet set apart and firm for my stance. But I knew before I finished my turn that the room was empty. There was no one there. And the door never opened.

*****

I didn't sleep for the rest of the night but stayed up in the living room, tennis racquet propped on my knees, eyes on the back door. I didn't believe in ghosts, or spooks, or any of that other bull crap, but I did know that someone had come visiting the night before, and I didn't want to be caught off guard if he returned.

I didn't bother to tell my sister in the morning. I had told her the first time, and the second, screaming at her to listen to me when she told me I was exaggerating. I hated it when she treated me like a child, but I acted like one anyway, stomping up to my new room and slamming the door hard enough to make the house tremble.

I didn't try anymore. Part of me knew that she wouldn't believe me this time either, and it would do no good to bring it up. But the other part of me had some maturity. I could see the way her face looked pinched and pale. I could see that the dark rings under her eyes weren't quite covered by the makeup she so skillfully applied. And I knew that she was at the edge, and it wouldn't take much to just push her over. She was all that I had, and I wouldn't risk that for anything or anyone.

So when I heard her stir above me, I took my racquet and my stiff limbs and climbed the stairs back to my room. I stopped at the full length mirror, caught by the picture I made. My hair was long in layers, blond on the top layers with my own natural deep mahogany beneath, now framing my pale face in chopped chunks but not helping my complexion at all. My clothes were mostly castoffs, vintage store treasures mixed with things I found at the Goodwill. Even my night clothes had the same flavor of charity and recycle with worn sweats, a lace tank, and tatty chenille robe. I had several piercings and a tattoo that I was particularly proud of on my hip, but in the grim light of day, I looked anything but cool. Young, lost, and scared. I looked vulnerable, and I hated that since it reflected in my eyes so clearly.

I moved away from the mirror and started rummaging through my clothes. There were heaps on the floor, the chair, the foot of my bed, and pretty much every horizontal surface. My closet, on the other hand, was empty and likely to stay that way. In the tight space under the slanted eave I had stuffed pillows and blankets, books, and stacks of magazines. It was my retreat for now.

I threw on a pair of black leggings and an oversized sweatshirt with my old high school logo emblazoned across my chest. I stuffed my hair back into a ragged ponytail and slipped down the stairs, hearing the clatter and step of my sister as she prepared her morning coffee.

"We're out of milk," she mumbled to me as she ate cereal from a measuring cup with her fingers. She was dressed in her business casual wardrobe, pressed slacks, tucked in blouse, and tidy sweater that matched the blue of her eyes. Her hair was a natural blend of warm brown and blond shades, and I envied that and her clear golden complexion. She needed little makeup to polish the look. She was a natural beauty, as my father had always said, and even tired as she was, she was still a looker.

"I'll get some while I'm out," I responded, digging my hand into the box of cereal. "What else do you want me to get?"

"As little as possible," she responded dryly, and rinsed her hands under sputtering cold water from the tap. "I'll get paid Friday and go for a big shopping trip. For now, get just enough to get by."
She pulled the cereal from my grasp and neatly rolled up the inner bag and folded the top closed.

I nodded and eyed her as she picked up her purse and brief case. With her business degree, we had been lucky for her to have found such a good job at the bank. The downtown office of Louisville Trust had needed someone in the loan department, and they weren't opposed to training if the person had the personality to sell. My sister did. She could sell ice cubes to Eskimos, my father had insisted.

"Tori," she said, stepping out the door, "don't get too upset if you can't find anything today. We can look in the ads this weekend."

I knew she was trying to make me feel better. But damn, at only four years my senior, she shouldn't have to be acting like my mom. I should have a job and pull my own weight. Even if I hadn't gotten my degree yet, I should have a job. But for now, well, I hated that I was a dead weight in our new life.

"It's okay, Liz." I sighed and walked to the doorway where she hesitated. "I'm going to wander around town a little and see what I can find. There should be someone who needs help around here." I shoved my hands in my ragged pants and watched her eyes skim my face. "I can get a few groceries and unpack a little more. I want to have all of this settled by the time I go to work."

"Just don't think that this is going to be a forever job," Liz said, stepping out on the warped porch. "Once the probate goes through and we get some of the money, you are going back to finish your degree."

It was a standing argument. Once we had our parents' legacy, Liz believed we would be able to live again. We could fix up the house, I would go back to school, and we would begin to build back what had been taken from us in a ball of flame and crushed metal. I wasn't so sure that I could ever get back to that girl that I once was. I had been fired by grief, and I wasn't the innocent anymore. I didn't want to be that trusting, that stupid and self-serving ever again.

"Later," my sister called, and slipped into the SUV that filled our driveway. I smiled grimly as she pulled away. The second hand SUV had been my doing. I had wanted to find something incredibly safe for us to drive after being taught the bitter lesson that a shiny sports car versus almost any other vehicle was bound to lose. If I could have, I would have bought a tank.

I waved her off and returned into the silent shelter of my covered porch. From here I could see our fabulous view. Great pin oaks sheltered most of the yard, leaving a lot of bare packed mud and rolling green moss. The lawn, devoid of most any grass, bumped against the sidewalk, which ran parallel to the snaking road. Across the road was the huge plot of stone fenced grounds that surrounded an impossibly quaint chapel, Duncan Memorial, complete with slate roof and stained glass windows. Marching around the chapel like so many worshippers were the gravestones. They meandered next to twisty walkways, huddled in little family circles, and clustered around stone benches, their names and dates forever carved in worn faces. Towering trees sheltered the grounds, stretching limbs out like fingers trying to link above the stones. In the streams of sunlight that heralded another beautiful March day, the place was picturesque in a Kincaid postcard kind of way. In the dim evenings when the air cooled to a biting 35 degrees and the meager streetlights added rings of glowing yellow to the hard pavement, it was creepy. Some nights they left the light on in the chapel, and that was better because it looked like a tiny church getting ready for Sunday services. But when it was dark, it was just an empty graveyard filled with the dusty dead rotting away beneath the rich earth.

I didn't like it. I didn't want to live at death's back door. I didn't want to see the rows of cars that signaled a new resident being laid to rest. Death had been my companion much too recently for me to be comfortable with it here.

With one last look over my shoulder, I pushed my way through the door, letting it slam back on its spring hinges with a satisfying bang. My feet sounded a steady squeak as I crossed the floor, and I stopped to listen to the comparative quiet of the house.

How did he get in? With all of the assorted noises that this house made, how had he gotten in unnoticed? It wasn't a stretch to think that someone could break into the place. The wavy glass windows, while atmospheric, would be easy to open, except for the two in the attic that were painted shut, and the door's lock was fragile and prone to slipping. I had locked myself out on two occasions, and had easily slipped through the window with no tools needed. I had been noisy, however, and if my sister had been home, I had no doubt I would have heard about my carelessness.

So how had he gotten in? And what did he want with us?

Back inside the sun streaked kitchen, I poured the remnants of coffee into my mug and leaned against the counter. The question was becoming not why or how he was getting in, but what to do about it. Instead of blind panic, I tried reasonably to think of ways to protect us and our home. As I ate toast at the kitchen counter, I kept the newspaper open in front of me. I needed money if I were to get some help with the house. We needed new locks on the doors and windows. Even if my mind insisted that the intruder hadn't gone through the back door to leave last night, I knew that the supposition that he had merely melted through the darkness was a joke, and I needed to be practical. Whoever this was had come in for a reason. Even if all he meant to do was scare me, and he had done a fair job at that, he was coming into my home, and it had to be stopped. The police were out of the question. If my own sister didn't believe me, it wasn't likely that they would. I needed a plan. New locks, that would help, and a better weapon, maybe mace or pepper spray. I wondered where I could get that in a town this size. A gun was out of the question. I didn't know how to shoot, and I certainly didn't need to give the intruder something that deadly to use against me. I had heard that one of the best ways to prevent someone from breaking in was a guard dog. It was a possibility, but a dog would come with a lot of responsibility, and I didn't know if my sister would go for it.

I sighed. I was a legal adult. I needed to act like one. I needed a job to start making money. Once I had a paycheck, I would have a greater say in what went on around here. Then I could afford to help update the place, to add security, and to get a dog if I wanted one.

I bent over the local paper and started circling the help wanted ads. I was going out today.

*****

My car was a late model American made gas guzzler that the government had tried unsuccessfully to get off the streets a few years earlier. Its V8 motor roared under the hood, and it rode like a barge through the streets. I parked at the dry cleaners in the center of town, and climbed out into the sunshine.

I filled out applications. I tried everywhere; at the little Crestwood Market, the Dairy Queen on the corner, the Hometown Pizza down the road a stretch, and the consignment store that stretched back next to the railroad tracks. I smiled politely, if artificially, greeted and shook hands, and did my best to appear like the all American girl, dyed hair, piercings and all.

At noon I slid into a booth at a diner and opened the paper menu. I had my cell phone on the table next to me and was keeping a close eye on it. It was frustratingly silent now. My stomach rumbled, reminding me that I needed to eat. I chose the cheapest meal on the menu, requesting only water to drink. The young girl who took my order seemed nice, but told me somewhat ruefully that they were not looking for anyone to work there.

The grilled cheese was excellent, creamy with a blend of cheeses that was a little unusual for a mom and pop diner, and I ate quickly, licking my fingers clean without embarrassment. As I was nursing my ice water, a middle aged woman with artificially bright red hair approached. Since she was the oldest person I'd seen working there so far, I suspected that she was the owner or manager. She moved with confidence and had the demeanor of someone who knew hard work and liked it. She was looking me over with sharp eyes, and I shifted uncomfortably in my seat. I wiped my hands on the paper napkin and looked back at her. I was a paying customer and had the right to be here, just like anyone else. Just because I looked a little out of place didn't give anyone the right to look down on me.

I was working on a simmering case of righteous indignation by the time she stopped in front of me. "I hear you're looking for some work." Her voice was smooth Southern with an edge.

I slumped back in relief. My sister had told me that I could be too prickly for my own good, but I had a hard time turning off the defensiveness. "I am," I responded, looking at her a little cautiously, "but I heard that you weren't hiring."

"We're not," she agreed. She cocked her hip and looked at me, head tilted slightly. "I didn't know if you were looking for anything in particular."

"I'm not picky," I said honestly, "I just need something to pay the bills."

"Don't we all," she agreed with a shade of humor. "Well, we don't need anyone right now, but the 7/11 is looking for a clerk."

I studied her, trying not to get my hopes up. "Is it close by?" I asked.

"Honey, around here, everything is pretty close. It's down toward Centerfield. Just a five minute drive or so."

I didn't know where anything in that little town was, but I didn't like letting on how out of place I felt. I nodded like I knew what she was talking about, and finished the last of my water. With a little more confidence, I thanked her and slipped out the door. I left a generous tip I could ill afford, but it wouldn't be good business to make enemies in a town of this size. Besides the diner, I doubted I could get a decent meal anywhere else, and since my sister and I were not known for our cooking, it would be nice to have a backup if our own culinary creations were not edible.

I immediately climbed into my oversized car and

reached for my phone. It was another luxury, but one that my sister insisted that we both have. The data plan for the phones was enough to make us short on groceries, but I was grateful for it now. I knew I had seen the 7/11 on my way into town, but couldn't recall its exact location. I wasn't great with directions, so trying to retrace my steps would do me little good. Instead, I started a Google search, found the address, and let the phone guide me to my next destination.

The little store was located at the corner of nowhere, and I parked outside and watched as locals fueled up their cars and busied themselves with buying 32-ounce soft drinks and miniature bags of chips. They were all going somewhere, had some goal in mind, and were absorbed in their own little lives. It hadn't been long since that had been me, finishing up high school, touring college campuses, and spending the daylight hours shopping with friends and wishing for summer.

I had been such a child. I grimly popped open my car door and stepped out into the midday sun. It felt good here, with a hint of breeze. I shut the car door with necessary force and strolled to the door, pushing it open and squinting in the contrasting dim interior. The woman at the cash register might have been anywhere from 40 to 100, the sun and hard living baking her skin into an even tanned leather. Her hair was caught up in a high ponytail, and her eyes stood out in her bronzed face, bright blue.

"Help you?" she asked with a hint of the South in her words.

I hesitated for a moment, and then went to the counter. The store was bustling with customers, but none had approached to pay.

"I'm looking for work," I said, forcing a smile. "I have some experience in sales. I worked for a card shop and restaurant in my old town." I paused and took a slow breath. "I heard you might be hiring, and wondered if I could get an application."

"Sure," she said slowly. "We're looking for someone who can do nights. That sound okay for you?"

I had a brief flash of myself standing in the kitchen at my house armed with sports equipment. If I wasn't there at night, who would be there with my sister? Could I really leave her alone? But it wasn't something I could refuse either. A job was a job. I licked my lips and nodded. I really didn't have much of a choice. "Nights are fine," I said.

She nodded and turned as an older man in a navy cap and heavy beard placed a huge Styrofoam cup and a package of beef jerky on the counter. She rang him up automatically, gesturing for me to wait. As she exchanged small talk with him, I glanced around. A mother with two toddlers was in the candy aisle, and she was already looking overwhelmed as her little ones pawed through the brightly colored wrappers. An older man had a cup of coffee and was picking up a box of doughnuts. Behind me I heard the shuffle of feet and turned to see a guy about my age, his pale blond hair and light skin fairly glowing in the overhead lights. Glowing? I blinked, thinking that he might lose some of his odd illumination on a second glance, and he did. I felt my cheeks flush and turned back to the counter. Great, now I was seeing things. I knew I had been staring, so I deliberately kept my eyes forward, ignoring him and everyone else in the line behind me.

"Okay, here's the application." The voice of the lady behind the counter had me looking up quickly. She held out a single sheet of paper and a pen. "You can fill it out real quick, and I'll give it to the manager when he gets in," she assured me.

I took the offered items and turned back to the door. Keeping my head down, I didn't look toward anyone in the little shop, but slipped out to my car. I dropped into the driver's seat with a rush of relief and sighed. After gathering my thoughts for a moment, I glanced around the interior of the car. In the seat next to mine was a magazine forgotten and months old, and I used it to write on. Name was easy, as was age and birth date. My address made me pause. It took me a second to recall the zip code, and I wrote my cell phone since we hadn't gotten around to getting our home phone hooked up. I wrote my educational history automatically and thoughtfully listed the skills I thought would best match their requirements for the job in the proper space provided. For references, I had few. I chose some friends of my parents and a teacher from my high school, praying that the manager would never actually call these people. I didn't like the idea of my old life and my new one rubbing elbows in any form.

With the paper completed, I stepped back out of the car. In the 10 minutes or so it had taken me to write up my information, most of the current customers had left. The lady smiled as I stopped in front of her, and she took my paper.

"He'll probably get around to calling you in a day or so," she said. "The manager is George Carvel, and he's a good guy to work for. I'm sure you'll be hearing from him."

"Thanks," I said, and smiled back. I hoped I didn't look as stiff as I felt, but there it was. I couldn't pretend that I didn't hate this. I hated looking for a job in a place I had never been before, depending on the kindness of strangers. I hated the small town, the sympathetic looks I got when people found out about my parents. I hated my stupid life. "Thanks," I said again, and turned back towards the door. I stepped through and paused as the door closed behind me, pushing out a puff of coffee scented air. Across the street was a rather beaten looking station wagon, the driver obscured by the sun dappled windshield. But the passenger door was open, and I could plainly see the blond guy from the store. He was sitting in the wide bench seat, knees a little close to his face, his profile a sharp edged nod to masculine beauty. Not that I was in the market for guys, that was for sure. And he was certainly not my type. Beyond being a little too pretty and a little too smooth, I would swear on a stack of bibles that he was glowing again. And crazy was a problem I didn't need.

Chapter 2

It's weird when you watch your path to insanity from the outside. While it's happening it all feels too real. At a distance, you know it must be smoke and mirrors, but when you're there, when you're in it, it doesn't feel like any kind of illusion

I had bolted from the 7/11 parking lot as though I had the hounds of hell chasing me, firmly believing that I was losing my mind and really needed to be home when I finally came completely undone. But by the time I had parked my car, sanity had returned, and I knew that I was just overtired, or overstressed, or just plain overwhelmed.

Dinner was spaghetti with canned sauce and white Bunny bread slathered with margarine from a huge tub. The groceries weren't the healthiest, but they would last us through the week. I still felt faintly off kilter since my return but bragged with artificial confidence about my applications and my firm belief that I would be employed soon.

"When did you say you would be working?" my sister asked, her attention hung on the term night shift.

"I don't know for sure," I hedged. "But she said it might be nights. It's fine though. It will give me time to do some things around the house during the day. I can run errands when you are at work. I can have dinner with you, and then head to work."

"What about sleep?" Liz asked, frowning.

"I'll sleep in the morning." I stood and picked up my plate. I had eaten every last bite without noticing the taste. I rinsed the dish and put it in the sink.

"I don't like the idea of you working nights," my sister

replied.

"It's not like the place is downtown. Or even in a bad neighborhood. It's in the middle of nowhere," I argued.

"That's just what I worry about." Liz stood as well and began helping me clear the dishes. "I don't like you being out there by yourself. I know you think of yourself as self-sufficient, but really…"

I held up my hand to stop her words. "I haven't even gotten an interview. I'll worry about everything else later if it comes to that."

"We will talk about this later," she retorted, starting the hot water in the sink. "I'm sorry, but I do worry about you."

I sighed to myself. As much as she worried about me working in the store at night, I worried much more about her being alone. Home alone with the stranger.

*****

But just when you are expecting trouble, oftentimes, you are disappointed in a very different way. The night was quiet and still. There were no unusual footfalls in the hallway, no creaks of doors, no rattles of knobs. It was as silent as the grave.

I slept when the sun was just starting to gild the horizon, and woke when the alarm went off for my sister. I ate breakfast with her, watching as she read the paper and listened half-heartedly to the local radio program. After we had cleaned up and she had left in her dependable truck, I went back up to my room and kicked off my shoes. The doors were locked, the sun was up, and I needed more sleep.

I woke to the sound of the phone ringing at my bedside. I looked at the number with blurry eyes, and pulled myself upright before answering.

"Hello?"

"Victoria McDowell?"

"Yes," I cleared my throat and pushed the hair from my face.

"This is George Carvel from the 7/11. I have your application here and wanted to know if you would like to come in for an interview today."

I sat up straighter, my grip tightening on the phone. "Sure. I mean, anytime would be fine," I said quickly.

"Good, good. How about 2:00 this afternoon? I'll be in and we can meet."

"Two would be great," I replied, still sounding a little breathless. "I'll be there, Mr. Carvell."

He hesitated for a moment. "Now you do know that this is night work, right? You don't have a problem with that?"

I felt a little slip of surprise. "No, nights would work fine for me," I said slowly, waiting for his response.

"Well, that's good then," he replied. "I'll see you in a while."

"Yes, sir, and thanks," I said, and listened as he hung up the phone. I sat for another moment with the silence washing over me. In the buttery yellow of the midmorning, my room looked cheerfully shabby. The clothes mounded on the chair added a splash of color, and the window curtains fluttered with the barest of breeze. It could almost be taken as a good morning. The weather was nice, I was feeling more rested, my sister was safe at her job, and I had an interview to go to.

"Crap, and what am I going to wear?" I said aloud, pushing out of my bed.

*****

At noon I gave up pacing and went out to my car. I had a few hours to kill, but I couldn't just stay alone in the house. I wasn't built for standing still, and I needed movement and a purpose. I decided to go out for lunch and thank Blythe for the recommendation. From her perhaps I could get an idea of what Mr. Carvel was like and what type of employer he was.

I pulled my car up in front of the little café and slid out, careful not to wrinkle my pants. I didn't have many dress clothes. My wardrobe ran from the ultra-casual to the semi casual. I was wearing my funeral pants. I had had to make a special shopping trip just to buy things to get through the few horrible days that marked the passing of my parents and my old life. When I walked out on the other side, I had three funeral outfits, my sister, and a huge hole where my heart had once been.

This was my favorite of the somber outfits that spent most of the time carefully stowed in my closet. The pants were long and close fitting, the shirt tailored and conservative, the flat boots still shiny with a smudge of dirt on the sole that I was sure was from the cemetery. I was overdressed for the diner, and probably for the interview, but I had been raised on the idea that you wanted to make the best first impression. In the sliding reflection of the glass front window, I could see that my tightly braided hair was still in place, and my pale face was clean of dramatic makeup. No earrings, nothing but a conservative necklace. Check. Perfect for small town America. I pushed the door open and went back to the counter where I had eaten the day before. It just seemed the thing to do, and I didn't question the impulse.

"Well, hey," the young waitress greeted me. She was still dressed in the same uniform of jeans and a white tee shirt from the day before, but today her soft blond hair was up in a clip. "Name's Anna. We met yesterday?"

She said it like a question, like I might have forgotten her face overnight. I smiled back though, pleased that she had remembered me. "Hey. I'm in again. I just didn't feel like cooking."

"Oh, I hate to cook," she admitted. "Lucky I don't have to do it much here. Sam does most of the short order stuff here, so I just have to do some of the finishing touches."

I couldn't really see the fabled Sam, but I could plainly hear the clattering of dishes that made me think he was hard at work.

"So do you know what you want?" she asked, leaning casually against the counter despite the slow trickle of other patrons coming in the doorway. "Special today is chicken salad, which is one of my favorites."

I thought of my new job hopes and the possibility of a paycheck. "That sounds great," I said firmly, and handed her back the menu.

Half an hour later I had almost licked the plate clean, surprised at my own appetite. I still felt nervous about the interview, but Anna had dropped by to chat several times, and her easy bubbly personality made me feel comfortable despite myself. Watching her greeting the other guests, smiling and laughing, I shook my head. She really wasn't my type of friend. She looked more like my sister's group that she had hung out with in college, all lightly tanned and white teeth. But Anna was funny in a 'catch you off guard 'cause you really didn't see that coming' sort of way, and I liked her.

As she slid by a third time and settled with her elbows on the table, I found myself looking around the emptying dining room. I was worried that she might get in trouble with her employer when the kitchen door swung open, but the other woman just nodded to us both and headed into the back. I put down my nearly empty glass, Diet Coke this time, and sighed with satisfaction. Maybe I wouldn't be able to eat as well for another two weeks, but this was almost worth it.

"Well you look all cleaned up," the manager said in greeting when she came out of the kitchen.

"Oh, yeah, I mean, yes. I have an interview today at the 7/11." I bit my lip and tried again. "I didn't introduce myself earlier. I'm Tori. And your tip paid off. They are looking for someone at the store. They needed a new person to work nights."

She nodded and held out her hand. "Blythe," she said in a matter of fact tone. "And I'm glad that you're happy with the job." I took her hand and shook it, feeling a little awkward with the gesture.

"Oh, I haven't gotten it yet," I said quickly. "But Mr. Carvel seems to be really nice. So I just hope I am qualified for the job."

"You should be," Blythe responded, leaning one arm against the counter. "If you know how to work the register and can do some simple stocking, you should be good to go." She hesitated, her eyes glancing my way, and then down at the floor. "But you said he wanted nights?"

"Yeah," I looked at her carefully. "But that shouldn't be a problem. I don't mind being up late."

She was frowning. "How old did you say you were?"

"Nineteen," I said, that familiar prickly feeling rising. "But I'm living on my own with my sister. I can do nights, no problem." I tried to keep my voice flat, mature.

"What about school?" she asked, and I tried not to feel

defensive.

"I graduated from high school last year but had to leave college. I'm waiting to get settled before going back to school."

She had transferred her full attention to me. "What are you going to study?" she asked.

Now I was feeling as though the questions were a little more intrusive, too personal. Small town life, I reminded myself, and took a deep breath. Maybe here, it would be common for everyone to want to know everyone else's business.

"I don't really know." I looked down at my hands, bare of rings. I was feeling jittery, like I was in another interview of sorts, and I didn't like it. "I like photography and writing. I was thinking journalism."

When the diner door swung open I breathed a sigh of relief as three men filed in, all in casual suits with loosened ties and flushed faces. "I'll get them," Blythe said, and left Anna and me at the counter.

Anna turned to me with a wry smile. "You have to give Blythe a chance. She has college age kids, and wants to mother all of us. You just have to be in the right age range, and you're on her radar. She doesn't mean to be," she paused to pick the right word, "bossy."

"Oh," I said, and watched as Blythe steered the men toward a table in the front. "That's okay. My sister is worried about the same thing. She doesn't really like the idea that I would be working at night, but I don't have a lot of choices right now."

Anna looked like she wanted to ask a question, and I could see it in her eyes. It didn't take long for people to register that I spoke about my sister, but not my parents. I checked my watch, but I still had some time. I didn't want to make up an excuse to leave, so I decided on honesty.

"My parents were killed in a car accident last year," I told her, flat out, eyes direct. "My sister and I moved here for her job. That's one reason I need to be working."

Anna looked uncomfortable now, but her eyes were soft with unspoken sympathy.

"It's alright," I said quickly. I dug into my purse for my wallet and pulled out some very crumpled bills. "Don't feel bad.

I'm not advertising what happened, so not a lot of people around here know about us. We wanted a new start. We're adjusting."

She took the money and looked at me closely. "I don't really know what to say. 'Sorry' seems so stupid."

I appreciated the honesty. "Like I said before, it's okay. No one knows what to say."

She nodded and moved toward the register with money and my check. I turned away and looked out the window into the parking lot, blinking hard against the tears that seemed to linger just behind my eyelids.

But Anna didn't come back right away with my change. I saw her slip back into the kitchen with the money still in hand. A few minutes later, Blythe was at the window, looking into the kitchen and giving the order for the seated men and then walking into the kitchen. I tried not to watch and wonder, tried not to feel a little betrayed. I didn't want Anna to go to Blythe and tell her my problems. I didn't want, or need, I thought stubbornly, sympathy from strangers. At this point, I just wanted to get my change and leave, but I sat there on my stool, playing with the straw wrapper, knotting and unknotting the paper strip.

"Your change." Anna was in front of me, smiling slightly. She put the money on the counter next to me and scooted onto the stool to the right of mine. "And I'm on break."

I looked at her in surprise, but then I felt a surge of relief and smiled back. So she hadn't gone in the back to tell my sad story to the rest of the staff. She was asking for a break. I dropped the twisted piece of paper next to my plate and deliberately relaxed my shoulders. This was good. Some small town conversation with a local, someone close to my own age. I needed this. And I knew that the time until my interview would go much faster if I had someone to talk to.

"So are you still in school?" I asked. Let's talk about someone else now, I thought grimly.

"Yep. I'm a senior. I'll probably stay at home and go to U of L when I graduate." She swiveled on her seat to look at me. "You want anything else to eat? It's on the house. I'm going to get some pie."

I shook my head and watched as she slipped gracefully off the stool and went behind the counter again, stopping in front of the glassed in cabinet. She pulled out a whole pie, its meringue rising a good three inches above the golden crust, and set it on the table. With practiced strokes, she cut herself a generous slice and dropped it on a china plate. After she had replaced the pie, she grabbed a fork and napkin and returned to my side.

"Okay, so I have an idea." I turned to look at her. She deftly pulled her hair from its confining pony tail, pulled it back in a tighter bundle, and gathered it up again in an elastic band. She glance toward the kitchen and pitched her voice low. "Blythe makes the best bakery goods in the county, and everyone knows it. She doesn't have the money to expand to another location, but I have been telling her that the real money is in delivery. You know, delivering for some of the smaller companies, offices, and shops. Like catering on a small scale. She could start out small with just a few clients, and then deliver for individual customers too." She cut a huge bite of pie and tucked it in her mouth, barely pausing to chew. "People could buy each pie by the slice or the whole thing and have it delivered. We could do cakes too, birthday cakes, party cakes." She waved her fork at me. "But she would need someone to do the delivering. I can't because my car is a piece of crap and I don't trust it to take me anywhere. Besides, I can't work full time until summer. But you could."

"Deliver cakes?" I asked.

"Deliver whatever," she said, and cut off another bite. "You can drive, you can work full time, and I told Blythe that you would probably be relatively cheap to hire, at least at first." She looked at me slightly apologetically. "I was just assuming from what you said that you would be okay to start small."

I wasn't sure of her definition of small, but since it was a darn sight better than none, I nodded slowly. "What did Blythe say?" I asked. I kept my tone neutral. I didn't want to hope, and dammit, I wouldn't be disappointed.

"She's thinking about it," Anna replied. "I mean, you probably don't want to miss your other interview, but don't jump at the job at the 7/11 just yet. Let me work on Blythe in the meantime."

Chapter 3

I was offered two jobs in one day. My decision was really a no brainer. I could work at the 7/11 at night, situated far from the warm lights of the little town, or I could work days with Anna in the diner, with half priced meals. Sure, I would have to drive my own car for the deliveries, and there was no mileage allowance just yet, but for me it would be worth it. And my sister was thrilled. For what seemed like the first time since we had moved away from our home in Chicago and into the creaky old house, Liz had a genuine smile on her face, and I was the reason. She took me to the Dairy Queen to celebrate, with Blizzards for dessert.

The following Monday had me preparing for work at the unholy hour of 6:00 AM. I dressed in the dark, my fingers clumsy and my eyes at half-mast. I knew Blythe had already been there for a couple of hours before I was due to arrive, but that did not change the fact that it was 6:00 in the morning, and my bed was a big warm nest of covers. On the good side, I had been able to sleep soundly for the past several nights, thanks in part to the "security system" I had rigged. It had taken me a little time to barricade the doors with furniture each night, especially since I had to wait until Liz was in bed and asleep. Then I had to be quiet enough not to disturb her. Not as easy as I had thought it would be. There were none of the city sounds to drown out my noises. Lastly, I added metal sauce pan lids to the top, teetering for balance but guaranteed to fall with a bang if pushed by someone trying to get in the door. My final line of defense was the large kitchen knife I had stowed between my mattress and box spring. All of this took some time and stealth, but I knew that protecting her was more important than pissing her off, so I was willing to take the blame if she ever caught me at it.

This morning, I grumpily moved all the furniture back to its proper place before Liz woke, and gathered my purse and cell phone. I was leaving out the front door as she shuffled into the kitchen. Her hair looked like something had been nesting in it, and her eyes were dark and sleepy, but she looked a little less haggard than she had, and I breathed a sigh of relief.

"You don't have to be up this early," I scolded. "I'm a big girl. I can get ready on my own."

"Brat," she muttered. "I was just going to tell you good luck, but now I hope you burn the cookies."

"No you don't," I retorted. "To you, burning cookies would be a sin. And I won't be doing any baking yet. I'm just learning the ropes this week."

She ran her fingers through her hair and began working on the tangles. "Well, good luck anyway," she said and smiled a little. "Do you think they would let you bring home any extras?"

I chuckled as I skipped down the steps. The yard was cool and still grey with early morning. The curvy road in front of our house had strips of fog painted across the rising air, and the cemetery beyond looked pretty much haunted in the dim light. I frowned and then pulled myself from my reverie. Soon the sun would rise, the day would begin, and, hopefully, I would be making a little money.

Blythe had opened the doors of the diner, but it was empty of customers. I could hear the soft shuffle of her feet back in the kitchen and called a hello. When she came up front, she was wiping floured hands on a red checkered apron. "Good," she said, "you're on time. Come back here and find you an apron. They're back in the back room. You can put your purse in the office. You can keep your phone with you, but no unnecessary calls."

I blinked in surprise, still trying to wake up. Then I nodded silently, keeping my mouth shut, holding in any smart responses I might have had. Mornings were not my thing.

For the next several hours, I learned the secret to baking the perfect pie crust, the highest and richest meringue, and the creamiest custard. I whipped, beat, stirred, swept, mopped, and sweated. I saw the diner take on a bustle of life, starting with a rush around 7:00 and again at noon. By the time Anna arrived after school at 3:00, I was dead on my feet. Anna looked at me and grinned. "Wow, so how has the first day been?"

I smiled back wearily. "Blythe can outwork me without breathing hard," I said and leaned against the counter.

"Yep, but that's true of everyone here. She can outlast any of us. We think it's her magic brew. She has coffee she makes in the office, and won't share it with anyone."

Blythe made a humph sound as she passed, and Anna grinned at her.

"You coming back tomorrow?" Blythe asked me, hands on her hips.

I looked down at my stained apron and my raw hands. The day had flown, and being busy, while tiring, had kept my mind firmly in the present. "Yep," I replied. "What time do you need me?"

Blythe nodded. "Six o'clock. Just the same. We'll do that schedule until you're trained. Then we can look at a later shift if you want. Anna here is nagging me about the delivery thing, but that can wait another week or so."

I nodded. "It's fine with me," I reassured her.

"Tomorrow then," she said, and turned back toward the kitchen.

*****

While I wasn't watching, March rolled into April, and the weather went from being damp and cool, damp and warm, to damp and hot in the midafternoon. I worked until the high school let out and Anna came to take my place, and then collapsed in my bed at home for an hour's sleep before getting up to start dinner. By the time my sister was home at 6:00, dinner was ready, and we ate together across the scrubbed wooden table. She helped me clean up, and we took turns washing dishes and complaining about it. It's sad when your greatest fantasy is having your own dishwasher.

In the evenings, we sat down in front of the TV and

watched without much interest, smirking at reality shows that looked nothing like reality, and sitcom comedies that weren't really funny. By the 10:00 news, we were already drowsy but stayed to watch the local stories. I think in the back of my mind I would have been grateful to see a story about some creep who was breaking into people's homes at night and whispering to them in the dark. But of course, that story never came.

After my sister went to bed, I would set up my alarm system and turn in myself, checking my knife and laying out my clothes as though that was just a normal routine part of getting ready for bed. After two weeks of working for Blythe, she let me make a few batches of biscuits by myself, and I began taking orders with her out front during the lunch rush. I knew she really didn't need me there, that she could handle the task just fine whether I was helping or not, but I liked talking with the people and learning some of the names. I soon got to know the usual customers. There were the people from the insurance company right next door who had cinnamon buns and coffee every morning at the corner table. There was the group of young mothers who dropped their kids off at the Catholic elementary school down the street and then came for a rather rowdy breakfast. There were the few health nuts who came in while jogging to get their chai tea and oatmeal. There were the older couples coming in after morning services at the church to have biscuits and scrambled eggs, whites only please, and sweet hot coffee. The sheriff was a regular, as were a few of the teachers from the surrounding schools who stopped by to grab something early before class.

And with that settled routine, the people of the town soon began to know me as well. I had tried to lessen my natural tendency toward the flashy and wore jeans and plain tee shirts, usually black, which didn't show coffee stains, or white, which could be bleached. I had started seeing roots in my multi-hued hair, and chose to dye it all a mid-brown shade with just a hint of red, not far off my natural color. My sister was rather shocked with the result, but I didn't want to use my hard earned money to get a professional dye job, and I didn't want to live with my style as it was. I wore several earrings, but as long as they were small enough not to catch on anything, Blythe didn't comment. I left my multiple rings at home, which was fine because my nails started breaking as soon as I began baking, and my hands looked rough.

I'm not sure exactly who shared my life story with the patrons, but I could tell that most of the regulars knew of my parents' death. At first their eyes just slid over me, like you do when you've seen an accident and don't want anyone to know that you are looking. But as they got used to my presence, they seemed to work around the discomfort. They asked me about my sister, my job, and my house but studiously avoided anything that could be construed as delving into my past life history. I was grudgingly grateful. I didn't like that people knew of my pain, and I didn't want their sympathy, but at the same time, I didn't want to be the one to awkwardly tell them about my loss. As it was, I was fitting in just fine considering.

When the weather warmed toward spring, the complexion of the diner changed as well. Anna was there each day, helping to take orders and man the register. There were more customers as well: the high school kids who wanted to hang out after school and the middle school crowd on their skateboards or bikes, looking for a bit of sun and freedom. Anna greeted most with enthusiasm. It seemed that there wasn't anyone that she didn't know at least by sight. I felt a stab of envy. Even before my parents' death, I hadn't been like that. I was too sarcastic, too prickly, too determined to be an individual that I forgot what it was like to be part of a group.

On Wednesday morning, I sat at my own kitchen table, sipping coffee. Blythe had told me that I could come in a little later since Anna was there and would take the early morning due to some random day off for the school system. I gratefully agreed. I had set my alarm for 5:00 and had stealthily moved the furniture back into place. Once the house looked back to normal, nothing left out to alarm my sister, I had climbed back in bed. I slept in 'til a sinful 9:00 AM and trudged down to have my breakfast. I had gotten used to eating at the diner, and I noticed that we were low on breakfast food. I wondered if my sister had been skipping breakfast again, and vowed to check on that. I stood, my fingers warm around the mug of coffee, and went to the front window. The heavy trees had finally filled out, thick with new green, but I still had a clear view to the cemetery beneath their ancient limbs. I wondered idly if that was why we were able to get the house at such a good price. Were there more people like me who were not thrilled with the idea of living so close to a bunch of corpses?

The gate to the cemetery was open, but there were no cars. I could see the sun slanting against the slate roof of the little chapel, but its doorway was in shadow. For a moment, it seemed as though the door was open. I blinked and leaned forward. Had I seen movement? The door was closed now, but I could see a figure moving down the side of the building, sticking to the shadows. I frowned. His posture seemed just a shade too stealthy. He didn't come out in the sunlight, like someone just visiting. He stayed under the eaves of the building, finally disappearing around the side. I leaned back and took a sip of coffee. Ridiculous to be concerned really. What bad things could be going on in broad daylight? There was the occasional car still rushing past, and I guessed that I probably wasn't the only person home in the little line of houses. Across the road and to the right was another older home that sat shoulder to shoulder with the cemetery. It was built with stone and whimsy, and had a little gazebo out back. I had seen life around there on other days. A man puttering in the flower gardens out front, and a woman sitting on the porch with an easel, painting perhaps. Surely they would notice if someone were lingering in the cemetery?

I stepped back from the window and took my coffee up to my room with me. With a slight shake of my head, I started snatching up clothes from the floor and dividing them into piles of those that could be worn again, and those that needed to head to the basement laundry room. When I had sorted them all, I dug through the ones left to find jeans and a tee shirt for work. I ran a comb through my hair and pulled it back into a pony tail. I wore only one pair of small earrings and took a quick 360-degree view to make sure there was no excessive skin showing. No big holes in the jeans, the tee was tight, but the tank top underneath would cover me if I had any excessive bending to do. The shoes were nondescript sneakers.

After brushing my teeth, I headed out for my car. The air was warm and smelled sweetly of some spring flower that grew wild on the property. I paused on the porch to lock the door and then turned, glancing back toward the cemetery as though pulled there. Nothing. But then I stopped and stared. On the porch of the house across the street were two figures. The light bathed them with the morning glow where they stood, one on the bottom step and the other sitting on the stairs, long legs out in front of him. The standing figure was tall and lanky, dark hair hanging in his eyes, hands balled and pushed in jean pockets. He was tense, from every line of his stance. The other figure was lounging on the steps, the full sun hitting the fall of his pale hair and making it burn. He was looking up at the other guy and gesturing, seeming to be reasoning, calming. The other guy made an abrupt shake of his head and quickly turned. He seemed to glare, unseeing, into the street, and then his eyes landed on me. He stood for a long minute, and I could swear that he was looking straight at me where I stood on my porch, frozen. Then he turned and headed up the sidewalk, toward me. My eyes leapt to the other guy, his companion, but he was still reclining on the steps, looking after the man as I was. Neither was looking at me now, and I thought about just running to my car and leaving, like the coward that I was becoming. But the dark man didn't approach any farther than the entrance to the cemetery. He turned and passed through the gates and disappeared out of sight behind the stone walls. I stilled and watched, keys in hand but frozen with some indecision, but he didn't reappear.

When I looked back toward the house, I could see the blond man rising. I knew immediately where I had seen him. He had been at the 7/11 weeks ago. It was easy to identify him. Even in the light of the morning, he still visibly and inexplicably glowed.

*****

I tugged open my car door and carefully reached in for the stack of white bakery boxes. The contents were still slightly warm, and the aroma was intoxicating. I paused to kick the door closed with my foot and turned to look toward the retirement village. It was so new the sod was still fresh, and the flowers in the generous planters were struggling to spread. The parking lot was newly paved with sharp yellow lines bisecting the dark surface. A few cars were lined up in the front lot, and I had parked close to the door so that I wouldn't have to walk far with my hands full of delivery boxes. As strange as it may have seemed, despite my attempts at rebellion against society in general, I was surprisingly comfortable with the elderly. I had grown up with a bevy of great aunts and uncles, and the familiar scent of Dove soap and Old Spice was a warm reminder of a relatively carefree childhood. As soon as I got in the door, I was directed to a dining area where I carefully juggled the boxes as I tried to get someone's attention. There were clusters of residents at tables absorbed in card games and gossip. One lady wearing a tidy sweater set of pale peach and lovely curled white hair approached me, hands outstretched.

"Let me help," she said, and took a box from the top of my stack. She carefully set the box on one of the covered tables and gestured to the rest of the stack. "They can go right here. You really have your hands full!" She took another box, and I carefully set the remainder of the stack down. "We'll open them up and put everything on plates for serving, but we'll have to move fast. As soon as the crowd sees what you brought, they'll be no stopping them." She smiled and flipped the lid back on the box. "Oh, and these are my favorites." She gingerly took out an iced cookie and took a generous bite. "I hinted to Blythe that I liked them, but I didn't expect all this!"

I smiled back at her obvious pleasure. "You are one of our first deliveries," I said, and flipped open another box. "Blythe added a little bit of everything."

"Oh, good. So I won't have to choose."

As she explored the boxes, flipping them open and bending to catch the luscious smells, I watched with amusement. Soon, the other card players started noticing the new additions. In minutes we were surrounded by older folks, unconsciously shuffling into a line. One lady brought out a stack of pastel colored napkins and another went in search of the coffee carafe. I went from delivering the pastries to helping arrange them on platters, filling the massive coffee pot, and setting out china cups and real silver spoons. As the crowd lined up to choose their treats, the first woman pulled me off to the side.

"I didn't even introduce myself," she said, slightly abashed. "I'm Thelma. Thelma Coffey."

I took her hand and grinned back. "You were a little busy. I'm Tori, or Victoria." Her hand was cool and fragile in my own.

"Oh, a lovely name!" She exclaimed. "I taught history at the high school for years, and I've always been fond of our Victoria." She smiled, but her eyes became more speculative. "And I know just about every young person in our town, but I can't recall ever meeting you before."

"Oh, I'm new, new to town" I said quickly. She looked a shade confused, but then her expression cleared, and she smiled again.

"Then that explains it," she said with relief. "You moved here recently?"

"Yes, my sister and I," I agreed, suddenly aware that I was talking to a school teacher who would notice any lapse in my proper English. "We moved from Chicago just a few months ago. My sister got a job in Louisville."

"And are you at the high school, or have you graduated?"

"I graduated last year," I replied. "Now I'm working with Blythe at the diner."

"That's nice," she replied. "I do love Blythe's cooking. I was afraid that after I moved here, I would miss out on some of dishes she makes." She glanced out the window, a little wistfully. "I had my own little house in the middle of Pewee Valley. But the yard was just too much to keep up with, and the leaves in the fall were just burying me!"

"I know what you mean," I agreed. "When fall comes, we are going to have a big job ahead of us trying to take care of our yard."

"And may I ask, where do you live?" she responded.

I described our little yellow house with the chipped paint and the covered front porch. When I mentioned the location, across from the cemetery, and Duncan Memorial Chapel, her eyes brightened in recognition.

"Oh, I know that house. Lucy Knox used to live there." She turned, her eyes scanning the crowd as they dispersed with their napkins and goodies. "There she is. She's the lady with the floral top and the purple glasses."

I followed her gaze and saw a woman with iron grey hair bending over the pastries with a serious expression. She was studying her selections with intense concentration, and I barely heard Thelma's next words.

"I'll introduce you. I'm sure she'd love to know who was in her house. She had to sell when she moved here, but she knew she couldn't keep the place up. Like me, she was alone by then. Her husband died probably 20 years ago, so she's lived by herself for a long time." Thelma started to move off with a brisk pace, and I hurried to catch up.

"That's okay, Mrs. Coffey," I said to her back. I wasn't sure when Blythe expected me back, but I hadn't thought I would be gone this long.

She turned and took my hand lightly, "I'm Mrs. Coffey in the school, but now I'm rebelling, and you can call me Thelma." Her eyes were gentle behind the glasses, her hands soft.

I nodded, but she wouldn't be side tracked. She pulled me along while I looked back toward the clock, wondering if Blythe was noticing my prolonged absence. I tried unsuccessfully to make my excuses, but Thelma wouldn't be satisfied until I was sitting at a table with Mrs. Knox, and she rushed off to get me a drink. "You can have just a little break," she assured me. "If Blythe asks, tell her that I insisted. I taught her a few years back, and all of her siblings, so I know the whole family." She actually winked, and I couldn't help but grin.

Lucy Knox, or Mrs. Lucy, as she insisted I call her, was as sharp as Thelma with a spicy sense of humor and a broad streak of independence. She settled in a chair, leaning her cane against the textured wall paper and settling a cloth napkin in her lap. She stirred her coffee slowly, and then set the spoon neatly on the side of the plate.

"So you're living at my old house," she started, her voice low and gruff and shaded with age, but patted my hand to soften the words. "Well, I'm glad someone is getting use out of it. I was so worried that they might want to just knock the whole thing down. I'm afraid that maintenance was getting ahead of me." I think I must have seemed surprised because she went on hastily. "Not that the place isn't still good. It has great bones and a beautiful setting! I just couldn't keep up, and John, that's my oldest, said, 'Mom, you have to sell this place. It's just not safe for you to live there alone anymore.' " She smiled a little ruefully. "I didn't listen and broke my hip going to the basement not three weeks later."

"Oh, that must have been awful!" I gasped. She seemed so fragile, brittle.

"I was down there for almost 12 hours until the postman came to deliver a package and heard me shouting. I never left the door closed during the day. I liked the sunshine too much. Good thing for me, as it turns out. If the door had been closed, well, I might have been a skeleton before they found me."

I grimaced, and she laughed, a loud, rich sound that belied her tiny frame. "I'm just teasing," she said, her mouth still quirked in a sly smile. "I'm sure I would have started stinking at some point, and it would have brought in the dogs. Lots of dogs in the neighborhood."

I gaped at her a moment, at a loss as to what to say. I was used to older people, and certainly had been exposed to many personality types, but none that had the humor and sharp wit like this woman had. "That's quite a story," I said, not knowing what else to say, and watched as Thelma approached, grateful for the company. She sat with her second cookie tucked in a napkin, while she placed a little china cup of coffee at my elbow, and a huge sticky bun with spun sugar and cinnamon clinging to the golden surface in front of me. My stomach rumbled in an embarrassing way, and I decided that this might as well be my break from work.

Thelma lowered herself slowly into the chair next to mine. "Well Lucy, you must have shocked the girl. She has that look," she said dryly.

"Just told her the truth," Lucy responded, and took a careful bite out of her iced cupcake.

"You weren't scaring her with your ghost stories, were you?"

Mrs. Lucy looked up quickly. "No," she said. "Now Thelma, why would I want to do that? They've just moved in. I don't want to scare them off so soon."

"Ghosts," I interrupted, my thoughts going to my late night visitor. There was no way I would believe that he was a ghost, but I could certainly believe that an old woman staying by herself in the house might interpret his presence as something supernatural.

"Thelma is just going on," Mrs. Lucy scolded, her voice still deep. "There are no ghosts around there. All the souls in the cemetery are happy to be in Heaven. They don't want to be hanging around some old lady's house peeking in the windows."

"Was there someone doing that?" I asked, and I knew my voice had risen.

"No, of course not," Thelma said, her gaze sharp on my face.

"But there were some things," Lucy said slowly. She looked meaningfully at Thelma.

Thelma was looking at me carefully. "Tori, I know you don't know us, but we do know this town pretty well. Do you want to tell us what is going on?"

I looked at her, my usual ability to fabricate momentarily lost to me. I couldn't so much as open my mouth to deny it. Instead, I looked between the two women and told them everything.

Chapter 4

I left the retirement facility almost two hours later. Like the teacher that she had once been, Thelma promised to call Blythe and tell her that they had kept me to set up and help serve. I don't know if it was my tears or their mothering instinct that made them want to care for me, but now I really had two unusual allies in my quest for the truth.

As strange as it was, my slow slide into insanity had been halted for at least a little bit. It seemed that the ghost that haunted me had also come to the house while Mrs. Lucy had been in residence.

"Oh, I never actually saw him, and I couldn't prove a thing, but a woman knows when someone has been through her things. I could tell someone had been in my house. And I had heard all of the old stories, about real ghosts that haunted the house. But I lived there all of my married life, and my husband's family before me. I knew the truth, even if no one else was ready to believe me. Whatever was coming to the house wasn't some phantom, and it wasn't a figment of my imagination. But I was scared, and that was the last straw. And that was when John started his campaign to get me out of the house."

"It was time for you to move," Thelma interjected.

"I know that. But that doesn't mean that I wanted to go." Mrs. Lucy looked at me with tightened lips. "Even if no one else ever saw anything, I did. And now you have. And you need to be careful. I don't know who he is, or what he wants, but it's not you or I. It's something in the house."

Even in the bright sunlight streaming through the

windshield, I still shivered as I recalled her words. I knew she didn't mean to scare me, but I was scared. Well, hell, maybe she had meant for me to be afraid, but it was for my own good. But to be honest, my fear was mingled with a relief, the knowledge that I wasn't alone. Even if her son hadn't believed it when she said that someone had broken into her house and gone through her things, she had continued in her belief, and she believed me now.

I swiped away a stray tear. I had cried so much in the last few months, I thought that all my tears were gone. Apparently I was wrong about that one.

At the diner, I ducked into the bathroom and ran a washcloth I swiped from the kitchen over my heated face. As rough as I looked, after crying on the ladies at the retirement facility and two cups of coffee combined with a monster sugar rush, I felt better. I brushed my hair off my face and fastened it more securely into a pony tail. I knew we had no more deliveries scheduled for the afternoon, but I wanted to work through my last half hour to try to make up for my longer delivery time.

But Blythe barely noticed my lateness when I returned and immediately set me to work icing some of the cakes for an evening pickup. She didn't question where I had been, and she didn't ask about my pale skin or red eyes. I did catch her looking at me once, and I hoped it wasn't sympathy in her eyes. But it couldn't be helped. I stiffened my back, shrugging off the remnants of my worry; it was work now and drama later.

When school hours were past, Anna came blowing in, dropping her backpack on the desk in the back office and filling the kitchen with chatter. I could almost feel the energy rise off of her, and smiled unwillingly. Anna reminded me of my best friend from elementary school, with her careless conversation and boundless enthusiasm. My childhood friend and I had gradually grown apart when we had gone to different high schools, and when she had called after my parents' death, I had barely managed to speak with her, my words bitter, sour in my mouth. I regretted it now. I knew that she had only wanted to touch base with me, to show me that she still cared about me and our friendship, but I had frozen her out with dry eyes and sharp words.

I had learned the hard way that it took some effort to keep up a friendship. Now, miles away from home, I had shut out the few close friends I had from Chicago, and lived with just my sister, just the two of us.

Anna came behind me and flung an arm around my neck. "The weekend it upon us, Tori," she sang in an off-key voice. "We have to do something to have some fun!"

I looked at her and raised my eyebrows.

"Oh, come on! We can find something to do!" she exclaimed. "We're getting paid! A little cash to burn."

"Very little," I said under my breath. Most of my money had to go for living expenses and the shiny new locks on the front and back doors.

"Okay, fine. Fun on a budget. How 'bout I come over to your place after I get off and we decide what to do from there."

I shrugged. It didn't sound so bad, someone to hang out with on a balmy spring night. "Okay, cool. I'll be there."

She grinned and moved off to pick up a stack of plates. I smiled unconsciously. Fun. It wasn't a concept that I was too familiar with just now, but what the heck. I needed to let off some steam, and I didn't have any other pressing plans. Okay, fun.

*****

Anna's version of fun was about as much excitement as I thought I could handle. Early mornings and late nights reinforcing my homemade security system had taken a toll on me. When she appeared on my front porch, she had two bags of takeout burgers and fries. I supplied the bottles of Diet Coke, and we ate on the porch in the cooling breeze. The moon rose, pale white and half full, and gave us some natural light. In the houses around us, dim purple blue lights shown through gauzy curtains in a flickering reflection of the television screen.

Liz had gone out for the evening. She announced, as soon as I told her of my plans to meet Anna, that she had plans as well. I looked at her with raised eyebrows, noticing that this was the first breath of a social life that I had heard from her. She explained that some friends from work were planning on getting together for dinner, and she was going to meet them. I wondered, with a flash of guilt, how many such invitations she had refused so that she could spend her evenings with me, the dependent little sister. I gritted my teeth and pushed the thought away.

Anna lived somewhere in Crestwood, in one of the older neighborhoods where each house was situated on at least an acre of land, and kids rode bikes at reckless speeds through the streets. Her house was 30 years old, old according to some of her other friends, but compared to my house, which had stood over 100 years, it seemed pretty modern to me. She lived with her parents and a younger brother that she alternately loved and hated. He was in middle school and was experiencing the quicksilver moods that make adolescence so much fun.

"So Butthead went through my room and took all of my CDs, my iPod, and even my old radio. He's put them up somewhere, and he won't tell me where. When Mom gets home, she's going to have to kill him. It's the only fair thing."

I grinned, and took a big bite of the burger. McDonald's had finally come to the little town, and in some ways it gave me a feeling of security. It seemed that even far away from Chicago, some things didn't change.

"Why didn't you just make him tell you?" I asked, digging out a napkin to wipe my fingers.

"If I hurt him, Mom will be pissed. I have to just let it go for now. I'm trying to talk them into letting me go to Florida over the summer with some friends. I don't need to rock the boat just now."

"Um, yeah, I can see the problem."

"You're the youngest," she continued. "You don't have to be nice to any annoying younger brothers or sisters."

"Yep, just my older sister, and she's not so bad." Our voices sunk into silence, and I thought about how tiny my family had become.

Anna finished her meal and bundled up her garbage. "Okay, so why don't we walk a little." She put her hands to her flat middle and exclaimed, "I am so bloated!"

I gathered my papers as well, and balanced my soda on the rail for me to pick up later. "Sure. Give me your garbage, and I'll throw it away." I took her bag and headed back in the house.

I didn't want to leave the house open. I was always so careful to lock it when I left, whether Liz was home or not. If she thought it was strange that I locked her in when I left in the morning, she never commented. With a frown, I went to the back door and locked it, both the knob and the top deadbolt, both brand spanking new, then dug my phone and my keys from my purse. When I came back out, Anna was still on the porch, leaning against the rail. I stopped and used the key to lock the front door behind me, flicking on the front porch light that bathed the porch and its surrounding overgrown lilac bushes with a golden glow.

"You're locking up?" Anna said a chuckle in her voice. "Don't you know we don't lock our doors around here?"

I shrugged. "Too much city living, I guess," I said lightly. I wasn't about to tell my new friend that I was sure someone was breaking into my house at night and then disappearing again without opening any doors or cracking any windows. It made my attempt at security, the new locks and shoving furniture around to block the doors, just a little ridiculous, but he hadn't come back for some time, so it must be working.

"Let's go across the street," Anna said, and headed off the porch.

"Where?" I asked, and hurried to catch up.

"Just over here," she responded, and started to step into the empty street.

The streetlights here were obscured by the budding trees, and the shadows stretched in long fingers across the pavement. I shivered a little, but caught up with Anna as she reached the gate.

"Are people allowed here at night?" I asked nervously.

"It's fine. I know the family that lives next door, and they're usually the people that keep an eye on the place. The mom is the art teacher at school. She's cool."

I still felt doubtful. The guys that I had seen arguing on the porch of the house that Anna was referring to hadn't seemed to be too friendly. Maybe they were brothers that lived there, and the people that I had seen outside were the parents.

"Are there any teenagers there?" I asked, trying to sound casual.

"Yeah, just Dot. Dorothy."

"Dorothy?"

"Um hum. Funny name, I know. But she's really nice. She's gone away to college right now. But she's in state, so you might see her around. She's an artist too. Like her mom." Anna looked at me with a slight smile on her face. "And before someone else tells you, and freaks you out, Dot's dad also used to be the funeral director. She caught a lot of crap for that growing up."

"Oh," I said softly, thinking of the guys I had seen on the porch arguing. Definitely not a Dorothy among them. Or a funeral parlor father.

The gate was closed, but it took Anna just lifting a latch to open it. It squealed in an ominous way, and Anna looked back at me and grinned, her eyebrows raised. "Ooh, spooky," she whispered.

I rolled my eyes in response. I wasn't really afraid to go into the cemetery; it just had never seemed to me like a place that I might want to hang out. My own house seemed far more haunted than this place. Now that I was here, surrounded by the wide lawn dotted with stones, and in the shadow of the little chapel, it wasn't nearly as creepy as I had anticipated. The air held a cool breath and a hint of flowers. The darkness was filled with sounds of birds settling in nests with soft tweets, and the scuttling of other night creatures. The lights from the street bled onto the lawn, and the glow of the chapel's exterior lighting drenched the grounds with illumination.

"Let's walk a little," Anna said, and led me to one of the paths that circled around the property. It really wasn't that big a cemetery. The chapel was nestled to the left of the entrance, the stone and traditional stained glass making it seem somehow timeless. To the right was a paved drive that snaked farther back into the gravesites, tracing off into the darkness. I followed Anna as she walked on the path, her footfalls confident.

"Have you done this before?" I asked, curious.

"A few times at night, but more during the day. I rode here on bikes with friends, or stopped by to walk around with Dot. She likes to check out the grounds occasionally to make sure no one is in dropping trash or messing around. We even came here as a class for a field trip when I was in grade school to do rubbings."

"Rubbings?"

"Sure, you bring a big piece of paper and a crayon. You lay the paper against the stone where you want to see the engraving. When you color over the surface, some of the writing or pictures show up. It's easier to see them in the rubbing than in real life. Then you take them back to class and you get to write a paper about it." She grimaced. "I liked the coloring, but the writing, not so much."

I chuckled. It was funny. I was a horrible artist, and could barely draw a stick figure, but I liked to write. Not that I loved writing papers, but I did love a good story and would write journal entries or fiction when the mood hit me. I slowed and frowned. I hadn't written a word in my journal since my parents had died.

"So you never did that when you were a kid?" Anna's voice interrupted my musing.

"I guess I really didn't visit cemeteries that much when I was younger," I said. "Now I really don't want to that much."

Anna steps faltered and she looked back at me, her expression pure embarrassment. "Oh, I didn't even think! I'm so sorry! We didn't have to come here. We can leave right now!"

Seeing the connections that she had made, straight to the death of my parents, I immediately felt bad. "No!" I responded. "That's alright. I really don't mind it here. It's quiet. Calm. I never did anything like this in Chicago."

"Tori, really, let's just get out of here. We can find somewhere else to hang out. It just reminded me of when I was a kid." She was backing towards the open gate, but I stopped her with a gesture. I didn't want to leave. I wasn't afraid, and I didn't want to be babied like that. I could take this, no problem. And the whispers of any spirit were silent. I felt a surge of regret, regret that I was so much more haunted than this place would ever be.

I turned toward the darkness, shaking off my melancholia, and paused. "We can walk around for a while. I really don't mind. Then when we get hungry we can go inside for desert. I have a brownie mix." My cheerful voice was forced, but she smiled with relief.

"Okay fine. If that's what you want. And then I'll tell

Blythe that you were using a mix to make brownies." The humor was forced on her part as well, but I took it.

I made an exaggerated face at her. "Not if you value your life! I don't want to hear her complaining about my baking! You know how many hours we have put in trying to learn her recipes!"

We were both smiling as we started walking down one of the paved paths. The lights from the street lamps just outside the wall of the cemetery cut patterns of orange and black in the darkness. The path that we had chosen was lit with the moon and looked like a slice in the earth caused by the deep black of new pavement. I doubted that very many people drove back there.

"It is pretty," I said almost to myself.

Anna, hearing me, replied, "Well, it's one of the most popular wedding places in the county. There are constantly people coming in and out on the weekend."

"Really?" I asked.

"Yeah, sure," she said. "On a lot of days in the spring and summer there are several weddings going on in a weekend." She looked back over her shoulder at the chapel, now in the distance.

I looked with her, trying to imagine the place as something different. Something romantic and lovely. I sighed. I guessed I could picture it. The trees were full and beautiful, and would be especially stunning with autumn gilding the leaves, and the lawn was mostly a smooth carpet of green up closer to the chapel. The chapel itself was quaint and charming in the artificial glow.

"So have you been to a wedding around here?" I asked curiously.

"A few," she replied. "They are usually fairly small because the chapel doesn't hold many people, and they usually take a lot of pictures outside. I think most people use it because they like the grounds so well. And it's nondenominational. It's nice that way. Anyone in the community can use it. There have been some people from other countries to come here too." I could hear the small town pride in her voice and smiled. It would be nice to feel that feeling again. The feeling of home, of pride in your community.

But I hadn't previously thought of this place as a tourist attraction in the town. Now I realized that it was a landmark for the county. I thought of the many times I had seen cars coming in and out of the drive. Often I had thought they were families of some of the deceased buried here. Now I wondered. I wondered how many of the people I had seen here were actually looking for a place to be married or to baptize or christen their child.

"Here," Anna said. "Let me show you something." She was walking a little faster now, veering to a path on the right side of the cemetery that had sunk momentarily into pure darkness. I hesitated, my feet unwilling to take me there. Not in that dark. The uneasiness that I have grown accustomed to in my house suddenly reared its ugly head. I was looking hard into the dark as the perspiration beaded on my forehead, but my limbs felt cold, as though a stiff breeze was licking hungrily at our heels. And around me, despite the huff of moving air, an unnatural silence has descended.

"Anna," I called, my voice a little too high.

"Tori, I'm just over here." Her voice was calm, no alarm coloring her words, and she stepped out from a grove of trees and turned to look at me. The moonlight cut a slice through the night, and I could see her reassuring face. "What's up?" she asked.

"Nothing," I called back, forcing confidence into my voice. Stupid city girl getting freaked out by some old stones and the wind. I could handle this. This was a true case of nothing to fear but fear itself, and I was determined not to let it get the better of me, or to let Anna see it. I murmured a curse under my breath and increased my pace until I was next to her. The ground sloped up a little, and before me I could see two small stone benches. In front of the benches was a quaint little well, just like someone might see in the fairy stories, with a shingled top and stone base. It was so charming, so sweet, and I almost believed the innocence for a minute. Then I saw the heavy grating over the top. It was like a heavy mesh someone had wrought from metal that was spread over the mouth of the well. The practical side of me knew that this was for safety. This was obviously meant for keeping young children from falling down the well, or to prevent some idiot teenagers from hurting themselves. It certainly wasn't meant for keeping someone or something confined in the depths of the well. But even though my mind insisted on the reality of this, the terrified girl who sat with the racquet in her lap and waited for the watcher, knew the truth. That well was meant for something else. And I wanted nothing to do with it.

Anna didn't seem to notice my hesitation or think that my behavior was strange. She had dropped to one of the benches and tucked her feet up comfortably beneath her. "You can make a wish if you want," she said. Her voice startled me. I had been caught up in the chatter of my own thoughts and the comparative silence of the cemetery. I realized that my hands were clenched before me, as though I were preparing to ward something off. I struggled to make sense of what she had said. "Some people say it's a wishing well. You can throw in a penny and make a wish if you want."

I shivered. I wasn't planning on getting anywhere close enough to throw anything down that black maw. Just the idea of approaching it, much less looking down into its depths, made me shiver a little more violently. "No," I said, staying behind the bench. "I'm good."

"Don't believe in wishes?" she asked, but her voice was light.

"No." I rubbed my arms for warmth, even though it really wasn't a cold evening. "Do you?"

She looked a little lost for a moment. "No, I guess not. I just always thought it would be cool. You know, if some of it were true?"

"Some of what?" I asked, momentarily distracted from my own discomfort.

"The unreal. The fantasies we had as kids. Wishes, dragons, ghosts, vampires, all those things that go bump in the night." Her voice held a trace of humor, like she was laughing at herself.

I sighed, recalling when I too had been that carefree. I had thought that anything with a shade of mystery would be fascinating, a great distraction from my own dull life. But not anymore. I wanted dull, longed for normal, and my wishes, if dropped in the well, would be for the past that I would never see again.

"I don't think that's something that I would speak too loudly about," I said softly. The night was staring at me again, its glowing eyes the glitter of damp against the tree trunks and the flutter of pale moth wings.

"Alright, maybe not ghosts," she conceded, not sensing my discomfort but rather noting our surroundings with a nod. "But what about aliens, telepaths, the Loch Ness Monster?"

"Let's go for the sea monster," I agreed. "He's not likely to catch a flight and show up here."

She laughed, but I shivered. I could feel someone watching. My eyes traveled over the shadowed terrain. There were dozens of trees to hide behind, clusters of stones that would easily conceal a body, and the roughhewn wall that surrounded the property and cut off the cemetery from the road and neighbors beyond. My gaze traveled to the house that hugged the side of the graveyard. The windows were dark. Doubtless, the girl that lived there was still away at school and her parents likely tucked in their beds. But they could hear us, couldn't they? If we screamed?

"Okay, I'm getting a little cold," I snapped quickly, jarring Anna from her soft mood.

"Oh, well," she slid to her feet somewhat awkwardly.

"Sorry," I said, and pushed my hands through my hair. "My active imagination is making me crazy tonight."

"Sure," she said, but the look she gave me was hesitant. "You want to head out?"

"Yeah, if you don't mind," I agreed, and turned before she really answered me. My hands were cold numb things, but I was fighting not to run. My feet seemed to gain some certainty, and I could see where the end of the path widened into the drive that terminated at the gate where we had entered. The shadow of the trees lumbered over the grounds, smearing in the darkness, and I unconsciously picked up my pace.

"Hold up," Anna called from behind me. "I dropped my phone." She muttered an expletive. I turned to see her kneeling on the damp earth, hands outstretched and skimming over the ground. My eyes skipped between the gate and the figure of my friend huddled in the shadows. I like to think that I would have never left her like that, alone in the dark, that I had the guts to stand by her, but I could honestly not be sure of myself.

I turned back towards her and took a few steps. I could see her pale hands as though they were floating over the darkness of the soil, but I couldn't see so much as a blink of light from the phone. "Where did you drop it?" I asked, forcing my voice to sound less intense.

"Around here. It might have bounced some, but it can't have gone far." She huffed out a breath and sat back on her heels. "I would lose it in the darkest part of the cemetery." She stood, her hands pressed to her forehead. "We need a light or something."

I pulled out my own phone and used the flashlight app that made the camera flash flutter to life. It sent a stream of pure white light over Anna's face, into her squinting eyes, until I hastily directed it toward the ground.

"Good," Anna said eagerly. "Hold it steady. My phone has to be right around here." We both leaned over to look more closely at the ground, and then Anna threw up her hands. "It should have been right here?" The question in her voice made a shiver run down to my fingertips. The search had made me forget my earlier unease, but now it was back, and even more intense.

"Could you have dropped it earlier?" I asked, moving the light to shine behind us, back toward the well.

"I guess I could have, but I could have sworn that I had it! I always keep it in my back pocket. I thought for sure that I remembered feeling for it when I got up from the bench. It's almost like an instinct, you know? I check for my phone, make sure my shirt isn't riding up, nothing stuck to my butt," she laughed lightly at herself.

"Well, it could have fallen out after you walked a little," I said, frowning into the dark. I was really glad she couldn't see my face, because I was sure my expression would betray my fear. I kept the phone light on, directing it toward the ground and then out into the night. The light was fine for walking, but illuminated little beyond our feet as we moved forward.

"Oh, duh," Anna exclaimed, and stopped walking. "You can use your phone to call my number! We can follow the sound!"

I laughed nervously, feeling stupid. "I should have thought of that!"

"Yeah, well, it took me a little while too." Anna turned and smiled. "We would have eventually figured it out."

I turned on the display for my phone and pulled up the keypad. My hands were cold and shaking, more from nerves than temperature. I held out the phone for Anna to dial her number. She took it and bent over the lit face, quickly putting in the sequence and handing it back to me. I pressed the send icon and waited for the familiar buzz. "It's ringing," I said, and tilted my head away from my phone to listen for the corresponding ring in the darkness.

"I hear it," she said, whispering now. "It doesn't sound that close." She moved off, back the way we had come. I followed close behind, holding my phone in front of me for light. We were moving slowly, and I heard the tinny voice over the cell phone that told me that the voicemail had answered. I flipped the phone back to face me and stopped. I found the redial, and listened again until I could hear the buzz. Somewhere off to my left, a strange sound caught my attention. It wasn't a footfall, or a rustle of some woodland creature awakened by the strangers in its midst. It was a soft sliding sound. The sound of something moving across the ground, close but not visible, terrifying and real.

I quickened my pace, my eyes flickering from the dim figure of Anna moving in front of me, to the sound somewhere out in the darkness. My heart added to the mix of noises, and the silly tune of Anna's phone as it called out to her.

And then I saw it. The dim lights of Anna's phone lit up and blinking with each ring. It was just before us, chest high, sounding its last ring before it melted into silence. It was perched on the lip of the stone well.

"How in the world did it get there?" Anna asked softly, reaching out and grabbing the phone before any sound could escape my lips. "I never even came this close."

I stood in silence, my eyes peering into the darkness surrounding us. "I don't know," I said, keeping my voice pitched low. "But it looks like someone put it there."

"Someone?" Her voice was curious. "What do you

mean?"

"You didn't ever stand next to the well. You were sitting on the bench. Someone found your phone and moved it." My mouth was dry as I whispered the words.

Anna cursed softly, one word, and backed away from the well and toward me. "You mean you think that someone is here? Someone is with us?"

I nodded.

"This is a sick joke," she hissed. She gripped my arm with one tight hand and pulled me back.

"I just hope it is a joke," I muttered, and flipped on the light of my phone again. I panned it around us, but the light told us nothing that we didn't already know. There was no one there. No one that we could see, anyway.

"Okay, then I'm done here," Anna said, trying to sound brave, and pulled me along, her long legs eating up the ground. I jogged to keep up but kept close all the same. By the time we made it to the gate, we were moving at a run. Our way was lit now by the street lamps, and the orange glow made the gates shine like they had been dipped in gold edging. And the gate was closed.

"Did we close this?" I asked, standing in front of the double gate and looking blindly at the scrolled words pressed into the metal.

"I don't know." Anna sounded scared now. "I don't think we did. I just remember opening it." She went to the gate and pulled at the latch. It protested loudly as it gaped open, and I looked around as though worried that someone might have been alerted by the noise. "Go on," Anna said in a low voice. "I'm going to close this again."

I stepped through but stayed close and watched as she closed the gate behind us and shoved the latch back in place. We barely paused at the side of the street, standing on the uneven sidewalk. We crossed the empty road at a jog, and then raced up the sidewalk on the other side and through my front yard. My fingers were still shaking as I took out the key, but I managed to shove it into the old lock, and pop the door open. Anna pushed me inside and slammed the door behind us. She leaned her back against the chipped door and put her hand to her chest.

"That's it! That was absolutely terrifying! Who would do that?!"

"Do what?" I said numbly, fingering my phone.

"Well someone snuck in after us," she said, her voice losing some of its fear, and gaining an edge. "Probably some jerk from school. They wanted to scare us, so they came in after us and closed the gate." She paced over to the table in the kitchen and placed her phone on the wooden surface. "Then they must have found my phone and laid it up there so that I would think some ghost or something moved it. There have always been rumors about the place being haunted."

"Why would anyone want to scare us?" I asked, and watched as she prowled to the front window and peered out onto the lit front porch. I was trying to ignore the comment about the haunted cemetery. I wasn't ready to even think about that just now.

"Why not?" She turned. "If they had just found us there, they probably thought it would be really funny to spook us out."

I nodded slowly. "Just a prank," I said softly.

"Yeah, sure. And they are probably laughing their asses off now. We took off out of there so fast, I'm surprised we didn't leave a trail behind us." Her voice was gaining some of its confidence. "Crap, Tori, we were running by the time we made it to the gate. We probably did look pretty funny."

I forced a smile. "We were really moving," I said, and dropped to the kitchen chair. "In fact, you were pulling me along so fast, I think my feet barely hit the ground!"

"Yep, we are brave," she returned, but she was grinning now.

"Okay, so maybe not so brave, but at least we didn't wet ourselves," I said insistently.

She started to giggle, and I felt my muscles ease as I smiled back. She looked at me with my hands at my hips in a hint of defiance and began laughing harder. I soon joined her and all my nerves poured out in a stream of laughter. Soon, the tears were rising in our eyes as we subsided into a wash of laughter.

Chapter 5

Three hours later, with two brownies polished off, we sat on the couch in the living room and switched off the television. The reception was terrible and cable, with hundreds of television channels and a hefty bill, was just a dream for my sister and me. Liz had returned an hour ago and retreated to her room. Her greeting was satisfyingly sleepy and content, and I waved her to bed after she dropped her shoes by the stairs and locked the door behind her. I had warned Anna not to say anything of our cemetery adventure, and she had agreed without questions, although I could see the lingering curiosity in her eyes.

"You know, there really aren't ghosts out there," Anna said, looking at me, her expression a little concerned. "I don't want you thinking that this happens all the time. This was just a really bad joke."

"I know that," I agreed, but my voice wasn't nearly as certain as I wanted it to be. I sat up taller and pushed my hair back. "I don't believe in all that spiritual stuff anyway," my mind went blank when I tried to think of a better term.

"Yeah, and if we did have spirits, I really doubt they are cell phone savvy. I mean, there are a few old stories about ghosts around here, but none of them have been proven," she said, and reached behind her to tug an old afghan off the back of the couch. I watched her for a moment as she spread the afghan around her. My mind was caught on the idea. Ghost stories? I hadn't really thought of looking up any existing legends to see if they would shed light on my problem.

"What kinds of ghost stories have you heard?" I was

unwillingly interested but covering with my finely honed pretense of nonchalance.

She pulled the blanket closer. "Well, the best known one is the one about the bride."

That sounded like a safe one for me. The visitor that I had felt certainly hadn't felt like a young woman. The voice had been male. Even at a whisper, I could swear to that.

"We used to tell each other stories when we were kids, just to see who would freak out first and turn the lights on," she confessed. "See, the bride was a young woman who lived around here, right across from Floydsburg Cemetery. It was during the Civil War, and she had two gentlemen vying for her hand in marriage," she laughed, "at least, that's the way my grandma put it. She must have been quite a catch at the time. The bride, I mean, and I think her family was pretty important in the community. Of course, the community was pretty damn small too. Anyway, she couldn't choose which of the guys she wanted to marry," Anna hesitated, her eyes traveling to the windows as though she was thinking of the night. "Then they went off to war, both of her men, and with the circumstances, she thought that her troubles would be taken care of." She shrugged.

"That sounds a little brutal," I commented, and Anna nodded in agreement.

"Unfortunately for her, both of the men returned from battle, so the decision was hers to make. She couldn't get out of it this time. And she chose one of the men. But the other guy didn't take the news well and came to her home and killed her the night before the wedding ceremony could take place."

"Oh," I winced. I had suspected that was where the story was headed. "What about the guy she was going to marry?"

"I don't know about him. I guess he wasn't the most interesting part of the story. But the legend says that the bride was killed in her bedroom, which overlooks the cemetery just across the street." She lowered her voice and intoned the next words in a whispered rush, "And now she walks in the cemetery in her wedding gown."

"Ha! You're funny," I said flatly.

Anna laughed and raised her eyebrows. "It's a good story though, don't you think?"

"Yeah, okay, pretty good. And you said she lived over here?"

"Well close," Anna said, her eyes wandering to the window again.

"And which house was that?"

Anna chuckled. "It's on this side of the street, but a couple houses down. It really doesn't look like much of a haunted house these days. And the people who live around here say the story about the ghost isn't true, or at least, none of them have seen her."

It was a good story. The kind I would have liked to tell when I was 12 and feeling full of myself. It was the perfect story to tell at a slumber party with a bunch of preteen girls, a little creepy, very sad. But I knew that it had nothing to do with my problems, and I was equally sure that what had happened to us out in the cemetery hadn't been the bride's fault.

"I'm not sure I believe in ghosts like that," I said, trying to avoid looking into the empty blackness out the windows.

Anna didn't comment, but looked thoughtful. After a moment, she gave in to some of her questions.

"You didn't want your sister to know about tonight, did you?" She asked, whispering as she glanced towards the stairs. "Is it because of the ghost?"

"No, no that's not it," I responded, and rubbed a hand over my tired eyes. "I don't like her to worry, and since my parents are gone, she wants to act like a mother instead of a sister. She has enough to worry about as it is." I smiled wryly. "I don't really think she believes in ghosts either, but she does want to watch out for me, and I have to be careful about what I do. If she knew I was out running around in the dark, she'd have something to say about it. She just can't adjust to the fact that we're not in the big city anymore."

Anna looked thoughtful and slightly sad. "So, are you and your sister just going to live here for a little while and go back to Chicago, or do you think that you'll stay longer?" She tried to sound casual, but there was an underlying seriousness in her tone.

"We're planning on staying," I replied. "Liz has a good job, and we've gotten a substantial reduction in price for the house. It was in such bad shape, I think they were just grateful to have a buyer. They wanted it sold fast. As soon as we get a little more money, we're going to do some work on the place."

"Oh, well, it's nice the way it is," Anna said, glancing around. She was trying to be kind, I knew that, and I also knew that she was being way too generous in her assessment.

"It's fine in the dark, but close to a disaster when you really look at it. The roof is okay, patched at least, but it needs new siding or at least a paint job. The basement leaks in one corner, so we'll have to address that first. And the whole place needs new paint inside, the floors refinished, and lots of work outside."

Anna sighed. "It is a pretty area, though. And I know that houses around here don't come up for sale often."

"So I've heard," I said, almost to myself. "But we want to make this place look decent, like some of the other houses. We figure if we take our time, we can get everything done."

Anna nodded her understanding. "But don't worry too much. This house has been in slow decline for a while. The lady that lived here just couldn't keep it up."

I nodded. "I met her. Did you know that she lived in the retirement village where I deliver for Blythe?"

"Really?" Anna sounded surprised, so I guessed that the small town rumor mill had broken down somewhere along the way.

"She said that she lived here all her life. And she knew that she wasn't able to maintain it, but it was really hard for her to think of moving."

"I guess I could see that. She probably knew most of her neighbors, was comfortable with the house."

"She was, and she wanted to stay as long as she could. She said her family wanted her to move but she wouldn't agree. Then she fell in the basement and broke her hip. She was stranded down there for a whole day until she could get help. After that, she had to agree to move. I'm guessing at that point she wasn't able to do any repairs, so the place hit the market 'as is' which probably accounts for the decrease in price."

"And the ghost," Anna said, grinning.

"The what?"

Anna looked suddenly uncomfortable, her smile melting off her face quickly. "Oh, I shouldn't have said anything. There are ghost stories about most of these houses, and it's stupid to mention it."

"You started it," I said, but forced a smile. "Besides, I really don't believe in ghosts anyway, in spite of how, um, fast we left the cemetery. I'm not going to get scared off by some old rumor used to keep kids off the lawn."

She looked doubtful. "After getting so freaked in the cemetery, maybe another story isn't a good idea."

"It's fine," I returned, and shrugged. "I like hearing old legends. It gives a place character. Besides, I've never been much of a believer in the supernatural."

She was frowning slightly, but I could tell that she really wanted to tell the story. I knew she was perfectly satisfied with the idea that some teenager had been pulling a prank on us. And perhaps a few months ago I could have agreed with her. But things were different for me now. I knew something of ghosts, even if that wasn't really what my intruder was. I knew that someone was getting into my house, going through some of my things, and leaving before I could ever figure out how he could accomplish that.

But it wasn't that I really believed that my current problems had anything to do with an old ghost story that predated Mrs. Lucy and her immediate family. I just wanted to know what had been said about the place, and I really wanted to hear the story from another point of view. I knew from Mrs. Lucy that she believed that someone had broken into her home. But I also knew that she wasn't sure what to believe, if it were a real intruder, or something of the more spiritual sort. She had apparently heard all of the old ghost stories herself, and put little stock in them. But the word of one older lady wasn't enough to go on at this point, especially since I believed that the visits had never stopped.

"So spill," I said, stuffing a pillow behind my back and tucking the blanket in around my feet.

"The story is about the family that lived here, but it must have been before Lucy Knox moved in." Anna paused and pulled her blanket up more firmly, tucking it under her chin.

"There was a family with two kids that lived here just after the place was built. The grandfather also moved in, and he had one of the rooms on the top floor. But he wasn't here all of the time. He was a traveler and professor somewhere, and he went on long trips all over the world and would come back with great stories to tell but I think everyone agreed that he was a little strange. Obsessive, maybe. He was one of those really adventurous men, they say, but, too passionate. He was interested in other cultures, other religions, and ceremonies, rituals. He had gone all over the world, but when he got older he settled somewhere overseas for one whole winter, and when he came home in the spring, he said that he wasn't traveling anymore. He was staying in the upper room in this house, keeping to himself, and he wasn't talking to the kids anymore, or his daughter and son in law. He had changed, and it wasn't a good change. He just stayed in the room, and the light stayed on all night long. Or I guess it would have been a candle, because they wouldn't have had electricity at that time. The family worried. He stopped coming down for dinner; he slept all the time. Then, one day, he just never woke up."

I looked at her carefully. I really didn't want to ask which room was his, in fear that it was the one that I now inhabited, but surely there was more to the story. I could hardly believe that such an anti-climactic death would result in a rumored haunting. "And," I said frowning.

"And that very night, the night that the old man died, the youngest kid in the family, a little boy, disappeared. He was never heard from again. But they said that the old man could be seen out walking the grounds and in the house, years later even, looking for the boy."

"And that's it?" I asked, disappointment coloring my voice.

"Yes, no, well mostly. The story goes on, but I'm sure the last part isn't true." Anna was twisting a lock of hair with her fingers, thoughtful.

"And what's that?" I prodded.

"Some said that the old man wasn't really a ghost at all. He was real. They said he kept coming to the house and wrecking it. He would turn over furniture; knock things off the walls, empty out drawers. He was looking for something."

"For what?" I asked.

"No one knows. Something to bring his grandson back?"

"Back from where?"

"From wherever he ended up. But that's a problem; no one knows where he ended up."

I sat up and sighed. "It's a sad story, but there are too many gaps. If the boy and the old man were both dead, why did the old man come back at all?" My eyes strayed to the window where I half expected to see a face pressed against the rippled pane of glass.

"I told you it was a stupid story," she said dismissively. "There really wasn't a good ending to it. And I don't know how true it is. I just thought it was creepy, you know, some old guy walking around looking for the little boy."

"Yeah," I agreed, "could be a little creepy."

"Speaking of creepy," she interrupted, "Do you want to hear a better one."

"Sure," I responded, and summoned up some enthusiasm. "This is kind of interesting."

"Are you sure?" She turned and shifted against the pillows.

"Yeah, but this time, let's make it about someone else's house," I teased.

"Okay, it's a deal," she agreed.

"So what's the next story about?"

"How about the one I heard," she said quietly, her voice dropping again into that spooky whisper, "about a place down the road in La Grange?"

*****

I felt it before I heard it. The soft slither of cloth against a slick surface, the brush of skin against skin. I knew immediately that he was there. Somewhere in the dark folds of the night he was moving and searching, looking for something or someone. I sat still in the center of my bed so quiet that I forgot to breathe. He was just outside my door. I knew just the sound when weight was placed on that single board that emitted that tell-tale squeak. I knew to avoid that board when I prowled the house in the dark, but he didn't. He couldn't. He was just a ghost, a spoiled figment of my imagination. Right? Wrong, my brain protested, and I swung my bare legs over the side of the bed and let the soles of my feet skim the wooden surface of the floor. I moved just slowly enough, balancing my weight so that the floor wouldn't tell on me. At the side of my bed was my tennis racquet, unused for the last several years except as part of my self-defense. I took it and wrapped my chilled fingers around the worn handle. I was dressed in soft knit shorts and a tank top, and wished I had thought to wear something more appropriate for this possible confrontation. I moved to the door in silence and stopped at the doorway listening through the panels. Nothing. No sigh of sound, no footfalls, no breath. But I knew he was out there and he was close.

I opened the door very slowly. I had deliberately oiled the hinges only two days before, and now it opened silently. My bare feet were a quiet brush against the old wood, but even that sounded loud to my ears. The wind was a hush of movement outside, and small stinging droplets of rain made a patter on the windows. At least it was warmer. The cool of March had heated to the warmth of April, bringing with it the rain and the damp. I moved soundlessly down the stairs and stopped at the base. Was that a breeze? I walked to the side of the stairway and looked back toward the kitchen. In the dim light, I could see the black outline of a door gaping ajar. It was the basement. Any owners had long ago judged the basement to be uninhabitable, and so it served as a storage space, a laundry room, a sort of workshop with a high rough wood tool bench, and a tiny room that had once been used to store coal for the furnace. The poured concrete floors were uneven and patched in places with multiple cracks that gaped just enough for a sprinkle of earth to seep through with the heavy rain.

I walked to the head of the black stairway and smelled the scent of fresh earth and wet concrete. I knew that I hadn't left the door open. We never left the door open because it obstructed the walkway between the other rooms. Besides, we were only down there to do laundry, and between the two of us, we really only did the wash on the weekend when time permitted. In truth,

Liz had taken over that chore and insisted on leaving tidy stacks of my clothes on my unmade bed despite the fact that I wasn't likely to ever put them in the drawers where they belonged.

But now the door was open, and that very fact beckoned me to go down into the darkness and explore. Was he down there? I had no way of knowing, but it seemed unlikely that the open door was an accident. It was like the hundreds of horror movies I had seen where the foolish girl follows the killer into the darkened room only to discover that he was indeed waiting for her, butcher knife at the ready, mask neatly in place.

So I decided to err on the part of safety. Forget bravery. I went into the kitchen and found the huge flashlight that we had bought for the frequent power outages that came with spring storms. I hefted it and felt the sturdy weight of its metal body pleasing in my hand. I wasn't about to bring down a butcher knife from the kitchen. I had seen those movies enough to know that that would not be a wise move. The flashlight would have to be enough.

I crept down the stairs, flashlight held high in one hand, my fingers skimming the wall with the other. There was no railing on either side, just the rough texture of unfinished drywall that someone had hastily erected when they had decided to make use of the space. At the bottom, my feet felt the stark difference between the unfinished wood and the concrete. I panned the light around the space before me, noting the squat square windows that butted up against the ceiling and provided an exit into the darkened lawn beyond. But they were all closed, and had been that way for years if the accumulated dust on the sills gave any clues.

The basement was cut up into several smaller rooms with the unfinished drywall, in some places revealing studs behind the wall and supporting its weight. There was a bare bulb hung from the ceiling in each room; in the main room it was accessible by an actual light switch at the base of the stairs. In all the other rooms, I had to walk into the center of the room to pull the string that hung just above my head to turn on the light. In the tiny coal bin, the pull chain was a short two inches and seemed almost impossible to find in the darkness. At the base of the stairs, my fingers traced the wall, scrambling for the switch.

The bulb lit up, harsh and white in the grey room. Our boxes were balanced on rubberized totes that held most of our household goods that we hadn't had time to unpack. For the most part, our things were still tidy and easy to maneuver around. The basement floor occasionally puddled after a hard rain, so everything stored in the basement had to be either suspended away from the floor or in a water tight container.

In the laundry room, the floor had remained dry. The washer and dryer were from my parents' own apartment, and were oddly modern in the battered surroundings. Three baskets of dirty laundry were shoved up under one window but undisturbed. After shining the light into the room, I followed and switched on the overhead bulb. Nothing. Even the dust motes seemed mostly frozen in the still air.

Next was another storage area, mostly empty but for the huge old tool bench made from barn wood. Stacked on the rough surface were a few of our tools and a small red toolbox my dad had given me when I was twelve and told him that I wanted to build a birdhouse.

When the light flickered on, the shadows under the tool bench showed in black relief. I shook my head, panning the flashlight beneath, and breathed a sigh. This room was empty as well. It only left the tiny coal bin with the sloped ceiling. We had left the awkward space empty, but the previous owners had lined most of the walls with makeshift shelves to hold their accumulated clutter. Now the shelves were empty. But there was something in that dark, something in the utter closeness of the space that I didn't like, and I tended to avoid the room even on the brightest days. And tonight, with no moon coming through the bare windows in the outer room, I wasn't going any further. In the squat doorway, I shined my light beam among the shelving, but did not step in. The place was too small to hold anyone, even if they had wanted to hide.

And it occurred to me then that I had been fooled. He had been there, no doubt about it. And I had followed him into the basement like a gullible fool. I hadn't even entertained the idea that he was leading me on. And why would I? What possible reason would he have to make me want to go down in the basement? A reason that I really didn't care for slipped into my mind. I could think of one thing, and it sent random shivers over my exposed skin. If he had wanted to keep me there, either with him, or without, he could easily close the basement door and keep it that way. Chances were the windows would be painted shut after so many years of neglect, and I would be trapped down here.

I quickly turned away from the dark coal bin and hurried on cold feet into the main room of the basement. The light still shone brightly in the laundry room and the main storage room, so I couldn't immediately tell if the door was open at the head of the stairs. I held my heavy flashlight, unlit for now, above my head as though to bludgeon the first person who came into my path. I felt foolish standing like that, but not so much that I was going to lower the light. With cautious steps, I slipped

My breath slipped out in a huff of frustration and not just a little fear. I hadn't seen anyone down there with me, but there were plenty of obstacles to hide behind. It would be easy for someone to sneak down the steps and slip behind a stack of box-es. With my heart beating hard and heavy in my throat, I backed up to the stairs and placed a tentative foot on the bottom step. Keeping my one hand wrapped firmly around the heavy flash-light and my other against the wall for balance, I carefully stepped up to the next stair, pausing at each to look up toward the closed door and down to the basement.

At the top I stopped. Either the intruder had tried to block me in and then fled through whatever egress he had en-tered from, or he was lying in wait for me on the other side of the door. I now doubted that he had ever even entered the basement. The open door had been a ruse to get me to go down there, thus giving him the freedom to explore the house any way that he pleased.

Liz. Her name came to my lips as my hand closed around the cool metal of the knob. Liz was upstairs, probably in a deep sleep, unaware again of any disturbances happening just below her. Or was she? What if he had finally decided to stop the game? What if he had come for my sister, and while I was wan-dering the basement, had hurt her? Or worse. The knob turned easily and without thinking of the possibility of the stranger hid-ing just beyond the door, I threw it open and rushed into the tight hallway space. The house was just as sleepy silent as before. I closed the basement door behind me, leaving the lights glaring under the crack of the door, slipped back to the main room, and hurried up the stairs, careless of the noise I was making. My sister's door was closed but for a tiny gap that revealed a sliver of flickering blue light. I put my hand on the knob and pushed, slowly, slowly, until I could see in the room.

My sister was lying on her side, the blankets pulled up around her throat, her hair spread out around her. The cold light from the muted television cast an eerie glow. Her face was turned toward the door, and when I opened it, her eyes blinked open, a look of blank confusion that only deep sleep brings.

It's okay," I murmured, and backed out of the room, closing the door completely behind me. My eyes unexpectedly filled with tears of relief. I could only handle so much, so much fear, so much loss. I wiped at my cheeks with the heel of my hand and slumped a little, leaning against the cool plaster wall. After a moment, I heard my sister flop back on the bed, and knew she would soon be sleeping soundly again. My mother had always teased and said that my sister could sleep through anything, and for that I was grateful.

I returned to the first floor and stopped by the curtained window, slowly pulling back the heavy fabric to look out into the night. The rain had let up into a fine mist. It made the streetlamps glitter against the damp pavement. The lights of Duncan Memorial showed warmly. The cooler light of the moon was hidden by the thick clouds that promised more rain.

I leaned forward and squinted. There. There was a movement out there by the side of the road. They weren't in the Cemetery itself, but on the rock wall surrounding it. A figure of a person, long limbed, dressed in dark clothes that shadowed against the lighter stone.

"Got you," I said, teeth clenched. My jacket was hung on a hook by the back door, and my shoes were carelessly dropped beneath. My purse hung from the hook, my sister's attempt at being organized, and my phone was tucked in the outer pocket. I pulled out the phone, slipped on the jacket, and shoved the phone in one of the voluminous pockets. The flashlight went into the other as I slipped my bare feet into the tennis shoes I normally wore for work.

It was crazy, but I knew I couldn't stop now. I went into the front room and quietly pulled open the door, stepping out into the night.

Chapter 6

I crossed the empty street, my shoes silent on the pavement. I felt a satisfying burst of confidence, that somehow my ability to sneak up on my unsuspecting target was giving me a power that I hadn't previously had. In spite of this, I kept my hand firmly clenched around the flashlight in my pocket. I wasn't that much of an idiot.

He saw me when I reached the sidewalk. I could see his pale face turn in my direction, and a subtle stiffening of his frame. He was actually sitting atop the rock wall, his knees at the level of my chest, his face almost lost in shadow above me. I didn't step close but stopped a few feet away.

"What the hell were you doing breaking into my house?" My voice was nice and firm, and I felt tough, proud of myself for a moment. "I've called the cops," I lied, still standing well out of his reach. "You're not going to get away with this harassment."

He slid in one fluid motion off the wall and took one step closer to where I was standing. "Break into your house? I have no idea what you are talking about." His voice was mild, but his words were crisp. If I hadn't been positive someone had just been in my house, I would have believed him.

"You know exactly what I'm talking about," I bit off the words and forced myself not to take a step back.

"I don't," he responded. He pulled his hands from his jacket pocket and crossed his arms over his chest, starting to look annoyed.

For the first time I felt a twinge of doubt. Sure, someone had been in my house just a few minutes ago, but I had no proof that this was the guy. The fact that he was so close to my house, and outside at this time of night, might not have spoken well for his character, but it certainly didn't prove anything.

"Okay, so why are you out here then," I challenged, continuing to stay just out of arms reach.

"I was out for a walk." He looked over me then, his eyes going from my tangled hair to my bare legs under the too large jacket.

"And I have to say, I think I have a better excuse than you for being out here. Are you sure you didn't just have some kind of nightmare?"

That cut a little too close to what my sister had said, and I bristled. "I didn't have a nightmare. Someone was walking around in my house. They went all through the first floor and opened the door to the basement." I looked at him closely, my face feeling hot but forcing myself to meet his eyes. "And I think it was you."

He shrugged. "I've been out here for the last half hour." His eyes slid behind me to where my house hunched in the darkness. "I haven't seen anyone coming out of the house except you. No lights either. And I certainly haven't been wandering around in your house." His eyes went back to me. "Besides, what reason would I have to break into a stranger's house? And then be stupid enough to stand outside and watch."

A breeze blew the damp air around my legs and I shivered. I was beginning to get the feeling that I had made a big mistake on this one. True, I had never gotten a close look at the man who was breaking into my house, I had only heard the whisper of a voice, but I felt sure that I would know him if I met him again. Despite finding this guy sitting in the graveyard just across from my house in the middle of the night, I now doubted that he had anything to do with the break in. But I couldn't admit to that. I wouldn't let my guard down, just in case I was wrong about this.

"What are you doing here, then?" I asked my voice a little too loud.

"Sitting." He backed up and leaned against the wall. I had a childish hope that he would get his jeans wet in the process. He just looked too comfortable for my liking, and I was angry, angry at myself for missing the intruder, for being afraid, and for making a fool out of myself.

"You know, the cemetery is private property."

He smiled. It made him look younger, a little closer to the boy next door, but still not completely innocent. "I know. My friends live around here. I'm just visiting." He looked at me, his head cocked slightly. "I'm Drew." He actually held out his hand as though he thought I'd shake it.

I looked at his hand as though it were something totally nasty and stood my ground. He withdrew his hand and shoved it back in his pocket.

"Who are your friends?"

He shrugged and leaned back against the wall. "Thomas and Thea." He looked toward the house nestled close to the side of the cemetery, the windows dark and still.

"Doesn't ring a bell," I said coldly. I couldn't swear he was lying, but the names didn't sound familiar.

"Thea," he said patiently, "lives there. Her real name is Dorothy. She lives with her parents. Thomas is my friend. They are both away at school right now," his voice was soft, his words slow, like he was explaining something to a child.

The name Dorothy did sound familiar. There weren't many with that name in my age bracket. I remembered Anna talking about the girl, saying that she was a friend, and mentioning that she was in college. Of course, just because he knew her name didn't mean he was telling the truth. But then again, I could check if I wanted to. And why would he lie?

He frowned, seeing my expression. "Look, believe what you want. It's not my job to prove anything to you. I'm sorry that you've been having bad dreams, but there wasn't anyone breaking into your house that I could see, and it sure as hell wasn't me." He glanced down the darkened road. "And if the cops do come, like you said they would, I'll tell them the same thing."

His frustrated pose, tall and stiff, hands out and fisted by his sides suddenly struck me as familiar. I had seen him before. And looking over to the old house next to the cemetery, I was suddenly sure I knew from where. I had seen him arguing with the blond guy on the porch that day, the blond guy that seemed to glow every time I saw him. My problem, not his, I reminded my-self.

"You were over at that house a few weeks ago," I said softly, aloud although I wasn't really expecting an answer. "You were talking with another guy."

"That was Thomas. Yes, that's what I told you."

I shook my head slowly. "Okay, so Thomas is your friend?"

"From forever. From elementary school. I was in school with both him and Daniel." His face took on a pained expression, his eyes narrowing and his lips tightening as though he wished he could bite the words back.

"Daniel?"

"That was Thomas' twin. He died just about a year ago." He turned away, his dark eyes wide, and I saw that his eyes caught the light, like there were tears lingering just behind his lids. He blinked and ran a hand over his face, and I was sure I was wrong. Only I cried in public, standing in the dark, no rea-son beyond the sheer awfulness of my life.

But just in case, "I'm sorry," I said softly. I blew out a breath and made a decision. "I'm Tori. Victoria. My sister and I live in the house just across the way, and we have actually had an intruder who has come into the house. I knew I heard someone walking around, and when I came down to look, there was no one still in the house. But when I looked outside, there you were. I just assumed that it was you."

"So you're serious? You think someone is breaking into your house? Have you actually called the cops?"

"No," I said quickly. "I haven't been able to prove it, and I don't want to raise a stink. I sort of made that part up in case you were the one."

He looked at me, his frown apparent in the dim light. "That's dangerous. You need to let someone know about a home invasion. What about your parents?"

I felt the familiar jolt, and shoved my hands deeper in my pockets, waiting for the stab of pain that radiated from my head and directly to my heart to go away. "I live with my sister. My parents are dead." It hurt so much to say the words.

"Oh." He paused, his face lowered so I couldn't see his expression. But he didn't say he was sorry. He just looked at me gravely. "Have you talked to your sister?"

"Yeah, sure." I stopped, my eyes down, avoiding his gaze. For some reason, I didn't want him to think that I was crazy, delusional. I wanted him to look at me like he believed me. I waited a long moment until a gust of wind threw a spatter of collected raindrops down on my head. I hunched my shoulders and tried not to show how chilled I had become in the damp night.

"Look, you're freezing. Why don't you go on in? I'll be out here for a little longer. If I see someone skulking around, I'll come to your door and knock."

I looked up at him, noticing how tall he was, standing there in the dark. It would be nice to feel like I had someone else helping me, someone backing me up. It seemed ridiculous that it would be someone that I had just accused of being the invader, but it felt right.

"Sure, great." I ducked my head in an automatic nod. "Thanks." I turned quickly and looked toward my house.

"Tori," Drew said, stepping forward slightly.

I looked at him questioning.

"Never mind," he mumbled, and I walked away. At the porch, I turned around and saw him standing still. He waved a hand, and I realized he could still see me. He must have had really good night vision because the porch was very dark, very quiet. I used the key in the lock, and shoved the door open with a shoulder, hoping the sound wouldn't wake Liz. But all was silent, and when I made my patrol around the house checking locks and lights, I saw nothing amiss. When I checked out the window again, I was surprised to see Drew still there, but I closed the curtains without acknowledging him or turning on a light so he could see me.

I slept in my jacket and shoes, an uneasy rest full of dreams of strangers, of identical twins who cried in the dark, tow headed boys who seemed to emit their own light.

*****

The next morning I lay in bed and looked up at the ceiling. In general, my life had taken on a reassuring rhythm that I had started to take for granted. That is, before last night. It had been weeks since someone had invaded our space, weeks since I had felt the electric fission of fear climb down my spine. With the absence of fear I had found some comfort. I had settled into my job with Blythe, the routine of late morning rising and deliveries, baking lessons, and the stern mothering that Blythe just couldn't seem to resist. She wasn't obvious about it. It was just the frequent doggie bags of dinners that seemed to appear next to my purse at the end of my shift, or the unexpected tune up of my car as it was parked in the back lot by one of her sons. It was the reminder of traffic snarls in the little town, and the caution of where it was best to shop, to get a cheap haircut, and to get good produce. She just wanted me safe and satisfied in my new life, I knew that now, and was finding it much easier to accept her gifts. With an effort, I smothered the temptation to bristle and learned the value of holding my tongue and accepting some help gracefully.

But that was all changed. My life had been disrupted by the ugly truth of the situation. Despite the long absence of my nemesis, he was still out there, still eager to explore my home, and still searching for something. My first urge was to go to the retirement home. As ridiculous as it was, I really liked being able to visit the older ladies, and there was something of a release when I could be honest with someone. And they believed me. Mrs. Lucy, while older, was no one's fool. She knew the truth of my story because she had lived it.

But there was really nothing that either of them could do for me. They were confined by their living conditions and the sheer frailty that came with time. Their advice was great, but they wouldn't be able to help me physically if it came to that, and I was determined to protect my sister, even if she was being a pain in the ass sometimes.

I slipped out of bed and grabbed my phone. Craigslist had its own app, and even though I knew my sister would kill me if she ever found out, I used it to search for my first line of defense. In the section under pets were dozens of adoptable mongrels that needed a home, and many were cheap or free. I paged back through listing after listing, rejecting the small, the old, and the lazy. I wanted a sharp dog that would put fear into the heart of the evil doer, and if the evil doer was breaking into my house, I wanted a dog that would bite the hell out of him.

I narrowed my search down to some of the surrounding cities. Louisville proper was just a quick 20 minutes down the road, one reason why the towns of Crestwood and Pewee Valley had grown to be so popular as bedroom communities for the larger city. Southern Indiana was just over the river, with its own thriving businesses. The listings for the area held literally hundreds of dogs waiting to be placed. I settled for two different entries.

The first showed a picture of some monster mutt that looked like a cross between a lab and some other thicker, tougher breed. It had the gentle eyes of the lab, but the ears were shorter and the smile just a shade broader. Its parentage could have been almost anything, and I doubted anyone would actually know what had fathered the beast. But the description was what sold me on the dog as a possible choice. He was a nine-month-old male pup named Jeffrey, who was full of energy, gentle with children, and protective of his family. The owners claimed that they could no longer care for him due to a new baby due in the summer, and they wanted a good home for him. I figured I could provide that, and emailed the post to find out more about the dog.

The second candidate didn't look quite so large, but it was hard to tell from the photo. He had long shaggy hair that hid his eyes, but the post claimed that he didn't shed, which would go a far way with my sister when I began to argue for the dog. He too had a doggie smile and a lighter patch of white on his chest which was the only thing that broke up the black of his coat. He also was under a year, a neutered male, who was good with children, but only those over three who wouldn't be knocked down accidently. He had rudimentary training, and like the other dog, was fully housetrained. I wrote a note for him as well and sent it from my phone.

That completed, I got dressed and headed out the door for work. I had a good reason for wanting to be early. I wanted to make sure I could catch Blythe before the lunch rush to get some information. Despite what I had said the night before, I wanted to know just who Drew was and how he might be involved in the trouble surrounding my house.

*****

To my surprise, Blythe immediately knew who I was referring to when I mentioned meeting Drew the night before. I conveniently left out the part about the late night and the break in. Instead, I glossed over the story, saying that I was out for a walk and met him by the street.

"Sure, I know Drew," she agreed, wiping her hands on the ever present towel over her shoulder. "He's a friend of Dot's."

"Dot is Dorothy, right? And Drew called her Thea. It's getting confusing."

"A stage she went through," Blythe said with a smile. "But I've known her all of her life."

"Have you known Drew long?"

She looked at me, her eyes squinted in thought. "For over a year, I guess. He was involved in that terrible accident. The one where Thomas was hurt and his brother…" she drifted off.

"His brother," I prodded.

"Thomas' twin brother was killed in the accident. Thomas was in a coma for a long time. Drew was the only one who walked away."

I let out a puff of air, shocked. "Drew was in the accident with the twins?" I asked.

She looked at me frowning. "How did you know they were twins?"

I realized how my statement sounded and explained how Drew had mentioned the brothers, but had said nothing about being in the accident, or what had actually happened to Thomas' brother, Daniel.

"He doesn't like to talk about it," Blythe said softly. "It was hard on all of them."

I waited for a moment to see if she would elaborate. When she remained silent, I asked, "But Drew wasn't hurt at all?"

"No," she said softly. "At least not physically injured. He was torn up about it, though, and came into town to try to work through some of it. He's been coming by every so often since then."

"He's not from here?" I had gotten the impression from Drew the night before that he was part of the small town.

"Oh, no. Both he and Thomas live up in Cincinnati. They used to come into Louisville for visits, but they haven't ever lived here. But the accident happened not far from here." She frowned. "I'm not sure why Drew chose to come here. I know that Thomas came by to meet with Dot, but that was after Drew had come and gone. Dot said she had met both of the boys when they were in for a visit. But that was before the accident."

"Strange that Drew would be here before Thomas," I said softly. "How long has he been living here?"

"I don't really know," Blythe said thoughtfully. "He seems to come and go. He's not in school right now, but he is working."

"Where?" The question was out before I realized I was going to ask it.

"He does odd jobs. He does some lawn work and handyman jobs for the Parish. He also has a part time job with some guys who are doing interior/exterior painting. For now, he's a jack of all trades."

I nodded, but my mind was still caught on the original question. Why had Drew come to the little town, even before his best friend had? What did he want here? And why was he staying? If he hadn't had the odd habit of hanging around the cemetery by my house, I might have dismissed him completely, but now…

*****

When I got home, I had several emails waiting for me. I had seen the information on my phone, but preferred to open them on the computer where I could see the pictures more easily.

The first email was bad news. The dog Jeffrey had found his for-ever home, and was no longer available. Good news for Jeffrey, not so good for me. The second dog, whose name I hadn't seen yet, was still available, and several pictures were enclosed. Most of the photos were action shots with the dog catching a ball, tear-ing through powdered snow in a little yard, or perching on a tiny front porch looking hopefully in a window. His hair was in vari-ous stages of disorder, some looking like an overgrown terrier, others like a monster poodle. But beggars can't be choosers, so I called the listed phone number and arranged to meet them in one of the many neighborhoods by Fern Creek on the outskirts of Louisville. We agreed to an afternoon, and I chose a location by the interstate, a Kroger shopping center where I would feel com-fortably safe.

In truth, I wanted that dog. I wanted something besides myself to be on the watch, and even if the thing would just bark, it would be better than what I was facing now. It was sad to ad-mit that I was dreading the night. I hated when the sun started to set in a rainbow of reds, pinks, and golds. My sister's presence was reassuring for only as long as she was awake, but once she had retired to her bedroom, I felt abandoned all over again, cold and too alone. I checked the windows, and then checked them again. I barricaded the doors with heavy furniture, and pulled out a can of hairspray with the vague notion that if someone came at me, I could spray them with the blinding liquid, or set it afire with a lighter. I would probably burn the whole house down with that stunt, but it was reassuring all the same.

I picked up Anna from the high school the next day. I had worked early and hard all morning to make sure that Blythe could spare both of us for a few precious hours. Anna was my navigator, and being an animal lover, was also my cheerleader for this expedition. She thought that buying a dog was a great idea, and despite her ignorance for my real reason, she even mentioned that the dog would make me feel safer at night. I knew she was avoiding mentioning the chances of ghosts, and although dogs were known to be more sensitive to the paranor-mal, it was real live spooks that I hoped to scare away.

The drive was a fast 20 minutes with the traffic on the 841 moving like each car was going for its personal best high speed. I didn't know where everyone was going in such a hurry, but it was obvious that if you wanted to get there fast, this was the route to take. I was happy to get off on the Bardstown Road exit and join the normal traffic. As I turned into the parking lot, Anna asked hopefully if we could stop and get a soft drink.

"Depends if you mind sharing with a puppy," I teased.

"Dog germs are not a problem for me," she assured me, and grinned.

We pulled through a fast food window to get drinks, and then went on to the parking lot to wait. It wasn't hard to find the car with the dog. They had already pulled over their first generation Volkswagen Bug and were standing outside. The woman was rather pale with thin features, blond hair, and a big smile. The man looked like he hadn't smiled for a very long time. Inside the Bug was a large fuzzy shape that was pacing the back seat, alternately putting huge paws on the windows, and licking the glass with a long pink tongue.

"Man, I thought you weren't going to show," the man said, his voice relieved. "Here's his leash. I have his bed and his food in the back. He eats from a partitioned bowl so he won't choke himself." He was rattling off information as he thrust a folded leash into my hand and took off to the back of the little car.

"Wait," I called, but to his back because he was moving so fast.

"I'm so glad you're going to give Monty a new home," the woman gushed. Her smile had grown, making her close to pretty. "Dave can't handle a dog this size, but Monty is a great puppy."

Anna had barely gotten out of my car, and no introductions had been made. The woman had stepped back toward her own car, and to my surprise, the man had gone to mine and popped open the back door.

"Well I'm sure Monty is just wonderful," I said breathlessly as I watched the man toss in the last of the dog supplies and slam the door. "But,"

"Here's his paperwork." The woman pushed the folder at Anna, and Anna took it fumbling a bit. I could see by the direction of her gaze that she was fascinated by the happenings within the car. The animal was starting to make some noise. At first it sounded rather like a teapot whistle, all high pitched and whining. But the next sound was a bark, the big booming shout of a large dog who is ready to tear into something or someone.

"Monty, heel," the man ordered over the barking, and opened the door. I expected the bundle of fur to take off out of the car and across the parking lot, flying like a deer into traffic and ending this whole fiasco.

Instead, the beast gingerly set one paw against the pavement and paused to direct his gaze through the heavy curls to the man standing by the door. When a second paw joined the first, the man grabbed the dog's collar and fairly tugged him out of the car. The dog stopped his barking and suddenly seemed to notice our appearance in the scene. A long tail, oddly curved with an obnoxious puff of fur on the end began a ponderous wag.

"Bye, Monty baby," the woman cooed, and smacked a kiss on the fuzzy head as the man pulled him past her.

"Sir," I said, stepping forward, but not in time to stop him from opening up the car door again and throwing something small into my back seat.

"He loves treats," the woman called, and I turned, shocked, to see her climbing into the tiny front seat of the VW.

"But!"

The dog had leapt into my car after the treat and the man slammed the door behind him and was headed back towards his car. "I'd move fast," he said shortly. "When he gets anxious, he chews your seats. Or your shoes. Or the steering wheel. Just depends on where you are really." He had the driver's door open and was folding himself inside when I remembered to close my gaping mouth.

"But," I said weakly and looked at the folded leash in my hands.

I could see the woman waving and smiling through the passenger side window as the car pulled away. I don't think I waved back, but couldn't be sure. It was like a waking dream, and all my mind could think of was what was that thing in my backseat?

Four miles down the street, Anna stopped laughing finally. The dog had lapped up most of her Diet Coke, something I was pretty sure was a really bad idea, and had eaten an old piece of gum he had nosed from the floorboards, wrapping and all. He was all smiles and wagging tail, perched in the middle of the back seat, butt on the seat, front feet on the floor, long neck extended and head with lolling tongue somewhere just next to my right shoulder. Every once in awhile, he would lick my ear and blow out a puff of wet breath on my neck. He licked Anna's face generously, clearing off most of her tears of laughter. If dogs could laugh, I'd think he was doing it with her.

"Sit Monty," I said grimly as he leaned his head against my shoulder.

"He is sitting," Anna replied. "Well, his butt is. The rest of him won't work that way."

I sighed. "Liz is going to kill me. No, she's going to throw me out, and then she's going to kill me."

Anna laughed. "He isn't so bad. We'll give him a bath and trim up his hair." She ran her fingers through the mop of curls on his head. "Then we'll get his bed set up so that by the time she gets home, he'll be all settled in."

"He's a horse," I said under my breath.

"He's tall," Anna agreed. "But he's really not very heavy. It's mostly fur."

"And mouth," I mumbled.

"Sweet boy," she said, and scratched under his chin. "You'll make a good puppy for Tori, won't you?"

His wagging tail swiped at the rear seat and I sighed. "I hope I don't end up regretting this," I said, and glanced at Anna. But she was smiling, and I didn't want to ask what she thought was funny this time.

When I pulled into my driveway, I was relieved to see it empty. It would have been just about the worse day ever for my sister to decide to come home early. We unloaded the dog things first, waiting until the car was empty to usher the dog out and clip on the leash. Whatever hesitation he had shown in the parking lot was gone because he jumped from the car and started sniffing and marking my yard. Every few steps he would raise his leg slightly in attempt at doggy masculinity. When he had checked out the whole front yard, I took him in through the front door and up the steps. Of the two bathrooms, only one had a shower, a one-piece unit that must have been added sometime in the '90s. It took Anna and me our full effort to shove the reluctant dog into the tub, but once the water began to flow, he spent a lot of time licking the moisture from the walls, the faucet, and our hands. He wasn't opposed to licking soap either, which made me worry for his safety and common sense. Once wet, I could see what I had gotten. For the measly price of nothing, beneath all that fur was a lanky animal with protruding bones, more from genetics than diet, and long furry ears. There were mats in his fur, hard tangles close to his pale skin, and he twitched his ears unhappily, but he seemed in pretty good shape overall.

We toweled him off in the shower, going through four full sized bath towels before he was just damp to the touch. When we let him climb from the tub, we were rewarded with our own shower as he vigorously shook.

"Scissors," Anna called out, like a surgeon looking for tools. "And his brush."

I gave her the requested items that she had carefully laid out on the counter, and held his head while she worked. Beneath the long hair in his face, his eyes were large and dark brown. He looked amused. As she trimmed and clucked about his fur, I rubbed his ears, murmured to him, and generally fell in love with him. After a very long time, I let Anna take him out on a leash while I cleaned up the hair. He might not shed, but there was a fair amount of clippings on the floor, and the tub was ringed with dark brown dirt. I scrubbed and wiped up, making sure that the bath looked as it had when we had started. No sense starting the relationship with Liz on a sour note. The less problems she saw with our new roommate, the more she would be willing to tolerate him.

The thrum of a motor, a large, powerful motor, had me looking up and glancing toward the window. A door slam and Anna's voice filtered through the glass.

"Liz!" She exclaimed. "Hey."

I couldn't hear Liz' reply, but I was pretty sure she was asking something about the dog. It would be hard not to start that conversation since he was so obvious.

"She's in the house," Anna said, after a moment.

"Tori!" Liz's voice was loud, but I had heard worse.

"Yeah," I called, and hurried down, taking the wet towels with me. I swung open the basement door and tossed them down, vowing to pick them up later.

"Can I talk to you?" So Anna was still close by. Liz would have a hard time completing skinning me if Anna was there to listen. That didn't mean she wouldn't get her point across, however.

"Sure." I came in, calm and cool, hands still slightly damp and smelling of the dog shampoo that the old owners had included in their care package.

"The dog," Liz began.

"Is for security. You know how dad always said we shouldn't be home alone at night." It was a bit of a low blow to bring up our dad, but it was true.

"Security." Liz's voice was flat.

"Yes, I got him for security. And company, for when you're not around or when I'm gone and you're here by yourself."

"I like being alone," Liz said firmly.

"Well I don't."

Liz seemed to pause, her face still. Then I saw a suspicious gleam in her eye, her scowl melted into a sympathetic frown. "Oh, Tori, you should have told me!" she exclaimed, coming forward, arms out.

I let her grab me and pull me into a hug. "Tell you what?" I asked, my voice muffled against her shoulder. My big sister would always be taller than me.

"That you were lonely. I wouldn't have minded getting a dog for here. We have a yard. We can handle something small." She pulled back. "But that dog you chose! He's huge! What is he?"

"I'm not really sure," I said slowly, but I was relieved that she didn't seem to be that mad. "He was free."

"I've got his papers," Anna called, and she and Monty came in. As soon as she dropped his leash, he rushed to us, all smiles and flying legs, losing his balance on the old wood, and skidding face first into the couch.

"Crap!" Liz exclaimed. "What was that?"

I laughed and dropped to a knee. He came to me then at a more sedate walk and dropped his chin on my shoulder. "Liz," I said formally, "This is Monty."

Chapter 7

"He's a half standard poodle, half giant schnauzer. He's a giant schnoodle." Anna looked up from the paper in front of her.

"A what?" Liz took another piece of pizza and sat down at her place. Monty raised a fuzzy eyebrow at the food.

"Standard poodles are the big poodles that you see in dog shows, the ones with the goofy haircuts. They can get to be about the size of a skinny lab."

"Ugh, really!" Liz shook her head. "They are the most ridiculous looking dogs. He doesn't look like them."

"It's because of the cut. My uncle is a vet. They only do that hair cut on dogs that they are going to show. It's expensive."

"And stupid looking," I mumbled, taking a drink.

"It was originally done for work, not for show. It dates back from when the dogs went hunting with their masters. They kept more fur on their joints and the areas they were most likely to lose heat. They were water dogs."

"Hunting?" I looked at the dog lounging at my feet and grinned.

"That's what they were bred for."

"So that's why his fur is so curly," I said, and bent to rub my fingers through his hair.

"Yep," she agreed. "It will take some work to keep it brushed and cut, but he won't shed." She looked at him appraisingly. "The poodle mix dogs are getting very popular because of their coats, but that means there are more in recues too."

"And schnauzers don't shed either," I murmured. "That will be good for keeping the house cleaner." I was watching for my sister's reaction, but her face was relatively impassive.

"What kind of schnauzer would end up looking like that?" Liz finally asked. "I thought schnauzers were little black or silver dogs. We had a neighbor with one when I was little. His name was Snoopy. Didn't match his looks, but he was a cute dog." She glanced at me. "He was before your time."

"Well, you're thinking of another size of schnauzer, but probably the same breed. They come in a couple different sizes, like the poodles. A giant schnauzer is not very common. They are some kind of guard dog, and I only know that because I saw one in a dog show. I haven't even seen any others." Anna was rubbing the dog's ears unconsciously.

I looked at my sister and could tell she was caving. "Can we keep him?" I asked softly.

"I guess we need to get him some supplies," she said with a heavy sigh.

"No problem. He came with a lot of his own!" I tugged his leash and we headed inside, Liz following at a distance. I was trying to look very calm and in control, but it was difficult when Monty insisted on dancing on his end of the leash.

"And where did you get him?" she asked. I was slightly surprised that it had taken her this long to ask that question. Soon I would have to admit that it was all planned, and I wasn't looking forward to that conversation.

"I got him from an ad I saw. But they were really nice people." If you didn't mind them dumping their precious baby and heading for the hills, I thought to myself.

"What about shots?" Liz asked, arms crossed over her chest, skeptical expression making her suddenly look older, and vaguely like our mom.

"He's up to date!" I exclaimed, smiling. Surely this would work. Surely she could see by my expression that I was determined to make this work.

"We can take him by to see my uncle this weekend," Anna assured us. "He can give Monty a quick once over to made sure that he is healthy. I'll let him look at the records too."

"That would be great," I said with relief sneaking a glance at Liz. I knew that vet bills could add up rather quickly, but very little about dog care beyond that. The little collie mix we had had when I was a child had been cared for by my parents with my sister and me reluctantly feeding her if my parents insisted. She had been a gentle thing with big brown eyes and long soft fur. When she had died, my parents had declared that we wouldn't get another dog until we could help care for it. We had never gotten another pet. This was going to be a learning experience for all of us.

Anna stayed for dinner, but stated that she had to leave soon after. She had homework to do, but was reluctant to abandon us with our new roommate. When we had finally gotten his bed set up in my room, his dishes laid out, and his leash hung on the hook, she slipped out the door into the twilight.

"I'll drop Anna off and be back in a few minutes," I told my sister, reaching for my purse and the car keys. "If you can just hold onto him for a minute?" I handed her the leash with the clip firmly latched onto Monty's collar.

I was grinning when I slid behind the wheel. This was going to work. Monty might be a little awkward, but he was sweet and tried to be obedient. I was sure he would grow on Liz, given time.

"Just watch him around your shoes," Anna warned, as we pulled up to her house. The windows, framed in white emitted a soft golden glow, and even at a distance I could see the movements of shapes within, the heartbeat of a family.

I nodded silently, but my smile had slipped.

"And call me when you can to tell me how it's going," Anna continued, unaware of my wistful gaze.

"Sure," I said, yanking myself from my reverie. "I'll call. And thanks, Anna, for everything."

She grinned. "You might not be thanking me in the morning," she called, slamming the car door behind her and strolling up the steps to the porch. When she swung her front door open, more golden light poured out, and with it the buzz of voices, kids yelling, her brother, no doubt. I rolled up my window to shut out the sound, feeling low and self-pitying.

When I pulled up to the front yard, Liz was standing in the glow of the porch light, Monty sniffing at the ground as though after a significant hunt. They followed me into the house, and for the next half hour, we cleaned up the dishes with Monty pacing around our feet, hoping for a dropped crumb. When we were finished, we went into the living room to watch some television. Monty stalked around the room like a clumsy shadow, and then settled at Liz' feet. I smiled as I watched her unconsciously bend to stroke his hair. When it got darker outside, I put the leash on Monty's collar to lead him out for a final potty break. Our back yard was fenced, but I wasn't sure how secure it was, so we went to the front yard again. I didn't want to leave Monty in the yard alone until I was sure that he couldn't escape. More importantly, in the dark, I was afraid his black coat would make him almost invisible, and I wouldn't be able to keep up with him.

Standing outside in the silence, I wandered the yard and waited for him to do his business. The cemetery was silent, the budding leaves making only the barest whisper in the wind. Monty would occasionally jerk his big head up, listening and sniffing the breeze. I licked my lips and looked around. Nothing spoke to me out here, and I was grateful. Monty nudged my hand and leaned up against me. I wasn't alone.

*****

The next morning, Monty was up with Liz as she got ready for work. I could hear her talking to him and the jingle of his leash as she took him outside. I was dozing again when she put him back in my room and closed the door. When I slipped out of bed later, Monty was calmly laying by the side of my bed. When he glanced up at me, his eyebrows raised like a comical puppet. He looked utterly content and calm, chewing on something trapped beneath his giant paws. Chewing on something? I scrambled next to him and pushed aside his great head, revealing a single tennis shoe minus most of the back half.

"Monty!" I yelled. "No!" I snatched the rest of the shoe up and held the damp mess in front of me. He had done a great demolition job. Even though I didn't wear them often, they were the shoes I was most likely to reach for if I were going to run outside in a hurry. I sighed and tossed the shoe in the garbage. Monty stood and stretched his eyes on my face. He didn't seem to be too upset by my outburst. He went over to the bedroom door and sniffed at the crack between the door and the jamb while I scooped up the rest of the bits of shoe from the floor. It seemed like a sign. If I were going to have a dog, I was going to have to change some of my housekeeping habits.

The sun was up, a warm butter yellow disk low in the sky. I threw on my clothes, jeans that I had found on the floor, but still smelled okay, and a super soft tee shirt. I found another pair of old shoes and slipped them on. I went to the back door this time, letting the old screen door slam closed in our wake. I was really hoping that the fence would be good enough to hold my new friend in. It wasn't going to be fun if I had to take Monty out on a leash every time he wanted to check out the local squirrel population.

He and I followed the fence line with slow steps. There were a few boards that needed to be replaced, that was for sure, and the gate was closed but not latched. With one good nudge with his nose, Monty would have the run of the neighborhood. But in general, the fence was in pretty good shape, and would do fine once a few repairs had been completed.

A far off woof of another dog had Monty prancing eagerly, and I gave him the run of the yard while I was there to watch. He rushed from one corner of the yard to the other, barking and yelping as he went. He was seriously over enthused, and sent his whole body into a wag when the other dog seemed to respond. I let him run for a while and sat on the back steps. I had slept well the night before, slept like I hadn't a care in the world. It had been a wonderful feeling, and if keeping Monty meant a few chewed shoes, but more restful nights, it would be worth it.

When it came time for me to leave, I looked at the giant dog with consternation. I hadn't really thought this part through. I needed to keep him from wandering around the house, snacking on our belongings, and possibly marking what he considered to be his territory. But I didn't have an enclosure or any kind of cage. I settled for locking him in the bathroom, after first putting all our toiletries from the tub and the shelves into the tiny linen closet and closing the door. I thought about giving him his bed, but then worried that he might chew that as well. Instead, I made him a little nest of old towels and left him his bowl of food, a second bowl of water, and a few of the hard rubber toys he had brought with him.

I grabbed his fuzzy face and held his eyes with mine. "If you want to stay here with us, you are going to have to be a good boy," I said firmly. "No eating the cabinets, or anything else. I'll be home in a few hours to check on you and let you out." I kissed his forehead and released him. When I closed the door, he let out a few forlorn barks and then grew quiet.

At the diner, Blythe had already boxed up several deliveries for me, and printed out addresses with directions.

"You've got a busy day," she said as way of greeting. "Try one of the scones while they're hot. Let me know what you think."

Blythe habitually had Anna or me "try" one of her new dishes. I think mostly because she knew that I usually skipped breakfast and that Anna was starving after her day at school and loved a snack when she got to work.

The peach scone was a perfect buttery blend, and I ate it while I paged through my deliveries. I was happy to see that I would be going by the retirement village to see the ladies. I was anxious to talk to them and tell them about my newest experiences.

"Heard you got a dog," Blythe said, putting a glass of milk on the table in front of me.

"Um, yeah," I mumbled over the scone.

"News travels fast around here. One of your neighbors saw you with it last night while you were walking and mentioned it over breakfast this morning." She smiled. "I think a dog is a good idea. My boys always had at least one. Kept them in line. They had to care for them, feed 'em, bathe 'em."

"I thought he would be good company," I agreed.

"Hal Masterson, one of your near neighbors, said he was a big thing."

"He is. Not heavy, but very tall. He's sweet though."

"And he barks. With you girls living out there by yourself, you need to have something that barks. Put out a big water dish with Brutus printed on it, and put up a 'beware of dog' sign. That'll make anyone think twice before messing with you."

I nodded. It was a good idea. Once the intruder saw that I had a dog, maybe he would give up. Not likely, given the number of times that I suspected he had broken into the house, but still, there was that chance. "I'll do that," I agreed. "But why Brutus?"

"Nobody's afraid of Fee Fee," she responded.

I was still smiling when I left with my boxes. I would do my deliveries, and then drop by the house before coming back to the diner. I checked with Blythe to see if that was fine with her, and she agreed easily. I felt warmed when I saw how she trusted me, and vowed to be fast so as not to take advantage of that trust.

*****

When I returned to the diner, I was much wiser than I had been, but not for the reasons that I had anticipated. My deliveries had been easy, and I hadn't really been able to speak with the ladies because of a serious, almost bloodthirsty game of bridge. I delivered to the orthodontist and dentist, laughing when they said the sweets helped with job security, and took the bank their delivery last, managing to arrive right at lunchtime, to the delight of the staff.

At home, I approached the bathroom door with more than a little dread. The booming barks coming from within were just frantic enough to cause me great concern, but the thump of a large body hitting the door was even more ominous.

"Monty, no!" I yelled through the door and pulled it open. He greeted me with two paws to the chest which knocked me back, but not all the way to the floor. The warm wet feel of his tongue on my jaw had me pushing him down, but when I ordered, "sit," his fuzzy bottom hit the floor and he gazed at me eagerly. "Good boy," I said and rubbed his ears for a moment. Despite my concern, the bathroom seemed relatively intact. The toilet paper had been unwound into one giant stream of white which puddled on the floor before being stretched into the tub and back out again. The rest of it was shredded into fine pieces and spread liberally around the room, even up into the sink and on the top of the toilet tank.

I hurriedly picked up the mess and thrust it into the garbage can which I placed outside the bathroom door. I led Monty to the back door and stepped out with him. He once again marked his area and returned to me with a look of doggie satisfaction. When I put him back in the bathroom, I made sure there were no paper products for him to reach. I left the garbage can in the hallway, and gave him a small amount of food in his bowl. He was so thin that I worried that he wasn't eating enough, but I also suspected that it was his energy level that was keeping him thin.

At the diner, I set about doing cleanup for the afternoon rush. I shoved my hair back, catching the tangled strands that had escaped my ponytail, and tucking them behind my ears. I was in charge of bussing tables and making sure all the dishes were taken into the kitchen. I was breathing a little hard after only two tables and frowned at myself. Anna cornered me after she had only been in for 10 minutes and stopped me in the kitchen.

"So spill," she whispered, barely holding back the grin. "Who is the guy?"

"What guy?" I asked, stepping back and peeking through the window into the diner.

"What guy?" she mocked. "The guy that came by and asked about you. Sam was telling me about it. He heard the conversation from the kitchen, but didn't know who the guy was."

"What guy?" I asked again, now a little frustrated.

"Didn't Blythe tell you? Some guy came by and asked about you?"

"No," I said slowly. The number of guys I knew in town was pretty limited. "I haven't talked to Blythe since I came in from delivery. We've been busy."

"Oh, not too busy for this," Anna exclaimed, and tugged my arm until I moved with her out into the dining area.

Blythe was in conversation with a couple sitting at one of the booths, their coffee having been refilled innumerable times while they sat around and gossiped. They were the kind of regulars that would come by almost daily, and Blythe could serve them without ever taking their order.

Anna strolled up by them and smiled angelically, waiting silently until Blythe finally turned to her.

"Girls," she said, looking at both of us. I suddenly felt 12 again, like I was standing before a teacher.

"Did someone come by to see Tori?" Anna blurted, careless of the listening patrons.

I stood completely still, chanting to myself, I wouldn't be embarrassed, I wouldn't blush, but I would take a piece out of Anna when I had the chance.

"Oh, not to see her, I think, as much to check up on her," Blythe responded. "Come on now," she said, nodding to the customers and gesturing us back to the kitchen. We followed obediently, but I felt a wave of anxiety. I didn't like to think that someone was asking questions about me, especially behind my back. It made me faintly ill. I tried to control my expression, to look casual, like I didn't care, like I wouldn't care. I was pretty sure I failed at that.

"Who was it?" I asked as the door swung shut behind us.

"Drew." Blythe crossed her arms in front of her chest and tilted her head. "Drew came by and said that he had met you over by Duncan Memorial. He said you seemed a little, um, upset, and he was just checking to see if you were okay."

"How did he know where to find me?" I asked, still feeling uneasy.

"I don't really know. He just said that he had met you, not that he knew that you worked here."

"You do know everyone, Blythe," Anna interrupted. "Maybe he just assumed you would know Tori."

Blythe shrugged but apparently read my expression. "Don't worry about him, Tori," she told me. "I've known Drew for a while, and he's totally fine. He's even run some errands for me when the boys were out of town," she said, referring to her sons in college.

"So you trust him?" I asked.

"He's a good guy. He's just had some hard times lately. I think he was really concerned about you when he came in here. I didn't get the idea that he was just trying to dig up information about you." She turned to make sure that no one else was listening in to the conversation and bent a little closer to me, her hands falling to her sides. "You are doing alright, aren't you, Tori? Drew told me that you said someone had broken into your house, and you had come out ready to take him apart because you thought that he was the one."

I laughed, a forced sound, and avoided Anna's gaze. I knew that I would hear it if she thought that I had been keeping this from her, especially with her accompanying me to get Monty. "I had a really bad, really 'real' feeling dream. I would have sworn something was going on in the house. I didn't actually see anything, but I had this bad feeling, you know, like someone was there with me. So I was searching the house. I thought I heard footsteps and went downstairs. When I looked outside, I saw someone out by the cemetery. It was the middle of the night. It was normal for me to be suspicious."

"It wasn't normal for you to go out there by yourself. Not when you don't know many people around here. Drew said you just ran out of your house, and that you were alone. What were you thinking? If it had been a dangerous situation, you would have been running straight into trouble." Blythe was looking at me like she was somehow disappointed in my actions.

"I know," I said softly. "It wasn't one of my smart moves, but I didn't stop to think. If I had, I would have never run outside that way. As it was, I was confused and angry and just followed my heart."

"You ran outside to catch someone that you thought had broken into your house?" Anna's voice was disbelieving, and I could tell by her expression that she thought I had lost my mind.

"I'm a big girl and I can look after myself," I snapped.

"Well sorry I cared," Anna said in a low voice, cheeks flushing.

I pushed out a sigh and tucked my hair back again, trying unconsciously to keep my hands busy. "Anna, sorry. I'm sorry for being such a bitch." I snuck a quick glance at Blythe as the word slipped out.

"It's okay," Anna sounded just a little sulky, but I couldn't blame her. "But did you really think someone had gotten in?"

"I didn't really," I said, guarding my words. "I think somewhere deep down, I knew that no one had been in the house." I said a mental apology to Mrs. Lucy for the lie. "I just saw someone out there and wanted to see who it was."

"Damn it, I should have never told you those stories about the house or the cemetery. I should have never taken you there!" Anna looked guilty and a little sick.

"It wasn't your doing, and you didn't exactly drag me there. I don't think my dream had anything to do with your story."

"What story?" Now Blythe interrupted our conversation that had slipped off topic.

"I told her about the bride in the cemetery, and I told her about the old man that haunted her house." Anna looked miserable. "We had been over walking in the cemetery and I remembered the stories. But I don't believe them, and Tori doesn't either, do you?" She turned to me, her eyes begging.

"No!" I exclaimed. "I told you, I don't believe in ghosts. I might get a little freaked sometimes, but it isn't because I think that there are really haunted places. I really dreamed that there was someone in the house that night. A real someone, a human someone. I didn't ever think it was a ghost. And when I didn't find anything inside, I saw Drew outside, and went to talk to him. I admit, I might have seemed a little crazy, but I wasn't really."

"He didn't say you were nuts," Blythe interrupted. "So don't worry about that. And I told him that you were just fine, but that I would talk to you to make sure you weren't still thinking that someone had broken in."

"I'm fine," I mumbled and crossed my arms in a tight X. I felt awful. Awful that I had admitted my fears to him and now he thought I was a hysterical woman, awful that I had caused Blythe to worry about me, and awful that I had not told Anna anything, making it seem like I didn't trust her.

"I know you are," Blythe said, her tone matter of fact. "And now you have a new pet, and you're settling in. You have new friends. You'll do just fine." She was so certain, so sure.

Anna seemed to catch Blythe's tone, and quickly agreed. "Sure, and if you worry about someone breaking in again, you'll have Monty. No one would think to break in with him at home."

I was tempted to agree, to say that that was exactly my plan, but I didn't want to see the pity in their eyes. Poor Tori, getting over the death of her family and still grieving. Grieving so badly that she's seeing things in the dark, and is carried away by nightmares in her own mind.

*****

I didn't think that it was a coincidence that I saw Drew that night. He was sitting on the wall again, this time much closer to the house on the right, long legs drawn up, arms twined around his knees. It was a balancing act, and I had the nasty temptation to sneak up on him and push him, hard. Of course, sneaking wasn't even in Monty's vocabulary, so as soon as he saw another human, he began his bellowing barks of alarm and greeting. When he saw us, Drew dropped from his perch and moved toward us at an easy lope.

"Hey," he said.

The light was still good; the sun was holding court on a throne of golden clouds just over the horizon. The odd light made the scene look like something shot in sepia, an old photograph animated.

Monty broke the spell by giving a tremendous leap forward and leaving me with his leash in hand, an empty collar coiled on the pavement while he put his paws on Drew's chest and thrust his long nose forward into Drew's shirt.

"Down, Monty. Get down," I said helplessly. The dog ignored me completely, thrilled to have this additional excitement.

Drew put a hand out and grabbed Monty's paws, lifting them off his shirt. Monty bounced down and pressed his face against Drew's leg, eyes rolling up to gaze at him hopefully. Drew buried his hand in Monty's fur and gave him a brisk rub down from head to shoulders, laughing when Monty nudged his hands for more.

"Monty, stop," I begged, but approached cautiously. I didn't want the mutt to bolt because I was pretty sure I would never catch him if he ran. And worse, I didn't know the neighborhood well enough to find him if he got out of sight. But he was showing no desire to leave. He stood still as I slipped the collar back around his neck, sliding it over his head and tugging his ears gently to free them. I was uncomfortably close to Drew. I could smell the scent of soap and mint mixed with a subtle sweetness from the clinging vines at his back. He was tall. I hadn't realized how tall until I stood this close and he loomed above me, face shadowed as he held Monty still for me.

"New dog?" he asked, his breath causing my hair to stir.

"We got him yesterday."

"He's friendly."

"I was hoping for a little threatening, but so far, he hasn't met anyone that he didn't like." I smiled ruefully.

"I think if he knew you were afraid, he would react differently. Or if someone came on your property." He cupped Monty's jaw in one long fingered hand and angled his face up. "You're just a pup anyway, aren't you?"

"He's nine months old," I said quickly. "He won't get much bigger."

"Maybe not taller, but he should fill out some." He ran his hand up to the collar where I was clutching it. "This is too loose. You need to tighten it so he can't escape next time." He ran his hand beneath Monty's chin until he found the buckle. I let go and backed away just slightly. If he let Monty go accidently, I would be back to a chase. I didn't want that, but standing toe to toe with Drew was making me jittery.

"There." Drew finished buckling the collar back in place and handed the loose leash to me. "He won't be able to run so much. It might look tight, but with all that hair, it's really not."

"Thanks," I said, wrapping the leash around my fist. The silence was an awkward pause. "So I heard you came into the diner."

He looked at me directly, and I realized that his dark eyes were more slate grey tonight. "I did. I wanted to see Blythe. Usually she saves some day-old desserts for me. And I wanted to see what she knew."

"About?" I prodded.

"About you, your sister, your situation. I didn't like leaving and not knowing if there really was a threat at your house. I haven't seen anyone lurking around, but that doesn't mean that they haven't been there." He cast me a curious glance. "Blythe acted as though you had never said anything to her about the break-ins. She was completely surprised."

I sighed. "I haven't told her. I didn't want anyone to think that I was losing it. I don't have any proof, and my sister is not so sure that I'm not going crazy anyway. I didn't want to worry her, and I was pretty sure if I told anyone else in town, it would get back to her."

"Well I..." He was interrupted by the slam of a door from the house next door. A girl came out, the golden light catching her curly hair in a wild disarray around a pretty face. She was looking at Drew and me as we stood there on the sidewalk, but was soon distracted when a long eared dog slipped out behind her and came racing toward us, long howls of barks heralding his arrival.

My hand tightened on Monty's leash, but he seemed to be thrilled to have a friend. He fairly pranced with eagerness to greet the new dog, and pulled hard on the leash. I called "sit" a few times but got no response. If he knew the command at other times, he was pretending he didn't now.

The girl followed the dog at a more leisurely pace. She must have been pretty confident of his behavior, because she was smiling when she reached us.

"Baxter has a new friend," she said, and bent to stroke Monty. "How are you, Sweetie?" she crooned in a voice we all save for puppies and babies.

"Hey, Thea," Drew greeted. He bent to pet the beagle who was sniffing at Monty, then at Drew's jeans, before going back to check out the other dog again. "Wondered if you guys were coming in."

Thea looked at him, smiling slightly. "Both of us, or just Thomas?"

"Really just you. Thomas is just a side benefit."

She grinned broadly. "That's better." Her eyes went to me and she waited for Drew to make introductions. When he didn't, she stepped forward. "I'm Dot, or Thea as these guys call me. I've been meaning to come over and say hi. I saw you all had moved in, but you must be pretty busy. Haven't seen you around home much." I gave her a tight little nod, but before I could respond, Drew spoke up.

"This is Tori. She lives with her sister over there," he nodded his head in the direction of our house. I could tell he was trying to avoid the uncomfortable question that followed, where were my parents? Where did I go to school?

"I'm glad you got Mrs. Lucy's house. It needs someone who can take care of it."

"It's a lifetime project for now," I agreed. "Did you know Mrs. Lucy?"

"Sure," Thea agreed. "You can't live around here for long before you meet all the neighbors. We pretend that we're not a small town, but we really are. You start to know the faces and recognize the names." She paused and looked back toward her house. "And I'll have to introduce you to my parents. My mom still works at the high school, teaching, but my dad is retired. He can come in handy if you have some problems around the house." She smiled slightly. "He can at least hold a hammer and attempt a quick fix."

I appreciated the offer, I really did, but I knew that I wasn't likely to take her up on it. I could tell by her words that she already knew my home situation and wasn't going to make me discuss it. It was a relief, but at the same time, her little family unit made me ache just a little bit more. Monty tugged at the leash as he tried to chase her hound, and I pulled him back, happy to be distracted.

"Did you get a new dog?" Thea asked.

"Just yesterday," I agreed. "We adopted him from a family that couldn't keep him anymore. His name is Monty."

"Hi, Monty," she said, giving his curly head another pat. "Well, this is Baxter. He's the neighborhood busy body. He's met pretty much everyone, and he thinks he owns the place."

I smiled and bent to brush my fingers over the other dog's slick coat. He immediately sat to enjoy the attention, and I chuckled when his eyes closed with pleasure as I rubbed his ears. "He's quite the watch dog," I teased.

"He does what I want him to. He barks when he's alarmed, and loves everyone else. He's great company."

I nodded. "That's really want I want Monty for," I admitted.

"I think it's a good idea," Drew began, but I sent him a warning glance. I was pleasantly surprised when he stopped and changed the subject. "Where is Thomas?"

"He's coming in tomorrow morning. He had a paper to finish for early Monday and wanted to get it turned in before he came home."

"Home?" Drew's eyebrows rose.

"To my home," Thea corrected, but I thought that her face seemed to color. "So what are you doing? Any new jobs?"

He shrugged. "I'm still doing a lot around the church. Just when I think I'm done, they think of something else that needs fixing or painting. They have even had me over at the old chapel, helping to clean out the basement. I didn't even know the place had a basement."

I must have looked curious because Thea clarified. "He does work for Father Joe and Father Ben. They are over at St. Benedict. They have a really old house that needs work just to keep it standing. There is also an older, smaller church on the property that they call the chapel along with the school and a few outbuildings. They've chosen Drew as their unofficial handyman."

"Oh." I could think of nothing better to say. Churches were not places that I would want to work at, and I had no desire to discuss religion. My baptism papers may have said I had faith, but my heart wasn't sure of anything any longer.

"I work some other places too," Drew said, his voice quiet.

"Um hmm," Thea said, and turned to me. "And you're working with Blythe? She said the delivery business has really expanded. She's really happy with what you have done to help."

"I'm relieved to hear you say that," I responded, genuinely pleased. "It's been a good job, but tough. I've gotten to know a lot of people around town too."

Thea grinned. "It is something of a local hangout. If you want to know something about the area, all you have to do is drop in and listen to the talk around you."

I nodded in agreement. The conversation turned to some of the local news around town, and I found myself relaxing into the evening. It didn't surprise me that Thea seemed to be familiar with just about everyone in town. She had grown up here, and considering how many people I had met in my few months of residence, I knew that the people around here liked to talk. I listened to the flow of words, gathering a few facts that I stored away for later. Drew was mostly quiet, busying himself between spoiling the two dogs. After a few minutes, he crossed the street into my yard with both of them and started tossing sticks. To my surprise, Monty could snatch a stick out of the air with ease and then return it mostly unscathed. He showed no signs of wanting to run off, so I felt comfortable with him off the leash. When the sun had truly set, I realized that I should head back indoors. I didn't want to leave my sister alone for long, especially without the dog to keep watch.

"I guess I'd better head in," I said, nodding toward my home. "I've got an early morning."

"Sure," Thea was smiling, hands tucked into her pockets. "I'm glad to have finally met you."

I nodded and moved reluctantly toward my home. The sun seemed to be setting too quickly, and I could tell that Drew was getting ready to leave as well. That part I didn't like. I had gotten used to thinking that he would be on watch outside my home, but I reassured myself with Monty's big warm presence.

"Maybe we can stop by Blythe's this weekend," Thea said as she climbed her porch steps.

"Sure, I'll be there," I responded and forced a smile. It was getting dark, and I didn't much like the dark.

Drew cast a wave, and I wondered if he would come by as well. I turned and headed back across the road, slipping beneath the shadows of the trees. Monty waited for me next to Baxter, both panting and sniffing. At a whistle, Baxter scurried across the street to his home, and I caught Monty's collar in one hand so he wouldn't follow.

"Later, Tori," Drew's voice seemed to catch on the air. When I turned around, they were both gone.

Chapter 8

I didn't mind working on Saturdays, but I hated missing out on time with my sister. She was spending her time off doing errands around the house, errands that weren't fun because they amounted to cleaning, scrubbing, and organizing as well as trying to start on the thousands of repairs that the old house required. On the other hand, I dreaded trying to clean my room, sorting through the mounds of clothes and debris that were covering the floor. It was much easier for me to clean up other people's messes. To work on my own was something I would continue to dread, however, because I was due to work in 20 minutes.

I finished putting my hair up in a headband and ponytail, making sure all stray stands were tucked away. My jeans were clean, but pale from laundering. Comfortable. My shirt was a plain pale yellow tee that could benefit from an iron, but since I didn't think we actually had one in the house, I wasn't that concerned with it. No makeup, a quick spritz of scent, and I was ready to leave.

My car started on the first try, and I had to grin as I pulled out. Monty was in the front window, black nose pressed to the glass, watching as I drove away. I was pretty sure he had already licked the glass. But he was standing guard over my sleeping sister, so I treasured him all the more.

At the diner, the weekday regulars were replaced by the weekend visitors. There were a few new faces, people in town who were going shopping in nearby La Grange, or attending a ballgame at one of the local schools. The scent of bacon and fresh biscuits guided me through the door, and I grabbed a quick snack as I pulled on an apron.

"Start some more coffee," Blythe told me as she passed. "And look to see how much cream we still have. I might have to put in another order."

I nodded. "Good morning," I teased.

"Hmm, we'll see," she replied, and disappeared back into the dining area.

I slipped out front to start a new pot of coffee, pausing to pour out the remnants of the old. My hands were sure and steady at the task, while my mind wandered to other places. I was developing a taste for coffee, with plenty of sugar and cream, as well as a taste for small town living. I felt sure now that if I were late for work, or didn't see Anna for a day or two, someone would call me on it. I was becoming part of a community, part of something bigger than my own diminished family, part of a larger circle. It was reassuring and at the same time, really frightening. I didn't want to let anyone down. I didn't want them to think of me as anything less than a hard worker, a good friend, an adult.

These thoughts were drifting in my mind when the door swung open and with that, I lost my sanity. He was there. I knew it was Thomas, friend of Drew, Thea's boyfriend, regular guy. But he was just not right. He was dressed in jeans and a tee shirt, just like Drew who entered behind him, and Thea at his side. His pale hair was brushed back off of his face and his golden green eyes were laughing at something that Thea was saying. But he was lit. Like thousands of tiny sparkles of light coursing under his skin, he looked as though he had borrowed a halo from some Renaissance painting and bent it around his frame. It was warm and gold and pink and something that wasn't white, but very close. When his arm touched Thea's, the light seemed to give around him, bending like liquid, but not like shadow.

As I stood there frozen, I realized in some small cold part of my mind that I had finally gone crazy. I had worried that the grief of losing my parents would one day cause me to melt down into a mound of sobbing flesh, unable to communicate, adrift until the control would return. But I didn't think it would happen like this. I felt sane. I felt normal. I saw everything else as clearly and as real as the coffee pot in my hand which had tilted to the floor, and then, as in slow motion, had slipped from my slack fingers and hit the wooden floor with a great crash, glass shards spraying out in a burst of hard shine.

The sound of the pot hitting the floor had Blythe looking up from the register, and the three coming through the door stopped. The words died on Thea's lips, but then she hurried to the counter.

"Tori, are you alright?"

I stood there in the suddenly silent diner. The tip tap of the register keys resumed, and Blythe called out over her shoulder, "Clean up in the front."

I knew that Sam would be out in a moment with dust pan and broom, doing what should be my job. But I also knew that I was still insane and unlikely to be able to help. Because as many times as I blinked and ran suddenly cold fingers over my eyelids, Thomas continued to glow like a ghost out of a B movie.

"I think I need to sit down," I said softly. But I didn't move. My feet weren't responding to my brain screaming, and my mouth felt dry, my lips numb. I felt a warm hand catch my elbow and Drew bent towards me.

"Tori, come on." At his words, my feet moved, following him, leaning into him until I could feel the steady heat of his body, the warmth that had completely seeped from my skin. Thea pulled out a chair, and Drew gently steered me towards it. His arm went around my shoulders and he eased me down to the seat. My eyes travelled from him, to Thea's worried face, and then beyond. No matter how many times I saw him, I still saw it, the odd colors and light. An aura, I thought.

And then he was beside me, and before I could pull away, he had taken my hand in his, his warm, normal fingers encircling my wrist, feeling for the racing pulse beneath my skin.

"Get a cloth for her head," he was saying, his voice smooth and mellow. "She looks lightheaded. Maybe she needs something to drink."

At his words, Thea disappeared to the kitchen, and Drew pulled a chair up very close to me. His arm was back over my shoulder, supporting me, and I leaned into him and closed my eyes.

"I'm fine. Just faint," I said softly, not, *I'm going crazy, call my sister, call a doctor.* I was going to try to get control of this.

"You probably should stay sitting for a minute." I could feel Thomas let go of my hand. "My sister has had a lot of problems with light headedness lately, and I've gotten to be something of an expert in the field. I think you'll feel much better after you've rested for a minute."

I opened my eyes and regarded him. Thomas was just an ordinary guy, pale hair, gentle eyes. He was just a little older than me. He was taller than I, but not as tall as Drew. He looked like nothing more than a normal college guy, home for the weekend, hair in need of a trim, and jaw in need of a shave. Except for the subtle lights that trembled about him.

Thea was back with a glass of orange juice and a biscuit with bacon peeking out. "Blythe said you're on break for the next 30 minutes unless you feel like you need to go home. She's not charging you for the pot, but she might charge you for the juice unless you finish it."

I could see Blythe across the room, her gaze sharp on me as she made sure that I was taken care of. "Thanks," I muttered, and took the glass, sipping carefully. I didn't really feel that bad now. I was growing accustomed to the up close vision before me. As long as I didn't think too hard about what it was saying about me, I could look at the pretty colors with a detached interest.

No one else seemed to notice my distraction. If Thea thought that I was looking at her boyfriend strangely, she must have chalked it up to my health. Drew kept his arm around me, and I didn't move away. I took little bites of the sandwich while Thea and Thomas pulled up chairs. Blythe brought them soft drinks after a moment, and put one cool dry hand on my forehead.

"Feeling better?" she asked, and when I nodded, she smiled slightly and walked away.

Thea seemed to take the situation in stride, and began to talk around me, including me in the comments, but generally filling in the silence. I was feeling rather ridiculous, but not enough to ward off the fright. I didn't know what was wrong with my vision, but I wasn't about to let on that it was anything more than what they suspected. My stomach seemed settled so I obediently ate the rest of the biscuit and drank the juice. I stood slowly, moving from the shelter of Drew's arm. He stood with me as though afraid that I might fall, but that was fine with me. I wasn't so sure that I wouldn't.

"Well, we were going to grab some breakfast," Thea said, her voice a shade too bright. "What's on the menu?"

I walked to the counter, gaining my balance, and settled with them on the stools. I felt better there, more in the center of things, my hands cool against the counter top. Blythe poured me more juice with a pointed look, and I drank it slowly. Thomas ordered a huge meal with eggs and bacon, a decadent cinnamon roll drizzled in icing, and hot coffee, black. Drew laughingly asked for a duplicate of the meal, adding that Thomas would take the bill as well. Thea held back with some highly sweetened coffee and toast, her eyes still checking on me.

By the time breakfast was over and the plates were cleared away, my break had stretched to an hour. I could feel Thomas' restless movements, and noticed the glancing exchanges between him and Thea. And although I had taken comfort in Drew's steady presence, I was now ready for them to leave. I wanted things to be back to normal, and more importantly, I wanted a moment alone to think. When they left, Thea asked me if I needed anything, and I knew she was hinting that I could escape with them. But I didn't. It was better, in my opinion, to stay and work it out. Better for me not to think of what was happening to my brain. Better to hide my fears for just a little longer.

I didn't have to worry for too long. My next delivery was at the retirement home. I helped Blythe pack up the assortment of bakery goods and sat in the blessed silence of my car. There wasn't a question about what I would tell the ladies. I might share my concerns about the house, but I wasn't going to ruin their confidence in me by adding that I was seeing auras. I was having visions, but not around anyone but Thomas. Just one. Why?

Mrs. Lucy was in front of the television, but her mouth was open slightly and she snored delicately. Her curls trembled with the sound. I stopped and stifled a smile before saying her name softly.

"I'm not asleep," she said, her eyes fluttering open.

"I can see that," I agreed.

"Did you bring anything good?" she asked, her eyes raking my empty hands.

"The good stuff is in the dining room."

She nodded. "Then we'll go in there to talk."

Over pastries and hot tea, I decided to ask her about the house. I wanted something to distract me from my own personal dilemma, and the subject seemed safe enough. Anna's story had been stuck in my mind, an unfinished tale. When I asked Mrs. Lucy about it, she nodded, unsurprised.

"It's one of those stories that people never get enough of. Mad scientist, stolen child, mysterious ghost." She wrapped her frail hands around the mug. "Which one did you hear?"

I returned her assessing look. "How about you tell me yours first?"

She laughed, showing a mouthful of straight teeth, too white and even to be her own. "Okay, I'll tell you. But you have to promise not to take it all too seriously. People tend to exaggerate things, especially over time. And many years have passed for this story. If they like it, it grows and changes, and before long, you don't really know how it started in the first place. That's how it is with this story. No one knows the exact truth, which is why there are so many different versions of it."

I nodded solemnly, repressing a smile. "I promise not to believe a thing you say," I teased.

She huffed, but grinned, the teeth again visible. "Well, my family has actually always lived in that house. It was built by some of my 'greats' generations back." She pondered her own words for a moment. "The old place has been passed down, uncles, cousins, and then to my parents, and when they passed away, my husband and I moved in." She looked at me sternly. "I have only good memories of that house, so you keep that in mind when you go looking for ghosts."

I shivered a little and thought longingly of a sterile little apartment in Chicago, close to traffic and the rumbling trains.

"One of my 'greats' was living there with his family. He had the house built before the cemetery was more than just the plots. It was before they ever built Duncan Memorial, and the cemetery was smaller. He decided to settle there, close to his business by the railroad and invited his father in law to move in. They did that, you know, kept extended family close. Not like now when so many of us end up in nursing homes." She frowned a little. "I don't know much about the man. I heard that he was a teacher at a university in Indiana, or maybe Virginia, and that he studied geography or maybe history." She took a sip of her tea. "He wasn't mine by blood, so I have to admit, I didn't pay him as much attention. He was just someone who moved in for a place to live, as far as my family was concerned."

"Do you know his name?"

She looked puzzled, but just a little. "You know, I don't. But I probably have it somewhere in my boxes. You know, they gave me a storage area in the basement to keep some of my things from the house. There were a few still available, so I took it. Lord knows that I probably won't ever go down there and look through any of it, but I hated to think that it would just be destroyed, and none of my own family was interested in it. I wasn't going to make my son live with all my mess," she said wryly.

In my mind I could picture a dank basement with stacks of old boxes, slowly molding and deteriorating. I wasn't sure that I would want to look around there if I were her kids, but now that I was in the house, the idea held appeal. Healthy curiosity, or was I becoming morbid?

"Well, anyhow, he was living in the top floor, one room for him to sleep in, and one room that he filled with books. The family that lived there only had two children, rare in those days, a girl and a little boy." She looked wistful, a little sad for this part of the story. "The father in law had a lot of stuff packed in every corner of the house, artifacts from his travels, papers from his studies, journals, and books. All of the personal things I kept at home, but the rest was just too much to handle. He had stacks and stacks of books that stayed in the house until I finally persuaded my husband to pack up the lot and get rid of them."

I pictured that as well, the family boxing dozens if not hundreds of old books to be stored away, or tossed in the garbage. "What happened to them all?" I asked.

"We took them to La Grange. There were some ladies there that were getting things together for a little historical museum. They took the books and anything else that we wanted to get rid of that was old enough. They have a little place still, I think. It's in one of the old houses on Main Street in La Grange, you know, where the train runs through."

I didn't know. I had driven to La Grange only a few times since we had moved to the area. I could vaguely remember a downtown area with a great brick courthouse that we had visited, flanked by older homes and stores.

"But you wanted to hear about the ghost story." She took another sip of tea. "The old professor was living in the house, but he was a strange one. He stayed locked in his room for hours without coming out or even answering the door when they knocked. I think they really believed that he had lost his mind, considering how he behaved. They took up his food, and he ate in his room. They were never allowed in to clean. And then one day, they knocked and knocked. He never answered. When they used their key to get in, he was dead, still sitting at his little desk, books in front of him."

I shied away a little from that image. Some mad scientist looking man, white hair like an earthly halo, little glasses perched on a bent nose, leaning back in his chair, book in hand but never reading again.

"But he was an old man by then, and people didn't live as long as they do now. They called the doctor to come, and after they took his body away, they realized that they hadn't seen their son. They wanted to tell the children about their grandfather, but couldn't find the boy. No one could say that they knew where he went." She looked pensive. "And no one ever found him."

"How old was he? The little boy."

"Not yet school age," she replied. "But that was where the ghost story started. The people around here said that they were sure that they had seen the old man walking down the road, even when the family swore he was locked in his room. In fact, some said that they saw him walking with the boy, and then later, looking for the boy. The reports continued, even a few days after the old man was found."

"That does sound like a ghost, creepy," I commented. "But he wasn't seen in the house?"

"Outside is all I have ever heard. And I never saw a thing. I think the family went a little crazy after the little boy disappeared. They didn't know what had happened, the father in law was gone and they had to care for his funeral and all of the arrangements. I think the mother of the boy was taken to the hospital for a little while, nerves, but I know that she eventually returned."

"She was able to come home?"

"I have a picture," Mrs. Lucy said. "It shows the family in front of the house. They aren't very clear, but it must have been after the little boy disappeared. He's not in any of the pictures I've seen. Just a girl, their daughter."

*****

When I returned home from work that evening, I had a bone deep weariness that I hadn't felt since we had first moved to the new house. I stopped my car and looked through the bug spattered windshield at the house before me. The yellow paint was still peeling, the yard had been cut but was mostly weeds struggling to survive in the shade of the trees. The porch listed a little, but my sister had added a little rocking chair next to the door, and that gave it character, at least. And there was a pot of flowers on the step, curtains in the windows, and lights shining through the glass.

When I stood, my eyes automatically went up to the upper windows, wondering which of those was the room where the old man had died. It shouldn't have surprised me that someone had died in one of the rooms. That happened in most old houses. I had a childish hope that the room wasn't the one that I slept in. As an afterthought, I included my sister in the hope. I didn't want either of us picking up an extra spirit, or worse yet, finding one in our bed.

I ate little for dinner. I had thrown together a chicken casserole that my mom had taught us to make, and used cornbread muffins to round out the meal. It was a definite comfort food, but I felt too anxious to find much solace. After dinner, Liz and I sat in the living room to watch the television. I couldn't concentrate. I went up to bed early, and sat up listening to music. I pulled up Facebook on my phone and flipped through the various entries. Most of my friends from Chicago were still updating me at a distance. I hadn't handled the change in my life well, but they hadn't either, I thought bitterly. Not one of them had tried to come and see me or seek me out in my new hometown. It made me slightly envious and irritated to see their status updates of what guys they were currently going out with at their new colleges or what dresses they were wearing to the next party. Spiked heels, nail polish, and boys seemed to be their primary interests. I felt a little pull of disappointment. But hadn't that been me a year ago? Hadn't I been painting my nails with patterns, buying the highest heels I could walk in, and agonizing over which guy I really liked and wanted to go out with? Granted, the nail polish may have been black, but still.

I dimmed the phone display and plugged it in next to me to charge. I stood uncertain and undecided. I knew that Liz would care for Monty tonight, and would put him in my room before she went to bed. I was glad that she liked him well enough to keep him with her, but missed his presence. I left the door cracked open so I could hear the drone of the television. I tucked my legs under the heavy blankets and slid down in bed. I doubted I would be able to sleep. I was thinking too much. I was worried too much. I couldn't slow down my thoughts, but…

I woke in the darkness, the meager lights of the streetlamps outside coming through my window. I was not alone. I could do more than feel the presence this time. I could see him. He was in my room. I lay as still as I could; my eyes squinted closed in case he could make out my face in the darkness, the glitter of my eyes. Through my lashes I looked at the still shape by the door. Tall and dark. That was all I could tell. I couldn't say if it was a man or woman, old or young, armed or not. I could see nothing except that there was someone in my room, and it wasn't my sister. I thought of the bat next to my bed or the tennis racquet tucked underneath. Then I thought of Monty. Automatically and without conscious thought, I turned my head to look for his long shape next to me on the floor. My heart pounded in my throat. I prayed the movement had looked enough like a sleeper's shifting that the watcher wouldn't know that I was awake. I squinted again, but did not see Monty's furry shape resting next to me. Had Liz taken him in her room? Had she left him out? And if he had the run of the house, where was he now? No, he had to be in her room. Why else would he have not barked or whined? Unless.

I realized that I couldn't see the watcher's shape as well. My shifting had put the doorway just at the far side of my line of vision. Fear made me sick. What had he done to my dog? Had he hurt Monty? Killed him? I saw the shadow shift and slip out the door behind him, pulling the panel closed. My breath escaped in a whoosh, but I stayed very still. I was shocked when I heard the sharp clicking of Monty's nails as he walked, calm, through the hallway and clattered down the stairs.

I jumped out of bed shoving the blankets free and to the floor. My feet were almost soundless when they hit the floor. What the hell? Why wasn't my loyal companion tearing into the intruder? How could he do that to me? He was walking with the guy, wandering through my house as though they owned it. Fury made me head to the doorway, but I stopped to grab the bat by the bed. I wasn't going unarmed. If my stupid dog wasn't going to protect me, I would take care of myself.

Downstairs I paused, completely silent. I was getting good at sneaking. Unfortunately for the visitor, Monty wasn't quiet. I could still hear his nails, in the kitchen now. He was probably hoping for a treat or a snack, the traitor.

I slipped around the corner and looked in through the doorway, still mostly concealed in my dark night shorts and long sleeved tee. I could see his shape now. He was tall. Much taller than I. For a moment I hesitated. It was a man, and he had me on size. If I didn't get a good solid whack with the bat, I was dead. My element of surprise was the only thing that was in my favor just now, and that was assuming that the guy had come unarmed.

Strangely though, I wasn't feeling the breathless panic that I had on the other visits. I was scared, heck yes, but I wasn't terrified. And I didn't feel that sick feeling now, the feeling of something wrong the feeling of evil that had permeated the air like a really bad stink.

I raised the bat and stepped forward. And then Monty saw me. It hadn't occurred to me that I couldn't sneak up on the idiot dog. I just figured that if he were stupid enough to align himself with the bad guy, he wouldn't notice me sneaking up on him. That was my first mistake. Whatever alerted him, also let him know who I was. He didn't bark, but turned on long legs and galloped toward me, suddenly all toothy smiles, and thumped his paws on my chest, snuffling his great black nose into my neck.

"Monty, no!" I yelped, falling back but not all the way to the floor, dropping the bat as I tried to get my balance. The figure turned. "Drew," I whispered.

"Tori," his voice was soft, weirdly so, almost airy.

"Dammit, Drew, what the hell!" I exclaimed, using up all my curse words in one sentence. I shoved Monty down and ordered him to sit.

"I can explain," Drew was saying, but he had his hands out and was keeping his distance. I wondered how scary I looked to keep him at bay so well.

"Why are you in my house?!" I exclaimed, my voice still in a hiss. How would I explain this to Liz? The guy that I had just met, and was starting to like, was the one who was breaking into our house?

"I was following someone. He was here," Drew's voice was quiet and strained. "You were right. Someone is breaking in. I got here just in time to see him, but then he was gone!"

"What?" I bent and grabbed my bat, stepping closer to him. "What are you talking about?"

"I'm saying that you were right. There is someone coming in here. I don't know why. But I saw him tonight. I was trying to catch him."

"But Monty," I started.

"Kept him from going upstairs, I think." Drew looked at the dog who had dropped down into a sit at my feet and was leaning against my leg. "He was blocking the stairs and growling."

"How did you get in?" I hissed. I still felt really angry, but I was beginning to lose the edge of fear.

He didn't respond, but the look that came over his face was something close to confusion.

"Drew," I said angrily.

"He's gone now, but you need to be careful. Keep Monty around. I think that's working," he was speaking fast now, and he had taken a step back, away from me.

"Drew, I really need to know how you got in. Maybe that's the same way that he's getting in!"

Drew's eyes settled on my face and his expression became pensive. "Tori, I'm really sorry, but I can't. We'll talk later, but now..." He stopped talking, and his eyes traveled beyond me.

I glanced back, looking for whatever had gotten his attention. My first thought was Liz. But there was nothing in the dark. Monty was still at my side, and all this registered before my eyes went back to where Drew was standing, or where Drew had stood. He was gone. The door was closed, the window closed, and there was no way he could have gotten past me without touching me. But he was gone. Like a really good magician, without the smoke and mirrors, he had disappeared from my kitchen as though he had never been there.

Chapter 9

I called in sick to work. I couldn't explain. What to say? I had totally lost my mind and was walking in my sleep? I had dreams so real that I found my baseball bat lying in the hallway downstairs? I had seen a man break into my home the night before but had lost him in a split second?

I slept in until 10:00 and dragged myself out of bed, feeling foggy and stupid. There was no excuse, nothing that seemed possible, or plausible. There was no way that I could believe that seeing Drew the night before had been a dream. He had been there, standing in my kitchen. I could recall the clothes he wore, the way his dark hair had been mussed, and that his eyes had been a midnight blue.

I put on the coffee, adding an extra scoop just to be a little stronger, and slumped in the kitchen chair. The light coming in the window was grey, a foreshadowing of wet and chilly weather. I took a mug from the cabinet and held it by the pot, waiting for the dripping to stop. I had a vague feeling that if I could just get some caffeine in my system, the mysteries of the universe would be revealed, and I would know what the heck was happening to me.

I added a lot of sugar and a fair dollop of milk. I wasn't hungry but pulled out a little container of yogurt anyway. Coffee on an empty stomach might make me regret it later, especially since stress was pushing up into my throat. I ate slowly, standing at the window. I was pouring a second cup of coffee when I heard a knock at the door. Monty barked from his station on the floor, and padded to the door. I followed, not even caring that my hair was uncombed, and I was still in my night clothes.

Drew. My first urge was to turn away and leave the door closed and locked. He was the last person that I wanted to see just now, but on the other hand, he was the only person I wanted to talk to. Or hit. A good punch to the stomach, or maybe a fist to that unshaven jaw, would have made me feel miles better.

I gave up and opened the door. "What?" I knew that despite my delusions, he hadn't been here the night before. I knew that in his mind the last time he had seen me was at the diner. Any rudeness that he got from me would be pretty much undeserved.

He ignored the comment and walked past me, pausing to pat Monty on the head. "Good morning to you," he said, and headed toward the kitchen as though he had been there a hundred times.

I wiped my hand over my face and pushed back my hair, feeling the tangles catching my fingers. When I made it to the kitchen, he was helping himself to the remainder of the coffee in the pot.

"Do you have any real sugar?" he asked, holding out the mug.

I silently got the bowl out for him and tugged open the refrigerator door. "Do you want milk too?"

"A little," he responded head down as he stirred his coffee with my abandoned spoon. "Look, I'm sorry about last night."

I stood absolutely still. Of any words that I had expected, these were the last. Sorry. Last night. He had seen me last night; he had been here. I wasn't crazy.

"You were here last night," I said flatly, resisting the urge to make it into a question.

"And I'm sorry. I should have talked to you about this before, but I wasn't sure what was really going on. If I had thought that you were in danger, I would have said something earlier, I swear. I just can't believe that he, well, that he is going this far now."

"He who?" It wasn't the question that I wanted to ask. I wanted to ask about Drew himself. How had he gotten in? Where had he gone? What was he doing in my home? But those words seemed stuck on my tongue, destined to remain unsaid.

"He is just this man, this parasite," his voice was bitter. "I don't know who he is, or what he wants. I just know that lately he is always there, like some kind of shadow."

"Where?" I interrupted.

"He turns up everywhere that I go. He's been by my home, he came while I was working, he stands on the corner and watches me, he comes here to the cemetery when I come, and he follows me." He stopped and looked me full in the face. "I don't want to freak you out, but there is something different about this guy. You should know that first. He has some ability. He can get into places. He doesn't need keys or open doors. He can just get in without even trying."

I must have looked disbelieving because Drew hurried on. "The reason I know what he can do is because I can do it too. I can go in places, places that I shouldn't be able to. And I can get out. Locks don't stop me. At least, not anymore."

"Like last night," I murmured softly.

Drew stood and put his coffee on the table. He went to the window and looked blindly out, not seeing the shaded yard. "I don't really know what to tell you, Tori. I don't want you to think that we're all crazy, but some crazy things are happening, and I don't know what to do about it." He rubbed his jaw with one hand and moved toward the living room. His restless pacing was making me nervous as well. I sat very still, forcing my hands to remain clasped in my lap. He stopped in the doorway, glancing toward the comparatively dim living room. When he turned back toward me, my breath caught. Oh, not another one, I thought desperately. But I could see it now, with his back to the darkened living room, I could plainly see that he had his very own glow. Soft and white, almost colorless, but there.

"Oh, God," I said, half in prayer. I hadn't been religious for a long time, but suddenly, the spiritual didn't seem quite so distant.

"Tori?" Drew's voice sounded worried, and I realized that I was staring at him.

"You're glowing," I stammered. "Your skin, your clothes! You're glowing like there's a light shining directly on you, or from you. Please tell me you see it!"

Drew came closer to me and sat carefully down in the chair next to me. He scooted close, but his eyes were wary. "Tori, I don't know what you're talking about. I haven't heard anyone say that I glowed before."

"Stop!" I cried out. "Stop right there. There is something more going on here, and you're not telling me! You say that you can get in locked buildings, like you don't control that. You act like this guy is stalking you, and you seem to be stalking me. Thomas was glowing, and now you are. I am not imagining it!" The pitch of my voice had risen until I was screaming at him.

Drew's face seemed to pale when I mentioned Thomas' name. "What do you mean? Thomas?"

"Don't deny it! There is something weird going on with Thomas. He looks like he's got an aura, a light surrounding him all the time, even when he's in the light, in the sunshine. I've never seen it with anyone else. No one. You want me to trust you, now you trust me!"

Drew sat forward, his brows drawn together over very dark eyes. He blew a slow breath, his shoulders slumping slightly. Then he put his hand out, his fingertips glowing just slightly against the darker wood. I looked into his eyes and knew what he wanted. I waited a long moment, hearing only our uneven breathing. Then I pulled my hand from beneath the table and slowly put it in his, feeling the warmth, the very human warmth of his skin as he held my hand.

"I believe you, Tori," he said softly. "Now we need to find someone who can help."

*****

I was only slightly surprised that his first call was to Thomas. It was a relief that he wasn't calling a shrink on me. And I supposed that Thomas took it pretty seriously because he said that they would be in town in a couple of hours. Drew didn't elaborate any further on the conversation. I just sat in uneasy silence. A couple of hours looked like an eternity, and Drew wasn't in a talkative mood.

I stood stiffly after my cup was empty. Automatically I turned off the coffee pot, put away the milk and sugar, and cleaned up the little kitchen. My mind couldn't settle on any one thought, so I tried desperately not to think at all. It wasn't until I was settled in the big chair and had propped my feet up on the table before me that I noticed that I still wasn't dressed. Flushing uncomfortably, I made my excuses and left Drew in the living room retreating to the quiet of my own bedroom.

I closed the door and leaned against the panel for a minute, just breathing. The whole morning had felt like a bad science fiction episode, something just brushing reality, but not really firmly situated in it. I wasn't sure if the arrival of other people would lessen the feeling. I already had problems with Thomas. Not that it was his fault that he glowed, but the very fact made me incredibly jittery when he was around, like I had chugged a whole case of caffeinated energy drinks. Thea didn't trigger any unease in me, however, and something about her usual calm seemed welcome just now. I moved away from the door and began rummaging in the piles of clothes on the floor. I finally settled for comfort and dressed in old jeans and a soft tee shirt, adding a sweatshirt because I still felt inexplicably chilled. Was I getting sick? Was this all part of some fevered dream? Man, I hoped so. I knew it wasn't. I knew that this was just part of my new reality, whether I liked it or not.

I headed to the bathroom on bare feet and looked at myself in the mirror. Face pale, eyes a little glassy, hair in tangles falling over my shoulder, nice look. I brushed my hair but ignored my face. I couldn't worry about what I looked like. I didn't have time for that. I brushed my teeth and leaned against the cabinet, just catching my breath. I returned to my room and grabbed my cell phone which I jammed in my pocket. Security. With a defeated sigh I closed the door to my room. I returned downstairs almost silently. Drew was still in the living room. He had sunk deeper into the couch, and his eyes were closed. I stopped in the doorway to just look. He looked different, somehow. Experience, rather than time, had marked his face early. He looked older than his 20 years. His face was tired, fine lines around his closed eyes. His hair was a uniform dark mahogany color except for a tiny patch of white at his hairline above his right eye. Grey hair? I had heard of people going grey early, but this was very early. I guessed stress could do that to a body. I shrugged my shoulders slowly to loosen the muscles and came into the room. Monty rose leisurely to come to me and pressed his wet nose into my palm. I supposed he was making up for earlier when he hadn't been the best guard dog. Or maybe he had been? Maybe he knew that Drew wasn't there to do me harm, so he had allowed him free access to the house. I couldn't really know what was going on in that canine brain of his.

I slid into the chair and pulled my legs up beneath me. Monty collapsed with an audible thump next to me. With a sigh, I leaned against the back of the chair and let my own eyes close. Just for a moment. Just a little rest. Rest while I wasn't alone.

I came awake at the brisk knock against my front door. Someone knocking? My brain felt dull still. Someone was knocking. Still blinking the sleep from my eyes, I watched as Drew walked to the door and swung it open. I was getting slowly to my feet when Thomas and Thea came in. Monty pushed past Drew and began eagerly circling the new arrivals, pushing his long nose against their clothes to catch their intriguing scents. Thomas paused to gently rub Monty's ears, calming him instantly.

"Drew," Thea's voice was cautious. "Are you both okay? Thomas didn't fill me in completely, but I figured this had to be important."

My eyes went to Thomas then as he stood framed in the doorway. There it was. The glow. In contrast to Drew's, Thomas glowed like a thousand tiny lights, not just one single point. His illumination had shades of colors and tones. It was beautiful as much as it was frightening.

Thomas, in turn, was looking at me, his eyes assessing. "Are you feeling okay?" he asked.

"Do you mean, am I going to run screaming from the room?" My tone was slightly bitter, like I was angry that he was making me face this, this abnormality.

"Okay, yes, are you going to?" Thomas was so calm.

"No," I said slowly. "No, I guess not."

Thomas dropped onto the rocking chair across from me, his gaze holding mine. I had the uncomfortable feeling that he was seeing right through me. Thea, noticing my discomfort, sat next to me. Monty slipped between us, resting his head on my knee.

"What do you see?" Thomas asked softly.

So I told him. I told him about seeing him that day outside the little store, seeing the shine even in the midday sunlight. I told him about seeing it when he was visiting Thea's house, and again at the diner. I tried to describe it for them, the faint shimmer that seemed to highlight his features.

"And you've never seen this with anyone else?" Thea asked her voice soft.

"Not until today." I rubbed my hands up and down my arms and avoided looking at Drew.

"But you do now. You see it on Drew." Thomas looked at me intently.

"Yes," I responded.

"And you saw Drew last night in the house."

I looked up quickly, surprised that I was almost forgetting that event. "Yes, he broke in last night!" I felt a mild resurgence of anger. "With everything else going on, I can't believe he was in here. I told him I thought someone had broken in, and then he did the same thing!"

Thea touched my arm gently, and I looked toward her. "He didn't exactly break in," she said firmly. "This is a whole lot like what happened to me last summer. And trust me, this is not something that is just going to go away."

"What do you mean?" I asked, and kept looking at her, the one person who seemed real and solid.

"All right, this is going to sound crazy, but hear me out. Then you can call the cops on us if you want." She paused and took a deep breath. "Last summer I was left alone at my house for a few weeks," Thea began. "My parents had to be out of town with my grandmother, so I stayed behind for school and work. That's when I met Thomas. I kept seeing him walking in the cemetery night after night and finally got up the nerve to talk to him." Her eyes slipped over to Thomas, and he nodded almost imperceptibly. "He was only coming at night, and he would only walk in the cemetery. I never saw him anywhere else, and no one else in town seemed to have heard of him. We talked, but he never really talked about himself. I knew something was strange about it, but I couldn't help but trust him." She smiled a little, but then her eyes grew very serious. "Then I found out about the accident." She stopped and glanced away, momentarily thrown from her calm. I saw her fingers clench in a double fist on her lap. "I found out that Thomas and his brother had been in a car accident earlier in the year. Daniel was killed on impact, but Thomas was taken to the hospital where he remained in a coma for weeks afterwards. While I was seeing him walking in the cemetery, while I was talking with him, he was lying in the hospital in Cincinnati in a coma."

I didn't interrupt, but I must have looked disbelieving.

"Trust me, I didn't believe it at first. But I knew that I had met Thomas. I had spoken to him. He was as real as you or I. Then I saw the article and read about him. I saw a picture, and all of a sudden, I found out that he couldn't be who I thought he was. I had to find out what the truth was. So I went to see him at the hospital. And I knew after seeing him there, in that hospital bed, that he just couldn't have been anyone else. When I first came to the hospital, he was still in a coma, virtually unresponsive. I knew then that he obviously couldn't have been sneaking out of the hospital at night. There was just no explanation that made any sense."

"It's called bilocation," Thomas said softly. "It's a phenomenon where one person can be seen in two places at the same time. When I was visiting Thea, I was aware of everything that was happening with her, but when something happened in the hospital room, I became aware of that too and lost touch with the other side. I really didn't know what was happening to me, because the only time I was really conscious was when I was here. And the accident caused something of a head injury, so my memory was wiped out anyway."

My eyes automatically went to Drew where he sat in silence. He wasn't moving, denying or agreeing. I would almost have felt better if they had grinned, laughed even, and told me that they were just kidding, so much easier to think that I alone was losing my mind and not the whole bunch of us.

"I saw it, Tori," Thea said, her voice surprisingly firm. "And I'm not joking or crazy. He was in that hospital, completely unaware of what was happening around him, while at the same time he was visiting me."

Drew still said nothing so I finally turned directly to him. His silence wasn't proving anything to me. He saw my expression and sighed. "I thought it was a load of religious hocus pocus," he said flatly. "After the accident, I ran as fast and as far as I thought I could. My best friend was dead, and his twin brother was in a coma. Their family was in shambles. Their sister was in a denial of her own. And I walked away without more than a few bruises and scratches. I didn't want to think of the accident, but in the end, I couldn't avoid it. So I decided to come here because I thought that I needed to solve a different problem. I knew I was avoiding Thomas and his family, but I couldn't face them, not then. I thought that if I could figure out why Daniel had brought us to this cemetery in the first place, I could somehow know the reason he died. Or at least what he died for."

I had gotten mixed up and overwhelmed somewhere in that speech. I looked at Thea for clarification, but she seemed lost in her own thoughts.

"So before the accident, Daniel brought you here for some reason?" I asked.

"A few times," Drew agreed. "We came during the summer to do some exploring. Daniel always had these ideas that he needed to 'research.' He was the adventurous kind of guy, and if he didn't have any excitement going on around him, he would make his own. He was always looking for a new plan, a new mystery, a new, I don't know, quest."

"So why here?" I looked at Thea since she was the local, but she just shrugged.

"That is the million dollar question. Or it was until all of this came up. Then the 'why' became less important, and the 'what now' became the real problem."

"Did Thomas come to you too?" I asked Drew.

"No. I found out about all of that after Thomas had woken up. When he regained consciousness, I gave in and came back home to stay for a while. We talked. I should have done that much earlier, but I probably would have just written him off as someone who got hit on the head one too many times." He looked apologetically at Thomas. "I'm not much of a believer in all that spooky stuff. Ghosts and miracles have never made sense to me. I believe in science, what I can feel, see, touch." He shrugged.

"What made you believe?" I asked softly.

"Because it started happening to me too," he replied, face grave. I shivered unwillingly and had to drop my eyes for a moment.

"And that's why you glow," I stated softly.

"No one has ever said that before," Thomas replied for them both. "You are the first person who has even seen us as different."

I looked at Thea sitting close to me on the couch. "You don't?"

"I don't see anything like you do," she said honestly.

"But you said you saw Thomas walking here even when he was really somewhere else." Even saying the words sounded ludicrous.

"I saw him, but he didn't seem any different to me. That was the part that was so scary. I saw him walking out here for weeks before I finally met him. And even then, we just walked and talked. I mean, sometimes it seemed like he was holding something back, but I never thought it was anything like this." She paused. "Later, after we had known each other for a little longer, I thought I saw him vanish in front of me. I figured it was my mind playing tricks. I've done this before, like you. I thought I was losing my mind. I thought that this whole thing was insane." She looked at me, her face very solemn. "I didn't know what was going on really, and then I found an article about Daniel in the accident. I knew I hadn't met a ghost, I mean, I knew that for sure, but when I read that article and saw the picture…" Her face looked a shade paler.

Thomas leaned over and caught her hand. "Daniel and I were close in more ways than just being twins. We did everything together, and we really did look identical, even as we got older. We thought it was really funny to fool friends, and we were good at it. I really could have been Daniel's ghost." His eyes flashed in pain.

"But then I found out that both of them had been in the accident, and I went to the hospital in Cincinnati to really see him. And he remembered me. There is no way he could have ever known me, but he remembered me."

"Does it still happen?" I asked suddenly. "Do you still show up in two places at once?"

Thomas looked uncomfortable. "I don't think so," he said. He frowned. "I know it sounds stupid that I don't know for sure, but I don't. All I know is that I have no memories of being anywhere else."

"And you?" I turned to Drew.

"I didn't even know what was happening until a few weeks ago. I woke up in my bed, but I had the feeling that I had been outside all night. Then when I was talking with a friend, I found out that I had been sitting out on his front porch for most of the night."

"Sleepwalking." I said firmly. "You were sleepwalking."

Drew shook his head. "Maybe that night I could have been, but when I came in here, I wasn't."

"Last night?"

"And before," he said. "I can't explain it, or how it happens. I just," he spread his hands, "I went to sleep. Then I was in your house. But I know that I was also in my room at the hotel." He stood and paced to the window. "I know that it doesn't make any sense, but I could feel that I wasn't just here. And I knew that while I was in the room at the motel, I was also in your house with no memory of how I got in. And then something pulls me, like being drawn from a dream, and I knew that I had left you here but never went through the door."

"And the other man you keep talking about? The man breaking in?"

"I think he's like us." Thomas and Drew exchanged looks.

"How many of you are there!" My voice sounded a little too high.

"I don't know," Thomas said from his place in the chair. He was still holding Thea's hand loosely, and she still looked white around her lips. "We don't know who he is, or what he is doing here. We just know that he's here, and he's watching. And now it seems like he can do what we can. Even if we have no idea how it happened, or why it happened, we apparently aren't the only ones it happened to."

"And Savannah," Thea said softly.

Drew turned back to them. "Savannah what?"

"Savannah?" I interrupted.

"My sister. She's our, I mean, my younger sister. Thea saw her do it too. Just once."

I couldn't believe we were talking about this so calmly. Saw her do it. Saw her somehow be two places at once.

"So you and your sister can do it," I murmured. "But Drew isn't related to you. Thea has lived here all her life and can't do it." I looked at Thomas. "What caused it?"

Thomas shook his head. "We don't know. It never happened before the accident, but Savannah wasn't even there. She wasn't in the accident. She stayed at home when we decided to come back here." He ran his hand through his longish hair, ruffling the pale strands. "And we don't know about Daniel. We don't know if he might have been able to do it if he had survived the crash."

I looked over at Drew, standing still and straight by the window. His face was turned toward the sun, but his eyes were closed. "You didn't tell me about Savannah," he said softly. "Why not?"

"I don't know, man," Thomas said, looking pained. "We have been really trying to keep Savannah out of this. She's had such a hard time with Daniel," he stopped and looked down at his hands. "She needs time, and she doesn't even know it happened. We haven't talked to her about it, so I didn't think it was fair to talk to anyone else."

Drew stayed at the window, but nodded slightly.

I interrupted. "So do you think that the reason that I see your aura, or whatever, is because of your ability?" I was asking Thomas, but my eyes kept straying to Drew.

"At a guess, I would say yes. But we don't have any information to back that up." Thomas looked over at Drew as well. "We have been trying to figure out what Daniel had in mind when he began bringing us here. Whatever his reasons, he didn't tell us. But he usually liked to keep secrets until the big reveal."

"He could be a real pain in the ass sometimes," Drew said on a sigh, opening his eyes and pacing toward the kitchen. "Did you find that flash drive I told you about?" He was directing his question to Thomas.

"What flash drive?" Thea was looking between the two, a frown marring her usual calm expression.

"No, but I haven't been home much lately." Thomas looked at Thea, and then back to Drew. "I was going to go through some things over the next break," he continued. "Most of his stuff is still sitting in his room. We haven't gotten much packed up." He didn't really say more, but we didn't really need to hear anything else. The part that was unsaid was the part about it being too painful to go through his things, to dredge up the memories. I knew that tune very well.

"We need to do that." Drew moved back to the living room and leaned against the arm of the chair. "We need to figure out what the hell Daniel was thinking of, and what has been done to us."

Chapter 10

At the end of the movie, you always kind of wonder what comes next. After the aliens land, are defeated, and little alien bits litter the suburban backyards like so many leaf piles, you have to wonder, now what? Do the people go out with their rakes and shovels and stuff the alien goo into large sized garbage bags to be picked up with the trash? Do they call the roofers to ask for an estimate for UFO damage when the alien ship parts skip across their shingles in the battle for world domination? Do the kids get a few days off school, like snow days but for alien infestation? And when they return, is it back to irregular verbs and algebraic equations?

I had always thought, if something like that happened to me, I would just curl up in a corner and rock myself into some sort of safe oblivion. I would not cope, I would not be able to pick up the pieces. But I was wrong. Life goes on, even when the paranormal lingers like the grim reaper on the next page of the novel you can't stop reading.

I went to work, helped pay bills, visited the grocery, got gas in my monster car, and enrolled Monty into puppy training classes at the kennel just five minutes away. My sister went out on the first date that she had had in almost a year, and I helped her pick out a pair of classic jeans with some trim boots and a soft sweater to wear. She borrowed my earrings. She looked wonderful, as usual. I was hovering by the front door with Monty as she pulled out. I felt a little criminal. No one would ever think twice about Drew coming into my house while my sister was away; I was an adult, but I still felt somehow guilty about not telling Liz that he would be there. But what would I say? I was having a friend over so we could figure out why he was able to be in two places at once, and why reality and the laws of physics no longer applied to him?

Drew came as I was ordering pizza to be delivered. Friday nights were busy for the few places that delivered in our area, but I could wait the 45 minutes if it meant that I didn't have to cook. Monty was at the door, his feet up at shoulder height and his nose pressed to the glass. At a distance, it would look like some messy haired adolescent was looking out the window, at least until the person saw the flash of canines and the long black nose.

He greeted Drew like a long lost family member, escorting him through the door and following at his heels into the kitchen. Drew fussed over the dog, giving in to the longing brown eyes and doggie devotion.

"Hey," he finally said to me after I hung up the phone.

"Hey." I put the phone on the counter, and leaned back. My feet were pale and bare beneath the slightly ragged hem of my jeans. My toenails were painted a glittering turquoise. My fingernails were short and natural. Too much manual labor to keep them pretty. I looked up at Drew as he stood in the doorway. Handsome would not have been an exaggeration. He had the natural good looks that came with fine bones and strong genes. He would look better as he aged, a little more silver to his hair and crow's feet at his eyes would only add to his allure. It wasn't really fair.

"Did you work today?"

"For a while," he responded, not elaborating.

"Have you heard from Thea or Thomas?" I still felt strange saying their names. Here we could pretend normalcy, but as soon as they were mentioned, all bets were off for the normal world.

"Thomas said they will probably have to stay at school for the weekend. They'll be home next week, though. He said they were going to look into a few things there. Research."

I nodded and felt bad that I was so relieved. Thomas still made me a shade uncomfortable, like he had some unseen shadow that clung to him. I didn't feel that same way about Drew, even though I could still see his faint glow in the dim lighting of the kitchen.

"So do you have a plan?" I asked, and tried to keep my voice light.

"We can look up a few things before it gets too late. Then I thought we'd go over to the cemetery once it's dark enough."

I repressed a sigh. He had already told me that he wanted to try to go to the cemetery with me once night fell. He had some idea that we could find out more in the night rather than hunting during the day. I had told him about my experience with the assailant in the cemetery and how Anna and I had both felt that someone had been out there. Drew still wasn't sure that it hadn't been some teenager enjoying an evening of fun, but I knew. I had that feeling, and I could recognize the fear well.

"Do you have a computer we can use?" Drew asked, sliding into a seat at the table.

"Upstairs," I responded, "I'll go grab it." I climbed the steps rapidly. The laptop lay plugged in and closed on my bed. I had been surfing the Net and looking up some social sites just after work, making faces at the status updates from my old friends, thinking of how mine would sound in contrast, something about ghost hunting, sleepwalking. Now I unplugged the computer and carried it downstairs.

Drew watched as I put it on the table in front of him, and I booted it up. The screen lit up with a soft whir of the fan, and a picture appeared. My sister and I, dressed in our childhood Easter finery, white straw hats and matching purses with daisies -- yellow for my sister, pink for me -- were posed in front of a blooming azalea bush, the blossoms like clusters of snow. Behind the bushes was the ledge of the front porch, and the door was just slightly ajar, showing nothing of the inside of the house. But I knew what was there. Inside in the cool interior, the smell of ham and simmering beans would permeate the air. On the counter would be the coconut cake that my mom made every Easter, and her purse with the little bouquet of jonquils that my sister and I had picked for her before we had to leave for church.

And behind the camera, behind the lens that we smiled into, was my father, ordering us to stand still, just for one minute more, while he snapped picture after picture of us frozen forever with forced smiles. But we were happy. We had been happy. And the photo, with the ghosts of my parents just outside the frame, was a reminder for me of what had been.

"Cute," Drew said, drawing me out of my thoughts. "All dressed up and nowhere to go?"

"We had just gotten back. Church. We went to services every Sunday, every holiday." I hoped my voice wasn't as bitter as I felt.

"Church? Are you religious?"

"I was," my voice was low, and I clicked on the Internet to get a search started.

"I've never been much of a church person," Drew said, his voice light and thoughtful. "But I've been working for the priests over at St. Benedict, and they bring it up sometimes. Makes me think."

I said nothing to this. If he was going through his own conversion, it was his business. My religion, or lack of it, was mine.

"I don't really believe in religion so much anymore," I said, but I knew my tone sounded a little belligerent.

"Yeah, but the more I've learned about all of this ..." his hands made an all-encompassing gesture, including the computer, the house, and the scenery out the window.

I shrugged and looked away. In some ways it was far easier to believe in the supernatural and not the divine. Hauntings could happen anywhere, there was a reason for it, and it was purely human in origin. Divine was a mystery, an unanswered question of why, and why not, and why me.

"What are we looking up?" I asked, glancing his way. His eyes were intent on mine. I felt my cheeks heat and looked away.

"I don't know. Let's start with the history of this place. If Daniel was coming here to look for something, or study something, he had to start somewhere."

I nodded and started the search.

By the time the pizza came, I was really hungry and starting to get frustrated. Considering how old the area was, there was very little written about the cemetery and the surrounding homes. There was the story of the ghost bride; she had scored a whole page on a website discussing historic features of the area, and another about the chapel and the man who had funded it. The history of the place, that the chapel had been in memory of his wife, was a little sad, but sweet, and that they ended up buried there together had a poetic feel to it. But nowhere did it mention anything else about the possibility of hidden treasures. There was some reference to the fact that there had been another church on the land before the chapel had been built, as well as a school house, but neither held much more interest than a quick blurb about their existence sometime in the foggy past. If Daniel had been coming here to see the chapel, or the cemetery around it, there were no clues to why in our reading.

The pizza was delivered by a boy a few years younger than me, and he stared at me for just a shade too long, causing me to lose my temper just a little. "Take a picture, it'll last longer," I said under my breath as he hurried away, cash clutched in his hand.

"He's just never seen you before," Drew said behind me. "Out here, either you're from here, or you're new. If you're new, you've got to be interesting."

"I'm not," I said darkly.

"He thought you were. Maybe he just thought you were cute."

"I'm not," I said again, and walked past him into the kitchen. Irritable. I was just a little too sensitive and irritable. I forced myself to relax, rolling my shoulders to ease the tension, and put the hot pizza on the table. I fetched some paper plates and forks from the drawer. "We've got Diet Coke and water. That's about it. We don't stock much."

"Coke is fine," Drew responded, flipping the pizza box open to examine the contents.

"I didn't ask what you liked," I said behind him. I was paying for the pizza. He'd damn well better not complain.

"I'm not picky," he said, as though reading my thoughts. "And next time, the pizza's on me."

Next time. I rolled the thought around in my mind for a moment. Did I want a next time? Would I look forward to seeing him again? My feelings for him, or about him, were so tangled in this mess of uncertainty that I couldn't really figure out what I thought of him as a person. My eyes slid to his tall figure bent over the table. So okay, he was cute. Handsome, I amended. He seemed to be a nice guy, honest if a little strange. But circumstances had thrust him into the strangeness, not by his own choice. And Monty liked him. Did that count for anything?

"So far, I guess we have a big nothing," Drew said slowly, dropping back into a seat.

I leaned over and helped myself to a piece of pizza. I got two cans of soda from the refrigerator and handed Drew one. He nodded his thanks, and I took my seat opposite him. "Nothing might be just what we find, but there might be something that we are missing," I said, dropping my napkin to my lap.

"So where else can we look into information about this place?" Drew asked, his voice just a shade distracted.

I felt Monty bump my leg and passed him a piece of pepperoni under the table. "We'll have to ask Thea. She grew up here. Surely they have some kind of historical register or something. There are those plaques everywhere, talking about the historical significance of everything."

He looked confused. "Plaques?"

"There are signs that list what the place used to be, and its significance in local history. I've seen a bunch in Pewee Valley. Someone must have records and know where everything is."

"Maybe in La Grange," he agreed, referring to the little city where the courthouse and government buildings were stationed for the county.

I nodded and finished my first piece of pizza. I hadn't thought that I would be hungry. I was still feeling more than a little nervous at the thought of going into the cemetery at night. I wasn't enough of a damsel in distress to think that just the presence of a big strong man would make it a safe place for me to be. In truth, I probably would have felt better with Thea at my side. She just seemed so calm, so comfortable with where she lived and her place in the community.

"So we can call Thea to ask about the historical society. Then we can see about getting some of their records," Drew was looking out the window where the day had grayed to an early evening. "Thomas can look into some of Daniel's things to see if he can find any records of what Daniel was up to before the accident."

"About that," I interrupted. "You acted like you thought Daniel had some information on him."

"He did," Drew replied, taking a sip of his Coke. "Daniel had just gotten a new cell phone. He was trying to get all of his information off of his old computer at home and put it on the new laptop he had at school. He had some of the information transferred onto his cell phone, but some of it was still on a flash drive. He showed it to me one day when we were heading back to school." He rubbed a hand over his chin, his eyes narrowed in thought. "Daniel was one of those guys with too much imagination and time on his hands. I really think he was brilliant, much smarter than I am. He had all of these ideas swirling around in his brain constantly. I think that's why he wasn't doing as well in school as he should have been. He would take us on these little trips to look into things all the time, stuff like museum shows, rare books, estate auctions, ghost tours, places that we ordinarily wouldn't give a second thought. He was always looking for the next adventure, and he was really interested in history, especially local stuff." Drew sat forward and folded his hands on the table in front of him. "When Daniel said he wanted to come to this little town outside of Louisville, I said sure. I thought we might catch a day at the Downs, maybe go down to Fourth Street Live for dinner, socialize. But he wanted to go hunting around in the cemetery. He took us to three while we were down here. All within a few miles of each other. One was the Confederate Cemetery, another I think is related to St. Benedicts. And he took pictures and kept looking at his phone. I thought it was the GPS he was checking, but when I asked, he just laughed at me. He was avoiding telling me something, but I wrote it off at the time."

"What was he looking for?" I asked. But I knew the answer. The problem was, no one knew what he was searching for.

"Don't know," Drew said, confirming my thoughts. "He wouldn't say. He just said he was checking out a theory. And he was looking for something, but he said he really wasn't sure what it was either."

"And now?"

Drew's smile was grim. "Now we look and see if we can figure out what it was before someone else beats us to it."

*****

The cemetery was quiet. The days had stretched just long enough that the yard was not in total darkness, but the sky was a dirty grey. Pale pinks and golds were just showing their fading outlines at the tree tops. The gate was still open, and Drew walked in confidently, as though he was familiar with the walk, and I supposed that he was. He had been something of a regular visitor for some time. Besides us, there was one other car pulled far into the cemetery, a late model sedan that was boxy enough to clue in to its age, but well maintained. An older man was hunched over a grave, standing like a statue in salute to solitude. His stillness made me shiver.

I had to keep my eyes down to watch the terrain. The stones were set in their own pattern, one I could not easily distinguish. They were all styles, from the tall monuments with columns and carvings, to the plaques sunk even with the ground. Drew was headed toward the largest clearing where the Chapel stood in its artificial glow. The stone and stained glass windows were classic and timeless. The spire reached high into the dusky sky, rising from a heavy slate roof. Arched columns followed the side of the building, but we went directly to the front. Drew moved as though he knew exactly where he was going, so I followed wordlessly. He stopped in front of the entrance and grabbed one of the handles. The door was locked. Drew muttered something under his breath and I leaned closer.

"What?" I whispered.

"They sometimes lock it, sometimes not. We must not have been lucky tonight."

"How are we getting in?" I hissed.

"We're not unless you have a talent for B and E. I don't have any magic keys. I've gotten in on other evenings when the place was left open. It's just not our lucky night."

I felt a surge of disappointment that washed over my anxiety. Even if I hadn't wanted to come, I had really hoped to find out something. I don't know what I really expected from the old place. Certainly not a sign that said, "Here's your answer!" but something. Drew tugged again at the door handle and then turned away and stuffed his hands in his jeans pocket.

"Now what?" My words hung in the air. A distant bang had us turning toward the approaching car, and we stood still in the shadows as the older man drove his sedan through the metal and stone gates. He paused at the street for a moment, the red of his tail lights garish against the grey of the evening, and pulled out in a billow of foul smelling exhaust.

Drew turned back toward me. "We don't have a whole lot of options. We can keep looking around here, or give up and go back to your house." He tilted his head slightly. "Didn't you say that the last time you were here and thought that you were being watched, you were over there?" He pointed to the opposite side of the cemetery, closer to Thea's house, where the old covered well sat shrouded in darkness.

"Yes, we went toward the benches," I responded, but my voice sounded uncertain, reluctant.

"Let's head over there and see if anything has been moved." He started without me, and I had a vague notion to just stand there. Would he notice? How long would it take for him to realize that I wasn't following? And why wasn't I following? I wanted to figure out what was going on just as much, and maybe more, than he did. I had a stake in this now. Someone had forced me to care. But I didn't want to go over there. I didn't want to walk any closer to that dark little spot where Anna's phone had been found.

I shook myself and forced my feet to move. My eyes stayed on the ground and on Drew's back, not looking beyond him. I had to hurry to keep him within sight; his strides were long, almost twice mine.

"Hang on," I finally huffed, as I realized that if I kept up the pace I was going to fall flat on my face. Fine for him if I fell, it wouldn't be him trying to nurse a broken leg.

"Sorry," he said seeing me lagging, and stopped on the gravel path. My shoes crunched over the ground rock and I slowed my pace slightly, pausing to dig a small piece of gravel from my shoe.

"Just let me fix this," I said, and squatted to replace my shoe. "Do you have a light? It gets a little darker on this side."

"Just my phone," he replied, and I saw him pull a slim phone from his pocket and the dull light from the screen momentarily lit his features. "This should be good enough. It's not even full dark yet."

I didn't respond. It wasn't that dark, but the shade was deceptive, and beneath those big trees, even the starlight was gone. I stood and shivered slightly. He didn't notice. When I started walking, he did as well, this time keeping pace with me.

"Tell me where you were when you thought he was watching you," Drew said, and his voice shook me from my thoughts.

"Okay," I said. "It was just ahead." We had gotten to the end of the larger path and had taken a smaller branch. It led away from the light, away from the chapel, and away from the gate. The stone wall seemed much higher from here, closer and heavier. I could hear the grass rustle against my shoes, feel the press of the air against my skin, and see the way the light had leached all the color from my surroundings. I was tempted to take Drew's hand, like a child, but forced myself not to. We approached the benches and Drew slowed.

"Here's the well. Isn't that where you found Anna's phone?" His voice was a welcome reprieve from my own thoughts.

"Yeah," I said softly. "It was here." The air seemed to press a little closer, and I felt a flicker of panic in the base of my throat.

Drew stepped up to the well and put his hands on the stone side. The metal grate trembled with the motion and let out the faintest of pinging sounds. "Wonder if people use this for a wishing well." His voice was low and thoughtful. "It's cold over here," he observed.

I felt the breath of cold too, like a slippery tide of wind, it seemed to brush at my cheeks and slip over my fingers. It was so cold, and so real, just there between where he stood by the well and where I hung back. And the dark. The dark seem to coalesce into the wave, something more like water and less like a cloud, more of damp than of air, pushing me back, and blocking me, blocking him. And the dull glow that I had accepted as just a part of him seemed to deaden. The light of him dimmed, and I could barely see the outline of his form. The panic that had been hiding in my throat was suddenly at my lips, tearing to escape. My feet were still, but my brain was screaming for me to run, run away, and don't look back.

"Drew!" The word was thin and high, not like me at all. He turned, and in that instant, I could have sworn he saw it too. His eyes seemed to focus, not on me but just before me, on it. There, in the ripple of dark and cold, there it was, something that didn't belong, didn't live, but somehow had a consciousness, and it suffered.

"Tori?" It was a question, or a response. I couldn't tell.

"Come on," I whispered, feeling my voice catch in my throat until all that escaped my lips was air. "Oh, God," I said in a prayer that I hadn't used for such a long time.

"Tori!" I could see his hand out, he was turning toward me, toward it, away from the open mouth of the well where the metal mesh kept it in, or kept something out. My feet moved then, and I started to go back, not looking, just sliding my feet back, heel first, in the damp grass. The air at my front was icy, at my back was the heat of the night. I could feel the earth breathe beneath my feet as though stirring in her sleep, and the gentle movement made me lose it. My balance went with my knees, dropping me to the ground in a hard slam with no hands out to catch me. My own hands were raised in front of my face, blocking my eyes, blocking my mouth so that I couldn't breathe it in, I wouldn't drink it in. The ice washed over me like a wave of cold black water. My eyes squeezed shut, and I held my breath, my hands over my face, my legs sprawled in front of me. And I went under.

*****

"Tori." The voice that beckoned was deep and rumbled in a chest that was pressed hard to my side. He was carrying me, like some kind of superhero character, holding me close to him as he moved with great speed. My eyes had just adjusted to the angle, when I saw that we were at the gate. It was still open, and he didn't stop there. No cars, no lights from oncoming traffic, just the silence of the dark, the grave, the night.

He carried me across the empty street and over my scarred lawn to the porch, and I wondered numbly if he would carry me across the threshold. But at the porch, he set me down in the old wooden rocker, catching it with one hand while he steered me into a sitting position with the other.

"You okay?"

The question wasn't really a question at all. He knew I was okay, but that wasn't the point. Would I be okay? Would I ever be okay?

"What was that?" I breathed. "What the hell was that?"

He opened the front door of my house and returned to my side.

"Do you need?" He held out his hand for support, and I took it. I wasn't going to be brave, and besides, there was a pretty good chance that my legs wouldn't hold me long.

"Lock the door," I muttered as we went through. Monty came to my side, but controlled his usual antics. He must have read it in the air, known that something had happened.

"You don't drink, do you?" Drew asked as he turned to lock.

"No," I said, and dropped to the couch. "It makes me sick." But I wished I could have something, some instant warmth. Drew paced the room for a moment, and then headed toward the kitchen.

"I'm going to check the other doors," he said in explanation.

I nodded silently and tugged a throw off the back of the couch. It was warm and fuzzy and dark blue, a present for my sister last Christmas. I wrapped it around my shoulders and tried not to think of that Christmas, that slice of before, when I really needed to deal with this, this after. Monty dropped to his haunches in front of me and laid his head in my lap. I absently stoked his ears and concentrated on my breathing.

"I got you water," Drew said, and placed the glass in front of me.

"Thanks," I took a sip, not because I was thirsty, but because it was there, and he had brought it for me. I kept my face down, my expression shielded. "What did you see out there?"

I heard him shift, and then he sat next to me on the couch. "I didn't really see anything. At least, I don't think I did. I might have seen something like fog, or, I don't know, something like a shadow. But it was cold. I could feel the cold, and it wasn't a cold spot like you hear on those TV ghost shows. It was a cold thing, a cold movement."

I was looking at him now, watching his eyes slide to the black windows as though he expected something to be looking in.

"Tori, I've been in that cemetery over a dozen times. I've walked through the whole thing and on nights a whole lot darker than tonight. And I've been in the other cemeteries too. I've been to the Confederate Cemetery, and some other ones around here. But I have never, and I mean never, felt anything like what I felt this time. Nothing."

I carefully set my water glass down on the table in front of me. "Neither have I," I said softly. "When I've felt the person in here, I've always felt like it was someone real. Not a ghost, just some person coming in. That feeling wasn't a person. It wasn't anything like what I've felt here."

"But when your friend lost her phone?"

"Maybe I felt it a little then. I was so spooked; I thought some of my panic was just me overreacting." I pulled the blanket closer to me, gripping it in a bunch under my chin. "But now I see the difference. I think that I felt some of it, just like I did tonight. I think it was there, but just not nearly as strong."

"Are you trying to say that the entity, or whatever, was with you the last time you were at the cemetery? Didn't you say someone took Anna's phone and put it on the wall of the well? Surely that couldn't be a ghost."

"No," I said quickly. "I don't believe that for a second. But I do think that someone was out there messing with us at the same time that we felt the ghost. And I think Anna felt it too. I think she didn't want to admit it, but she was as scared as I was."

"And maybe you feel it more?"

I nodded slowly. "I think I saw more than you did, but considering that I'm seeing auras too, that isn't a really big surprise. Maybe Anna felt what you did. Not as much as me, but still..."

"It was pretty bad," he said firmly. "I saw that, whatever it was, and felt it. Then I saw that you were backing away, and the look on your face wasn't good, not good at all. And then you fell, and I was sure that you were dead." He stopped. His words had sped up, and he was looking a little pale. "When I felt you breathing, my only thought was that we had to get out of there. And I've never felt that way before."

I licked my lips and pressed my hands tightly together, relishing the feeling of life in my fingertips. "So none of this has happened before? No one has talked about being chased out of there by a ghost?"

"The best ghost story we have is about the Bride, and I've never seen her, that's for sure. She's the only legend that I've consistently heard of that comes from the cemetery. And this place gets a fair amount of traffic. It's used for weddings and people visit all the time. It's not known as being a bad place, a haunted place."

I nodded. It was nothing that I hadn't heard. I knew Thea had lived happily next to the cemetery all of her life and had never been frightened of it. It was only with the experience with Thomas that she ever had any supernatural occurrences happen to her. If the place was inherently evil, or consistently haunted, surely she, or someone else in the neighborhood, would have said. And for that matter, Mrs. Lucy's family had lived here in my house for so many years, and she hadn't shown the slightest fear about the place. Even when someone was breaking in, she hadn't left. She had truly believed that her intruder was a real flesh and blood person, not some kind of ghost.

"So what has changed now?" I asked softly, to myself, and to Drew.

"You have," he replied, and looked at me, his eyes dark and soft. "Things have changed a little, with Thomas and his brother, but this, well, this is new. This came with you."

Chapter 11

When spring break for the colleges finally came around, I was relieved to have Thea and Thomas with us, helping Drew and me in our pursuit of …what? I was working in the daytime, seeing Anna on my occasional evenings off and then meeting Drew later that night. Anna asked me about my new distractions since she noticed that I seemed busier in recent weeks, but I was a little reluctant to involve her. She was my friend, my normal friend, my regular, carefree, happy friend, and I wanted to keep her in a bubble for as long as I could. Which wasn't easy.

"Tori, are you sure you don't want to go with me on Saturday?"

Anna was going to a party held by one of her classmates. It promised a lot of loud music, gyrating bodies, the heat of people, and the pure unadulterated joy of being young. I had seriously mixed feelings about it. At home in Chicago, I was known to enjoy a party, trying not to get busted, just to have fun. But here, with all of my new life complications, I wasn't sure if I could work myself up for a party. I put it off, tried to put Anna off, so she wouldn't ask me again, but in the end agreed to go. And why not? I had been working hard, being responsible, up to my neck in things I didn't understand, but I was continuing to live on as though this was normal. A night out would be good for me, I supposed.

I dressed in a short skirt and leggings that clung. My shirt was dark, my hair up in a careless mass, and my earrings brushed my shoulders and jingled faintly when I turned quickly. Anna came over and I helped her with her hair, pulling the heavy honey colored locks into curls, but leaving most of it cascading down her back. She was like my sister, lucky to be pretty in that natural way that wouldn't fade with time.

Liz dropped in and scowled at my skirt. "Can't you pull that down just a little?" she asked, sounding much older than she was.

"No," I said, and looked over my shoulder. "You can't see anything, and the leggings hide what you can." I looked at her speculatively. "Maybe you should come along."

She sniffed. "No thanks. I'm staying in. Monty is here for me."

"Anyone else coming by?" I asked. I suspected a relationship with someone she had met at work, but she was being close mouthed about it.

"No. Well, maybe," she amended.

I looked at her with raised eyebrows and she colored just a little. So something was going on. I had been so embroiled in my own little drama, I had missed out on what was happening with my sister. I vowed to get the details when we were alone.

"Okay," I said slowly. "Well, we won't be loud when we come in," I said.

She scowled at me and I grinned back. Anna interrupted our silent argument when she dropped to my bed.

"I guess I can wear these shoes," she looked doubtfully at the heels that she had brought.

"You're feet are going to be killing you in half an hour," I warned.

Liz ducked out as Anna and I debated foot wear, and she was nowhere to be seen when we left for the evening.

The party was being held in someone's field, just far enough out of town to allow a huge bonfire on the 20-acre tract of land. The house was a shadowing hulk behind us, one of the larger new constructions in the area. Parents were home, supposedly, but the house was dark and warned that intruders would not be welcome. This was an outside party, and it was meant to stay that way.

A pulsing beat met us as soon as we cracked open the car doors. Flashing lights like beacons from a landed alien ship lit up the field in an array of colors. The fire was already burning brightly, its warm glow almost overcome by the artificial light. A long table was set up, loaded down with cold finger foods and snacks. Drinks were placed on a smaller card table to the side with buckets of ice. No liquor was evident, but I knew that didn't mean that it wasn't there. Not that I cared. I had experimented just enough to know my limits, and when I was seeing auras and dead people, I needed to be at my sharpest. No reality altering substances for me.

Anna pulled me along, teetering uncomfortably on the heels. The points sunk into the soft earth, and she stopped, snagged. She yanked off the other shoe and pulled the offending partner from its place planted in the ground. I resisted the urge to tell her what I thought. It wouldn't help.

"I guess I should have brought a different pair," she said, her voice low.

"Hmm," I murmured back, noncommittal.

"Let me introduce you," she said enthusiastically, and dropped her shoes on the ground, walking in bare feet.

The crowd was extensive, and ever moving. Some people came, some people went, melting into the darkness like wraiths themselves. They were the local kids, the high school heroes, the geeks, the requisite members of the football team. They were a blur of orange lit faces, smiling, drinking from red plastic cups. We mixed in for a while, winding among the people, feeling the beat of the music in our bones.

My heart stuttered to a stop when I saw a familiar face. Thomas. He was sitting in a small group of shadows, but his illumination was unmistakable. I looked around to see if anyone else seemed to notice anything about him. Guy glowing, no, they just didn't notice. But there he was, and that meant…

"Hey!"

Thea's voice was a warm bubble of sound. I felt her hand on my arm, solid.

"Hi," I responded, and turned toward her. She looked like any of the other kids, face flushed and tendrils of hair curling gently around her face.

"Didn't know you were coming," she said, but she was smiling.

"Anna brought me. I couldn't refuse." I couldn't help but smile back.

Anna stumbled to my side. "I wish I had other shoes," she moaned, holding her shoes up by the narrow heels. "I've stepped on more rocks and sticks." She focused on Thea in front of us. "Hi, Dot. You in from college?"

"Spring break," Thea responded. "How's Blythe?"

"Tough," Anna replied, but her voice was warm. "You know how she is."

I stood back and watched the exchange. I watched as Thomas came up to meet Anna, watched her smile and laugh at something he said, watched as my worlds collided. I was staring at them, all so normal, when Drew came up. He was unmistakable. Even without his height, his dark hair and handsome profile, he was glowing like something lit from within. His skin had a shimmer to it, his very fingertips seemed alight.

"Victoria, nice to see you again," he said, and stopped next to me. He was smiling playfully, but it wasn't his expression that registered with me.

"What have you been doing?!" I exclaimed, louder than I should. Anna and Thea looked at me in surprise; Thomas was looking back toward the other partiers.

"What?" Drew stepped back, his astonishment mixed with apprehension.

"You know," my voice had dropped to a hiss. "You know exactly what I mean."

"Tori, what?" He asked, keeping his voice low.

He reached out, and before I could pull it away, took my hand. I saw Anna make a move toward us as he pulled me away, but Thea caught her with the muttered "lover's quarrel."

I let him lead me away, but my feet weren't entirely willing. I stumbled along, muttering unkind expletives. He didn't scare me. But his appearance, like some being from another dimension, chilled me. After we were standing away from the crowd, I yanked my hand from his grip and crossed my arms protectively over my chest.

"You've been doing it again. And you've done it more than once. Are you crazy? Don't you worry about what this might do to you? What if you got caught? What if someone found you, or found out? You would be put in some kind of hospital, never getting out, like some kind of lab rat!" My words spilled out in a deluge of concern, my breath quick, my cheeks hot.

He caught my shoulders in his hands, his warmth sinking through my thin top. "Calm." He commanded it as though I were some sort of trained dog. "Shut up for a minute."

I put my hands on his wrists, holding him still as he was holding me. I cleared my throat and looked at his shadowed face. "Okay, so explain."

He dropped his head for a moment, but when he looked at me again, his face was clear. "I have been doing it, but I have been very careful. I always make sure my door is locked, and no one can come in on me while I'm 'away'," he raised his eyebrows at the last word, and I frowned.

"Sure. That sounds perfectly reasonable," I responded, my voice cold. "I'm sure if someone finds you, they are going to take that into account. He's a freak, could be dead, but at least he remembered to lock the doors. "

"It's something that I have to do. I don't expect you to understand. But you have to trust me. I'm doing what I need to, nothing more." He took one hand from my shoulder and ran his fingers through his hair, ruffling the curls.

"You're doing too much. I can tell. You're like a beacon!" My throat felt tight. "I need you to take better care of yourself. I need you to be alright." I thought I might cry. "I just need you," but I couldn't go any further, and I realized that I didn't want to.

His warm hands went to my cheeks, framing my face gently. "I know what you are saying. I understand." His voice was a deep whisper. And he bent close, eyes dark and intense, focused just on me, and on this moment. I didn't move, afraid. Of what? That he would stop? His lips touched mine with a soft brush, barely a breath. And then he touched me again with more passion, more feeling, more heat, and there was nothing I could do but go with him and enjoy the pounding of my own heart. Alive. I was alive and warming, experiencing the sweetness if his embrace. He pulled me close, cradling me against his solid form for just a few moments, steadying me. Then I heard a sound, the unmistakable sound of feet wading too loud through the dry grass.

I pulled away and stepped back, my eyes toward the intruder and not Drew.

"I was getting something to drink and was checking to see if you wanted anything." Anna was lying, but doing it kindly, checking on me in a protective way.

"I guess I could use a drink," I agreed, feeling clumsy and a little lost. Anna waited for me to draw closer and turned back toward the group, walking slowly while Drew followed us into the light.

Thea had several people gathered around her, and seemed to be making sketches in the air with broad gestures. Thomas registered our presence with typical calm. As Thea finished her story, Anna and I escaped to get a cup of ice. I could see the questions in her eyes, but with so many other bodies crowded around, we couldn't really talk. But as many questions as she had for me, I had many more for Drew. He had acted on impulse, on some foolish idea that trying the impossible would give him insight into what made it possible. He was being stupid and putting himself at risk for what reason? I wasn't going to let him get away without answering me.

*****

"You are in such trouble," Anna said quietly as she dropped her purse in the office at the diner. "I'm sure that you were planning on telling me about the new guy. I'm sure you wouldn't dream of not telling me about something so important."

"I was," I said, and sighed. "But don't read too much into what you saw last night."

"I saw him kiss you. And that wasn't a meaningless kiss, so don't even pretend."

"It wasn't meaningless," I mumbled. "But it was a surprise."

"Really!" She exclaimed, and I had the definite impression that I was forgiven.

"Yes," I sighed. "Come on, we need to work. I'll fill you in later.

My explanation was edited, that was certain, but I clung as closely to the truth as I could. Yes, I had known Drew for a little while. Yes, I had met with him a few times. Yes, it was strange to meet someone at the cemetery. Yes, I trusted him, partly because he was such a close friend of Thomas' and by relation, Thea's. Yes, I thought he was fairly gorgeous, but no, we weren't dating. No, we had never been out, not like that. No, I wasn't hoping to have his babies. With the last question, I turned away to grab my keys.

I had deliveries to make, and I was meeting Thea and Thomas after work to talk about the problem at hand. Thomas had taken a day at the beginning of his spring break to go home and visit family. While he was there, he had also taken the opportunity to look through his brother's things. Since they shared a room, and had since they had been little children, it was easy to gain access to Daniel's belongings. And no flash drive had been among his things. So the flash drive, along with Daniel and Thomas' cell phones, were missing since the accident. And that made me wonder. What had happened to those pieces of technology? Thomas had been certain that both he and Daniel had had their cell phones on the trip. They were like every other young adult; they never went anywhere without them. Much less on a longer trip when they might have needed the phones. But the records from the accident didn't list that any cell phones had been recovered and kept by police, and there hadn't been any among the effects that had arrived at the hospital with Thomas and his brother's body.

"Look," I told Anna as I opened the back door to the diner. My hands were full of boxes, and Anna held an extra one for me to take as well. "I will be seeing him tonight. I'll call you later to tell you how it went."

"Okay," Anna agreed. "But I want details."

I laughed and enjoyed the moment of carefree talk. "I will give you details that I decide are appropriate for you to hear."

"Like there'll be anything more than that to tell," Anna scoffed, and I grinned back.

*****

My last stop was the one that I had been waiting for. To my surprise, I had been asked to drop off some pastries for a fundraiser tea that the Oldham County Historical Society was going to have that afternoon. It was a great coincidence. The tea would be an opportunity for sponsors to come and get a look at the offerings that the Historical Society boasted. It would also allow me to go in and look around myself. I wasn't sure about the relationship between my situation and the history of my house or the cemetery, but I wanted to at least investigate. And now I had the perfect reason to be there.

I took 146 instead of the interstate, enjoying the passing scenery. I saw long stretches of road populated only with homes or small clusters of commercial buildings. There was a large campus for several of the Oldham County schools, and the broad expanse of ground, enclosed by a stone wall with tall fences beyond, that surrounded the penitentiary. I probably wouldn't mention that particular landmark to my sister; I was pretty sure she wouldn't like to know of its proximity to our home.

The city of La Grange, when approached from this route, wound its way through some residential streets with impressive older homes tucked side by side. In the center of town was a large brick courthouse with a park like yard. Behind the courthouse was a street split by a railroad track, still in use. As I sat in my car, checking directions, I was astonished to see the train rumble through, just feet from the busy buildings lining the quaint street. I forced myself to look away from the retreating beast, and I turned behind the courthouse and followed the tracks.

The Historical Society was well placed in a lovely old home in the center of the city, tucked in the shadow of the courthouse. I parked next to the larger building and walked across the street, my hands full of pastry boxes. I had gotten really good at shutting my car door with a swift kick but had to wait for someone to come to the door of the house.

I stood on the picturesque porch, my eyes scanning the gingerbread trim on the railings, my mind elsewhere. When the door swung open, I was startled from my thoughts.

"Come in," the middle aged lady greeted as she held the door for me. Her smile was warm but she too looked a little distracted. "You must be from the restaurant. You can put the boxes on the counter. I'll move them when the table is ready."

She bustled around to the main room and gestured to the counter, obviously the office area of the building. I placed the boxes on the plain white surface and looked around in mild surprise. The large room had been partitioned off with walls and glass cases, the contents organized to show bits and pieces of local history.

"Would you mind if I looked around for a minute?" I asked quickly.

She seemed to notice that I was still there and smiled a little absently. "That's fine," she said, "let me just get the lights. There are more exhibits upstairs, too, if you want to go up there."

"Great, thanks," I said, and slipped around the first partition to see a little viewing area with a couple rows of chairs and a blackened screen. The cases were laid out with photographs of different local sites, labeled, and documents tracing the growth of the county. I found myself engrossed in some of the black and white photos, a window into the day to day life of the rural community.

And then there was the article and photos of Duncan Memorial. The story of the building was retold, about the land first being used as a small cemetery with an adjoining church as well as a one room school house. Next was the expansion of the cemetery and the eventual building of the chapel itself as a commemoration to a much loved wife.

There were charming pictures taken there, women in full gowns parading in before a wedding, the chapel façade almost engulfed in greenery, and shots from the interior, displaying gorgeous stained glass windows.

No mention of the well was documented, and although I thought that I had seen a photo of my own house in one of the sepia toned pictures, there was no mention of the family, the missing boy, or the events that followed.

And my time was up. I had to get back to work, my head stilled filled with memories from someone else's past.

*****

I walked in on a conversation, and my first thought was to turn around and walk out. Thea was sitting across from Drew, knees almost touching, at one of the diner's tables. Both had coffee in front of them, but I suspected that it had grown cold long ago.

"If he wants to go, I don't see that there is anything you can do to stop him," Drew said, but his face looked uncommonly grave.

"I know, but I'm just worried about how this will affect him. He doesn't think it will, but with him having no memory of the accident…"

Drew nodded, and looked up to see me standing there. "Come on. Sit down. Maybe you'll have a better idea," Drew said. He stood and pushed his chair back, picking up his cup of coffee. "I'm going to get a fresh cup. Want any?" he asked, looking from Thea to me.

"No, I'm fine," Thea replied, and I just shook my head.

"What's up?" I asked when he had walked away. I slid into the seat next to Drew's and dropped my purse on the floor next to me, bending over the table and leaning on my elbows.

"Thomas still hasn't found the flash drive. He's getting a little desperate about it now. He really feels like he needs to know what we're up against, and I don't blame him. He and Drew think it's all tied up in what happened the night they came here with Savannah. And they might be right." She shook her head slowly and rubbed at her eyes. "I don't know what to think."

"I thought that Thomas had forgotten most of that night."

She sighed heavily. "He has, but he has enough memory to make him want to know more. I mean, they knew that Daniel was taking them out here to look for something. And they knew that he believed it was either in the cemetery or close by it. And he had hinted that it had some kind of historical value, which for Daniel could have meant a lost Beatles album or a piece from King Tut's tomb."

"And Drew? He was there too. And he remembers it all. What does he say?"

"He doesn't recall Daniel ever really saying what he was after, and he says he was just going along for the road trip. He didn't know it was some kind of research."

"So what do they want to do?"

"Thomas feels sure that Daniel had the information with him, either on his cell phone in a file, or on that flash drive. He has been to the crash site with Drew, and they combed the area there, but it's been over a year now, and there really wasn't much left. The evidence that did remain after the accident has probably been taken by the police. But they know that the flash drive has to be somewhere, and the police don't have it, so that leaves…."

"The car," I said softly. Drew had mentioned it, and I had thought it a really bad idea. To go back and see the remains of the car, even if they were cleaned up, would be traumatizing. And they didn't really know what they would find. None of them had seen photos from the accident scene, and Thomas' parents didn't discuss it. "How do they know they can find it? Don't they eventually crush those things into scrap if nothing can be salvaged?"

Thea shrugged. "Thomas called around and finally found someone who knew where the car had ended up. It's in a junk yard in Louisville. We don't know what shape it's in, but Thomas is bound and determined that he wants to go there."

Drew returned with a new cup of coffee and a pastry on a plate, complete with napkin and fork. "This is for you," he said, and pushed it in front of Thea. "Blythe said that you were to eat it or she would call your mother. I don't think she was joking."

Thea smiled and accepted the plate. "I was telling Tori about your plan."

"And what did you think?" He looked at me, his eyes very close and very dark.

"I don't think that you can stop Thomas from going," I said, thinking out my words as I said them. "I guess the question is, who else will go with him, and how can we help him?"

Drew nodded. "Okay, so we'll go with that plan," he agreed.

We were on the south end of Louisville the next morning. Rain was predicted, but we didn't have time to worry about getting wet. Spring break would only be for this one week, and then Thomas and Thea would be back in Lexington, leaving Drew and me on our own with the problems we had dug up.

"What I wouldn't give to be in Florida right now," Thea said her voice wistful.

"Along with half of the state? No thanks, that's too many for me," Drew replied. He deftly steered the car around a turn, sliding into the lane to exit the interstate.

"So where would you like to be?" Thea asked a little sharply.

"Still in bed," Drew responded, and looked back out the rain spattered window. Only Thomas remained unfazed by the weather and the moods of his companions. His look was distracted, thoughtful.

I felt a stab of sympathy. I never wanted to see my parent's wrecked car, or the place where they had taken their last breath. I had purposely avoided going by the spot, detouring in order to avoid the road completely. He didn't have that luxury of choice. It was like facing your worst nightmare and finding out that it was true.

The gate was open when we pulled up, so Drew drove on, stopping the car by a small utilitarian building. A man in heavy coveralls came out, a huge mug of coffee in one hand.

"You all here to see the Toyota?" he asked by way of greeting.

"Yes," Drew replied for us and stepped forward.

"You're in luck. Found it yesterday and had 'er pulled up. She's not much to look at, you know? But I heard the story so…" His eyes flickered past Drew and settled on Thomas. I could tell by the expression on his face that he knew some of the circumstances. He pulled Drew off to the side, their heads close in a quiet conversation. Drew nodded, agreeing to whatever the man was telling him, and I wondered if there were rules to this. The car was no longer evidence. The accident had been labeled just that. Did anyone care what became of the car?

Drew returned to my side, his face looking older than I had seen it. "The car is just around back. We can go through it, but if we take anything, we need to let him know." He stopped and looked at Thomas. "You good?" he asked.

"I'm okay," Thomas replied. He took Thea's hand in his and started walking over the uneven gravel, his shoes making a slushy sound on the wet surface. Thea kept her head up, but her face showed some of the strain. I wanted to turn around and huddle in the warmth of the backseat.

The wrecked car was covered by a tarp, the heavy plastic shielding it from the worst of the rain. Drew went directly to the side and lifted a corner of the tarp, revealing the scratched surface of the rear door. Shrugging his shoulders, he pulled harder, the tarp slipping over the roof of the car, but snagging on the hood. Thomas came to help him, and it was clear then what the tarp had been snagged on. During the accident, the car had slid off the road at an angle, going across the oncoming the lane and ending up in a ditch, ensnared by tree limbs. The rear of the car was relatively unscathed. Clearly, this was where Drew had been since the back seat was the only part of the car that hadn't suffered significant damage. The rest of the car hadn't fared as well. The front hood was gone, ripped off in the accident, perhaps, but missing from the body of the car, as was the driver's side door. The frame, engine, and guts of the car were shoved from the front left fender into the driver's seat, the press of metal so close to where the seat should have been that it was apparent that the driver would never have made it out alive. And Daniel hadn't. I closed my eyes for a moment and shuddered. I could only pray that it had been fast.

The passenger side held less damage, but the existing parts of the windshield were bowed out, clearly showing where something heavy had impacted the glass from within the car. No wonder that Thomas was plagued with headaches. Just seeing the damage made me slightly nauseous.

"Damn," Drew muttered.

Thea put her arm around Thomas' waist as though bearing some of his weight. He was lucky to have survived the crash, that much was clear.

Thomas brought a hand to his face. A spatter of rain had us looking up toward the slate grey sky. "We need to go ahead with this," Thomas said, his voice grim. "It's going to pour, and then we won't be able to see much." He turned to Thea. "You still have the flashlight?"

She nodded and pulled her purse open, the huge bag easily holding three small flashlights and one larger one that she handed to Thomas. The others she gave out to us.

"I'll start at the driver's side," Drew said firmly. "You start in the trunk." He was looking at Thomas, and I knew what he was thinking. He didn't want Thomas to have to see where his brother had died, and Drew feared what might be left there.

"I'll look in the front passenger seat," I told them, and hurried over to the side, stepping over the tarp as I went.

"I guess I have the backseat," Thea said, and flicked on her light. "They always use these in the crime shows. I thought it might help us to see under the seats."

"It was a great idea," I agreed, and forced a smile. She looked back at me gratefully and yanked the back door open.

Drew couldn't find any kind of trunk release in the mess that had been the front console, but the trunk had been pried open sometime in the past and popped open easily. I hunched over the front seat, feeling a little faint when I saw the dark brownish puddle that had dried in copious amounts on the floorboards and ground into the remaining seat where Thomas had been. Gloves. I hadn't thought about it until now, but we really should have had gloves for this. I frowned and shined my light over the cracked plastic that had been the dashboard, the glove compartment with the door hanging open, and the floor with the mats shoved back against the base of the seat. Nothing there. No, that was wrong. There were papers, bits of pencil stubs, receipts, a loose car manual with a ripped cover, an old tennis shoe with broken laces, a wadded tissue, and an open pack of gum. But I found no phone, no flash drive, no bits of clues that would help explain what had happened there.

"Trunk's cleaned out," Thomas said from the rear of the car, slamming the lid back down. "Looks like someone had been in there before."

"Maybe the police," Thea noted.

"Maybe." Thomas shrugged and went to the other back door opposite from Thea's hunched form. It was jammed. The impact from the front collision had shoved the frame back, and the door wouldn't open. The driver's side lay open like a gaping mouth. Thomas didn't even look toward the front but walked over to stand next to Thea.

"There's a ton of stuff that's rolling around in here," Thea said, her voice muffled.

"We didn't clean this thing out enough." Thomas sounded lost.

"Well, it's good for us. At least we know that it hasn't been disturbed in here." Thea bent double, her flashlight beam reflecting bits of broken glass.

"Maybe," Thomas replied, but his voice still sounded unsure. He stood up, pushing longish blond hair from his face, and looking toward Drew at the front of the car.

"I see something in the floor by this seat," Thea was saying, her head so low that her hair was brushing the floor. "It was pushed against the side of the seat, back here at the bottom."

"Let me see," Thomas said, and waited for her to move. He took the larger flashlight and shined it beneath the back seat, wedging himself further in the car.

I glanced at where Drew was standing by the driver's side. He was frowning, and when I looked toward him he slowly shook his head. The destruction had been too extensive for anything to have survived the wreck there in the front. Anything or anyone.

"Here," Thomas straightened and held out his hand. In his palm was a black plastic case, the metal plug of the flash drive just visible. It was hooked to a blue lanyard with white lettering. "This is it."

"Are you sure?" Drew abandoned his place and came around the car.

"Positive. Daniel kept this with him all the time. He used computers in lots of places, and he didn't trust his documents to email or anything. He just kept it all together on this."

"Let's hope it didn't get broken," Thea said, taking the flash drive gingerly and looking at it closely.

"And no cell phones," I said thoughtfully. "But I guess the phones wouldn't have survived the crash. Probably broken. Would the police have just thrown them away?"

"Doubt it," Thomas said with a small grimace. "But they're not here anymore."

"Then we can head out," Drew said, his eyes going to the darkened sky.

We turned together, away from the wreck, the remains of the car, but Thomas stopped. "I'll be there in a sec," he said, and his eyes told us that he wanted to be alone. We walked slowly back to Drew's car, a sudden solemn silence settling on us. I glanced back to where Thomas stood, his hand on the hood of the car, his eyes down. I felt the sudden pain of the loss, fresh and real, and had to gasp. All I had lost, all that I was, and all that had changed. I doubted that he or I would ever get over this.

*****

We returned to the cemetery as the rain misted the grass like fog. Thea insisted that she wanted to go back to the grounds, and we all agreed to go. Her purpose for the return visit went unsaid, but there was an ache there, and none of us wanted to question it. With general consensus, we parked the car just outside the gate and stood in the shelter of the wall, close to Thea's house. I felt a shiver when I looked toward the well and backed away slightly. It was day, and while the light was filtered through the grey of the clouds, it was still safe here. But I couldn't shake the uncomfortable feeling. I forced myself to look away from the well and over the damp grounds, wondering what it had been like for Thea to find him, a ghost wandering in the night out here among the headstones. I looked to see Thea, her hands cupping her own cheeks, her eyes welling with tears. I wondered what she was thinking of. What was she mourning?

"Thea?" I said softly.

She turned her eyes on me and wiped at her cheeks. "I'm fine," she lied. I looked at her curiously, but she just looked away. I felt a little sting, but forced myself not to dwell on it. We all had our ghosts, and Thea was entitled to her own.

"Wish I knew what he was thinking," Drew said, his voice low. "Daniel." He had his head down and his damp hair fell in his face. He looked like some painting of emotion, of brooding, all dark and tense. Thomas stood leaning against the damp wall, hands tucked in his pockets. I figured that the flash drive was safely tucked in one of those pockets, and Thomas didn't want to give it up.

"Hopefully, we can get some answers," I said firmly, proud that my voice was so steady. I cleared my throat and wrapped my arms around my middle. "I am really surprised that we found the flash drive. It was a long shot."

Drew nodded and turned slightly. Rain fell with a little more force, beading his long eyelashes. His eyes went to mine, but I couldn't find anything else to say.

When the rain started in earnest, we trudged through the damp and ducked into Thea's house. She gave us a few old towels that we used to dab at our faces and hair, and then huddled in the kitchen while she put on the coffee pot and found some homemade chocolate chip cookies that her mother had left wrapped in foil. Her mother was working at the high school, and her father was on one of his trips to the store looking for more gardening equipment. The house was silent but for the steady patter of rain on the roof and the snuffle of her dog Baxter as he rolled over in his sleep.

"Let's go in my room," Thea said softly against the silence. "I'll get the computer going." She turned to face us. "Are any of you good with computers? They're not my thing. I always have my friend Lindsey help me when she's home." She pushed a stray curl out of her face. "Heck of a time for her to go to D.C. We could have used her help."

"Does she know?" Drew had dropped to the side of Thea's narrow bed, leaving room for two empty chairs at the computer.

"She knows most of it. She helped me last fall." Thea took the seat at the little desk. "She took all the weird stuff really well. Didn't think I was crazy at all." She made a wry face.

I stood in the doorway and studied the room. Where my space was buried in clothes and papers, open books, pens, pencils, and nail polish bottles, Thea's was neat and clean. Her books were stacked, her clothes obviously tucked in their proper places. The only thing that was completely out of character for the rest of the room was a massive flower arrangement that sat on a trunk at the foot of her bed. It looked like a sculpture, but it was formed from what appeared to be dried flowers and was molded into a shape that looked eerily like a face. Her room was like little girl meets Goth artist with a sprinkle of dog toys and a poster of some Dali print on the wall.

"Wow," I muttered, but she grinned at me.

"I haven't done much redecorating. Haven't had time or money."

"Is that yours?" I asked, nodding toward the flower sculpture.

"Yep, I made it a couple of months ago for one of my sculpture classes. Got an A." She shrugged. "I would have made it anyway. It was one of those things."

"Thea is really talented," Thomas said, animation finally finding its way into his features. "She's won awards and had her own show locally. Does some business too."

"It was a little show," Thea said, "in La Grange. But it was awesome."

Thomas put a hand on her shoulder. "It was awesome." He slipped into the seat next to her, leaving me to sit with Drew on the bed. I awkwardly dropped next to him, leaving room between us. We hadn't spoken about the kiss, hadn't acknowledged that it had happened, but it wasn't far off my mind. Now my feelings felt like a tangled ball of string somewhere in my solar plexus.

"I'll get this thing going, and you can try to read the flash drive," Thea told Thomas. The screen flickered blue in front of her and then went through the familiar loading sequences. Once the desktop was ready, Thomas took the flash drive from his pocket and plugged it in. Thea scooted over and handed him the mouse, and we all watched as he opened the file labeled "Daniel's papers." The single file yielded a string of many more, some image files, some Word documents, and many scans and PDFs.

I felt a subtle letdown and frowned to myself. Had I really expected there to be a file labeled, "all the answers you ever needed about what the hell is happening to you"? Drew had leaned over to see past Thomas' frame, and his arm brushed mine, momentarily pulling me from my musings. Another situation with no easy answer.

Thomas was clicking through the files, his eyes scanning and discarding pages faster than I could register. He hesitated on a few, leaning closer to look at the text. "These are papers from some book. He must have snapped a picture of them with his phone and then turned them into PDFs. He wouldn't have done that if they were books that he had, so they had to be from somewhere else." He leaned forward again. "I can't even read some of this. It's too old, too blurry. It looks like whatever it came from was quite an antique." He opened up another file folder on the computer and leaned close. "This is more of the same. It's a different book, but old. I doubt these are in print anymore. They must have been from someone's collection."

"Or a library," Thea murmured. "Enlarge that one. It should be clear enough to read."

Thomas obliged and they both leaned in, heads close and blocking the screen. "Really formal writing," Thea said softly. "Looks like an article." She put her fingertip against the screen. "That looks like a bookplate. It usually names the owner of the book. Edwin Morrison. I can't say I've ever heard that name before. Do you think he might have loaned Daniel the book?" She studied the article for a moment more. "This one seems to be about some religious figure. Saint Francisca."

"Do you have some kind of encyclopedic knowledge of saints?" Drew's voice was a shade too dry.

"No," Thea said slowly, "but I know someone who might."

*****

Religion was not my strong suit. I had gone to church at the insistence of my parents, but as soon as the last candles had been blown out after their funeral service, I had left the little Methodist church and never gone back. And it's not as though the people didn't try. There were casseroles and hot buttered rolls, calls to check up on us, prayers and cards to fill our mailbox, and phone calls: insistent, kind, battering calls that made me irritated, then angry, and finally bitter. I was so glad to move away from all of those kind hearted people, away from their soft eyes and Jesus words.

In this new little town we had no religion. There was no God figure standing on his high cloud judging us. He was back to being some safe concept that others could live with, but not me, never me again. Thea's proposal that we go to the local Catholic church to talk to the priest there made my stomach roll.

"Are you absolutely sure that this is a good idea?" I asked Thea as she walked up the slightly listing stairs to the covered front porch of the old house.

"I've known these people all my life," Thea said, her voice determined. "This is no big deal."

I shoved my hand through my hair and then hastily smoothed it down again. This was an argument that was getting me nowhere. "Whatever," I mumbled under my breath.

Thea turned to me at the door and frowned. "Look, if you have a medical problem, you go to a doctor. If you have a spiritual problem, you go to a spiritual person. If you have someone better, just let me know."

Apparently I had hit a nerve. "No, no, you're right. Sorry. I'm just being stupid."

Thea nodded and knocked on the door, three sharp raps with her knuckles. She wasn't giving me any slack. I was wrong, she was right, and she knew it.

The man that opened the door was not what I pictured when I thought of a priest. He wore jeans, a plaid shirt buttoned up over a tee shirt, and soft leather shoes. No clerical collar, no black.

"Dot!" He exclaimed, his face lighting up. "What a nice surprise."

"Father," she smiled and took his offered hand. "I hope this is okay. I wanted to ask you about something, so we came without calling."

"It's fine, fine. I'm going out to the nursing home later, but I was just catching up on a little reading."

He ushered us into what had once been a rather large and grand house. With age, it had settled into shabby comfort, but still held some of its original beauty. Someone had taken the time to decorate it with antiques, and although I knew little about old furniture, I suspected some of the pieces were the same age as the house.

When we stepped into the kitchen, Thea dropped into one of the chairs tucked around the table as though familiar with the seat. The good Father sat across from her and held out a hand in a welcoming gesture.

"I've done it again. Forgot the introductions. Dotty, who is your friend?"

Dot smiled. "Sorry. Tori, this is Father Ben. Father, this is Victoria."

I took the offered hand and felt something, a little flicker. It was like a soothing wave of warmth had slipped from his fingers, a spiritual flutter. Was I feeling his aura? What was going on with me? I forced myself not to draw back, to jerk away from the contact. He looked at me calmly, his smile still welcoming. So it was just me. He showed no sign of noticing anything different about me, and for that I was grateful. I stowed the thought away as something to consider later.

"Nice to meet you, Victoria."

I nodded, still feeling a little shaken.

"We had a question for you," Thea said frankly. "I figured if you didn't know the answer, you would know where to find it."

Father's face grew more serious. "Of course, I'll try," he assured her. His eyes went between us, assessing.

"We wanted to ask you about some church history. Have you heard of Saint Francisca?"

The priest's brows knit, but he didn't look like the name had set off any internal alarms. "There are several by that name that I can think of off the top of my head. I'm sure there are others that I can't recall. Do you have any other facts about her? What exactly were you looking for?"

"We are looking at anything we can find about her, but especially where she was from, where she died, what her history is, what she's known for."

"Okay, well we can start with one of my old reference books. Wait for a moment while I find it," he said, and slipped out of his seat. I could hear the steady pace of his steps as he retreated further into the house and looked at Thea.

"So what do you think?"

I was surprised by the question and looked at her with raised eyebrows, my expression a question.

"I could tell something when you took his hand. What did you think?"

I blew out a breath. "Do you study people for a living?" I asked and sneaked a look behind my shoulder.

"You are really easy to read," she said in an undertone as the steps heralded the return of the priest.

The book he dropped on the table was incredibly thick and bulky, more a tabletop book than anything meant for a life on a shelf. The binding was heavy, the gloss worn away with age, the pages gilded on the edges.

"Here we go. This is a fairly comprehensive collection of our more well-known saints. It isn't the most recent volume, but you weren't interested in someone from our recent history?"

"Right," Thea agreed, leaning on her elbow to look closer at the book. "We know that she was from Spain or an island off the coast. We know that she lived in the 1600s."

Father opened the book to the index and ran one finger down the list of names, easily finding the one they were looking for. "Saint Francisca, born in 1672 in Spain. Known for her service to the poor," his voice softened as they leaned together to read the text. In a moment, he sat up straight and looked at Thea. "This gives us a general idea, now I can search for something more specific. Come this way."

We stood and threaded through the kitchen door, deeper into the house. We went past closed doorways and curtained windows, stopping across from the dining room where the double doors had been closed against the draft from the front door.

"The library," Thea exclaimed. "I've never gotten to come in here!"

I stopped in the entrance and just stared at the packed shelves. Bookcases ran from floor to ceiling on three of the walls, parting only to allow a narrow opening for a window. A huge desk complete with clawed feet and scarred top dominated one side. On the other side was a small fireplace, framed in carved wood molding, and a pair of chairs, old by the looks of them, but most likely comfortable. The books themselves filled every horizontal space, marching in lines over the shelves, in stacks on the desk, and even small towers of them on the floor next to the chairs. I looked closer, curious of the subject matter. Besides the extraordinary number of religious texts, there were many secular works as well to my surprise -- British mysteries, biographies of political figures, tomes of poetry, and many with spines worn until the words were mere shadows.

"Pull up a chair," Father said grandly, "and welcome. We'll find what you are searching for."

*****

"The answer has to be in here somewhere." Thea laid out the stack of papers that we had accumulated. We were at the table in my little kitchen; Liz was out again for the evening. Drew was to my right, Thomas to my left. I had spent a long day at the diner, delivering to three different places before I could head home. The pastry business was booming, but it was exhausting to me. I had spent too many sleepless nights worrying about the stranger breaking into my home, about the totally insane idea that people, people that I knew, could be strolling outside of their bodies with perfect deliberateness, and I was scared of the life that I would be left with when this was all over.

Thea was looking a little stressed as well. They would be returning to school in a few days, and the distance would slow down our progress by quite a bit. While I had been working, she and Thomas had reviewed the documents and notes we had gotten from the religious texts as well as the Internet, and now they seemed ready to talk about what they had found.

"Saint Francisca was born in 1672. In Spain," Thomas started.

"Or an island off the coast of Spain." Thea pulled out her cell phone. "Yes, here it is." She held out her phone for us to see the tiny map. "And according to this," now she tapped one ink stained finger on a photocopy," she was from a wealthy family, a lineage with lots of land and lots of power. She gave it all up when she was just a teenager."

"She went into the convent?" Drew asked.

I knew the answers to the easy ones. "She entered the convent early, but they did in those days. She left home, left her family and comfortable life, to join a religious order. The order was devoted to Mary, the Mother of Christ. They were known for their service to the poor, the local troubled. They were a self-sufficient group, doing some gardening to help feed themselves and the rest of the community."

Thea took up the story. "Saint Francisca was known for her generosity, especially in her small town." Thea flipped over some photocopied pages, one a black and white pencil sketch of a bucolic farm scene, notable for the slight figures of women in habits tending to some plantings.

"But here is where it gets interesting. When Saint Francisca was in her 50s, she met up with a well-known privateersman named Juan Madino. This guy was like a pirate, a really corrupt character who stole from ships and redistributed the cargo to the highest bidder. He didn't have any problem working completely outside of the law. But I guess even pirates respected the Church."

"The nun and the pirate?" Drew said thoughtfully, now fully engaged in the discussion.

"It was written in one article that the two were distantly related, and somewhere else, it said that Juan Madino's own sister was in the order with Saint Francisca."

"Interesting," Drew murmured, drawing out the word.

"Okay, but here's where it relates to us. On one occasion," Thea continued, ignoring his comments, "Saint Francisca was in the convent, praying with the rest of the sisters. I mean, she was surrounded with other people. But at the same time, she was seen by a whole ship load of pirates. The legend said that she stood between this pirate," she pointed to the illustration before us, "and another pirate captain who was going to attack. She just appeared between the two and saved the pirate's life. It apparently changed him, amazed him so much that he became a legitimate sailor and highly religious man."

Thomas slowly picked up one of the photocopied papers, a picture of a woman in full habit standing between two threatening figures. "She saved his life and his soul," he said softly. "This had to be the story that Daniel was chasing, but I still don't understand why."

"The pirate outlived the nun, and eventually died in his personal island hideaway, but by then he had become known as a religious figure himself. His body was interred in the local Catholic chapel. Many of his belongings were buried with him in the church on the island, including a cross that was said to have come from St. Francisca."

My eyes followed the penciled sketch, copied from one of the priest's books, to another article in one of the newer tomes from his collection. "His grave was robbed," I said, flipping the article to the second page. "The church was desecrated, and the building was stripped of all of the significant artifacts. The thieves picked up anything that they considered to be valuable, including some of the treasures buried in the coffins themselves. His coffin wasn't the only one opened, but it was probably the most valuable." I skimmed the article again. "In the end, his body was returned to the coffin and then reinterred. No comment about all of the valuables that were taken."

"But if the cross was among them," Drew said thoughtfully, "and it had been Saint Francisca's."

"There is still no connection here," Thea said, her hands open on the papers. "How does a religious artifact from off the coast of Spain end up in Kentucky?"

"Wait," I said and looked over at her. "Mrs. Lucy was talking about the history of my house, and her family. In the ghost story about the old man, she said the grandfather that lived here at the time that the little boy disappeared was some kind of historian. He had come back to this country after traveling. She said that he had collected lots of artifacts from all over the world. After he died, they had to take some of them and box them up just because he had so much. What if he somehow ended up with the pirate's grave goods?"

"Or a gift to the pirate from the saint?" Thomas moved his hand over his face slowly. "What if the saint somehow transferred some of her abilities into the gift?"

*****

It was insane. It was ridiculous. I didn't know religion that well, but I was pretty sure that religious relics weren't like magic talismans. But we had no better ideas. I rolled over, tugging my blanket closer. The weather was cool for the spring, but the jonquils had already begun to bloom with brilliant yellows, and the season was changing. I wouldn't open the windows to the breeze, to the sweet scented wind. I wanted no chance that he would come.

I slept heavily and dreamed of pirates with gold teeth and gold necklaces, the weight of their plunder pulling them deep into the sea.

"Tori, wake up, girl!"

"Later," I mumbled, "just a few more minutes."

"Tori, now. Tori girl, wake up. Get your sister!"

"Dad," I said, my voice in a whine, "not yet." Then a moment and my eyes flickered open. "Dad?" My eyes stared into the darkness. I could smell it, the distinct scent of him, his aftershave and the soapy scent he favored. I sat up. I could still smell him, oh God, I knew he was there. "Dad," my voice choked. "Where are you?"

But now I smelled something else, smoky, sour. My feet hit the floor, and I rose, tossing my blankets to the foot of the bed. I tripped over the mounds of clothes blocking my way and yelped. Monty was at the door, a high pitched whine in the back of his throat. When I yanked the door open, I realized that the smell was much stronger. Monty arrowed out, his feet sliding on the stairs, his bark bellowing back my way. I ran down the hall, heedless of his noise and jerked my sister's door open.

"Liz" I shrieked, "fire!"

She sat up abruptly. "What?"

"Fire, downstairs!" I banged on her open door with my fist, adding noise to my hoarse cries. "Do you hear me? Get up! I'm going downstairs!"

My feet pounded down the stairs, the wood squealing in protest with each impact. I stopped in the doorway, staring into the dimness. A flame bloomed on the back of the couch, spreading upwards into the curtain. The cool air fed the fire, the yellow red dancing higher. Smoke settled like a dirty cloud at the level of the ceiling, clogging my breathing.

My sister stopped next to me and I realized that Monty was at her side. In her hand was a mini fire extinguisher, a gift from Blythe when she first guided me through baking cookies.

"Stand back," she bellowed.

"I'm calling the fire department," I said, rushing around the corner. My phone was in my room. Crap, I had left it there. I raced up the steps and down the hall, sliding a little on the floor. At my doorway, I grabbed the doorknob and then stopped. The door was closed. I hadn't closed the door. I had run out of my room, never even thinking to pull the door. I froze. He was here. He had done this. He had set my house on fire! Now he was in my room. I held my breath. I couldn't let my home burn. Liz's phone, where was it? Probably in her purse, and that was downstairs. I couldn't wait. I jerked my door open and ducked behind the doorjamb. What was I doing? I stood up straight and looked in my room. Still dark, still quiet. And there was the figure, the terrible darkness, the man shape, the image of something that I had never really believed in reality.

"It won't do you any good," he hissed. "You can't stop me, and if you try," his voice melted, and with that, his shape did as well.

*****

Liz sat next to me and took my hand. I could feel her cool slender fingers around mine, and all that I could think of was my dad. I had heard him, he had been there. A tear slid warm and salty down my cheek, and Liz gently pulled me down until my head rested against her slender shoulder.

"It's going to be okay," she said softly.

I nodded. The firemen had arrived, horns blaring, lights flashing, familiar faces under scuffed helmets. We were sitting on Thea's porch, but the fire was extinguished. It was mostly trapped in the living room, and the damage had been limited to that room as well. But the front window was like a black maw full of darkened shards of glass teeth. And my mother's couch, my father's side table where he rested the TV remote and his wallet and keys, the throw rug that had been tucked snugly in the entry of our old house, all were ruined by flame and smoke.

"Was this a mistake?" I whispered. "Should we have stayed home? Lived in the old house?"

Liz sighed. "We couldn't afford the old house. I didn't have a job there and didn't have any prospects either. This is a good change. We just ran into a bump."

"A bump?"

"Sure, a bump in the road. You know, the road of life and all that."

"Feels more like a pothole," I whispered.

"And now we're rolling out of the hole."

The door muttered against the doormat, and Thea's mother stepped out. She had a tray, a plastic one painted with beach balls, and held it in both hands while she used her hip to prop the door open. Coffee cups, cream, sugar, and a pitcher of hot coffee were on one side, a plate full of Oreos on the other.

"I didn't have time to bake," she said, and put the tray on the floor next to us. She smiled, her face pale, her eyes concerned.

"Thanks," Liz said, and started pouring herself some coffee. "Thanks for everything."

I smiled and nodded, but my head was far away. As my tear filled eyes glittered with the reflection of headlights, my mind was moving into a happier place, a place where no one was breaking into my home, setting fires, or trying to terrorize us. I longed for home.

*****

In the misty morning light, my house looked like a specter itself, shrouded with the remnants of smoke and fog. The windows were all dark, like eyes to an empty soul, and I felt like a little part of the house had died with the fire.

"Come on," Liz said softly, and I followed her across the street. The firefighters were cleaning up, packing away heavy equipment and hoses, their heavy boots making ominous thuds against the old wood of the porch.

"You girls be careful. Haven't gotten to inspect the structure yet, so we don't know how sound she is. You might just want to run in and get what you need for a few days. It'll take some time to get her back to being habitable." The fire captain's face was smudged with soot, his eyes reddened from the smoke. The fire hadn't eaten away too much of our lives, but it hadn't given up without a fight.

"Thank you so much," Liz said, stopping to take his big hand in her own. I passed behind her, through the door and into the smoky interior.

The smashed window held evidence of how the fire had been started. He hadn't needed to bilocate to get in this time. He had started the fire with a thrown shaft of wood soaked in some type of accelerant, and then retreated to the back to slip inside. We had predictably rushed downstairs, clearing the way for him to come in and explore without interference from us or our dog.

The couch was a loss; what hadn't been burnt had been water logged. The fire had spread up the cheap curtains, leaving a sizable hole in the ceiling surrounded by a great black ring of ash. You could plainly see where the fingers of flame had spread upwards and out, trying to reach farther into the room. The ceiling was soaked and dripping, the floor sagging from the weight of the soaked furniture, the sticky feel of ash and damp on every surface.

Upstairs, the smell of smoke permeated the rooms. There was no water damage to be seen, but the floors would have to be examined by someone more knowledgeable about structural integrity. My door was closed again. I stood there in the doorway. He had been in there. He had come into my room, and for what? I stepped into the dim recesses. I had no valuables, I had nothing that he might have wanted, or did I?

It took a moment for my brain to process the whole picture. My house was where we had sat around and discussed our thoughts about what we had found in our research. We had spread all our evidence out on the table like so many cards. The papers were here, the books borrowed from Father Ben, the computer that we had done research on, and the flash drive… where was that? Had Thomas taken it with him when he had gone home the night before, or had he left it plugged into the USB? I couldn't remember. I hurried across to my desk where my computer had always lain. But it wasn't there. My eyes slid to the floor and I stepped back in surprise. The computer was lying open at my feet, the keyboard pried viciously from the body of the laptop, the plates of electronic bits stamped and spread as though torn by furious hands. The stack of documents that had sat beside the computer was gone, and if the flash drive had been in the computer, it was obviously gone as well.

"Tori," Liz's voice traveled up the stairs. "What are you doing up there?"

"Nothing," I said quickly, and then realized that it sounded stupid to say. "I'm getting my things together." I looked at the mangled computer and felt a surge of anger. Now what? That bastard had broken in for one thing only. He wanted the information we had, and he had decided to prevent us from learning any more.

I pulled my phone from my pocket and sent a quick text to Drew. Then I yanked open my closet door and pulled a duffel bag from the shelf at the top. The material snagged and I tried to jerk it to pull it free. When it remained stubbornly stuck, I let go of the material and dragged the desk chair to the closet. I could see the catch now, a nail that stuck out a little too high. I leaned forward, head and shoulders in the closet, and tried to untangle the material. It would not give, the canvas too sturdy. I leaned a little further in and grasped the nail head. It felt sharp in my fingers, but irritation kept me trying, and with one upward pull, it came loose. A hollow bump and pinging sound followed, and I stepped off the chair to look at the floor. A wooden block, plain and grayish with age was sitting on the floor, and next to it, an old fashioned key, a slip of yarn looped in the top. I puzzled over the two pieces. I could see the imprint of the key on the wood. Had it been nailed up there? Had someone sandwiched the key between the shelf and the wood and nailed it into place? How strange was that?

I heard my sister's steps and dropped the key into the duffle bag. I threw the bag on the bed and grabbed my garbage can from beneath my desk. My hands were shaking as I stuffed the broken computer parts into the garbage and then tied the top of the bag closed. I couldn't let Liz see this, at least not yet. It was ironic that now that I had real evidence that someone had been in the house, I didn't feel like I could show my sister. I had let things go too far, had covered up too much of the truth to go back now.

I dropped the garbage bag back to the floor and started shuffling though my clothes. Without much thought, I started stuffing worn jeans, tees, and jackets into the duffle bag. I yanked open my drawer to find some underwear and dropped a handful of them on the top. I realized that my breath was coming too fast and dropped to the side of the bed for a moment.

"Chill," I murmured to myself. I put the duffle on my lap and slowly rummaged through the contents, taking a moment to think about what I would be needing in the next several days while we waited for our house to be inspected and declared safe to return to.

I added a few of my favorite dog eared books and a notebook that I had turned into a journal. I stood and went to my jewelry box, lifting the wooden lid and looking at the tangle of costume jewelry I owned. There were only a few pieces I cared about. I pulled out a pocket watch from my grandfather, a little locket from my mother's mother, and the charm bracelet. My mom had gotten the bracelet on her sixteenth birthday and had added to it over the years, with her marriage to my father, the birth of her children, her graduate degree, and our little successes depicted in tiny soccer balls, an artist palette for my sister, and a peace symbol from me. My dad had added a cross and a tiny book that really opened, reflecting my mother's interest in religion and in reading.

I stopped to fasten the bracelet around my wrist, and took the other sentimental pieces to put in my bag.

"Have you gotten your stuff from the bathroom?" my sister asked, peering around the doorjamb.

"No," I zipped up the outer pocket of the duffel bag to secure the jewelry. "I'm going there next. And I need to pack for Monty."

"About that," Liz said, her voice a little tentative.

"Don't worry. I've arranged for Thea to watch him for a few days. Hopefully we can move back in next week."

Liz nodded. "Insurance will pay for a few nights at the hotel, but I know it is a little farther for you to drive."

"It's okay, but I'll need to run a few errands before I can meet you at the hotel," I said and slipped past her. The hotel was close enough that I would be able to get to work with ease, but I wanted to be closer to the house to finish looking into this most recent crime against my home for one more day. Leaving Liz safely in a hotel for a little while would be a relief. I took one last look into my room and headed for the bathroom to finish my packing.

A few minutes later, I stood on the porch. Liz had run out to get some supplies, and I had the duffel bag and my crushed computer tied up securely in a garbage bag at my feet. I could see Thea pulling in, and Drew was out almost before the car was in park.

I watched him lope over, his long strides eating up the ground. His dark hair caught the wind, and a slant of sun made his beard stand out against his skin. His hands were in his pockets, and he ducked his head as he walked. He skipped up the steps and stopped next to me.

"Hey," he said, and looked at the closed trash bag at my feet. "That it?"

"Yep, $300 worth of scraps. He did a number on it. But at least Thomas had the drive, so we still have most of the information."

"I'm sorry about your computer. And your house. And everything." He pulled his hands out of his pockets and put them gently on my shoulders.

"Yeah," I said faintly, the words lost in my head.

He pulled me gently against him, and then more firmly, pressing me close, toe to toe, my face against the warmth of his chest. "Can't catch a break, can you?"

I shook my head silently. What to say? If I spoke I might cry, and if I started crying, I might not stop.

His hands traveled up and down my back, soothing and gentle. I made myself relax, give in for just a moment. I could feel his breath on my neck as he leaned in close. His lips were a warm brush against my cheek.

"We're going to get him," Drew murmured in my ear. "And from now on, you're not going to be alone."

I pulled back slightly and looked into his face. "You can't be everywhere."

"I don't have to be," he said softly. "Just at night. And I can come and go just like he can."

"You don't need to do that."

"I do," his eyes were dark and fierce. "And I will. He's not playing anymore, and we're not either." His hands moved to my face. "You were worried about me? Well I am taking care of you. I love you, Tori, and I'm not going to let you get hurt."

I stared at him, my eyes damp, my vision a little blurry. It was one of the worst moments of my life, and yet his words had made it one of the best.

"I love you too," I said, my voice choked and weak.

He smiled a crooked smile and leaned in to kiss me. And it was so sweet.

The throat clear from behind Drew had me stepping back, but he held me to him. Thomas didn't look even a little apologetic. "Okay, so we have some work to do. You'll have time to snuggle later," his smile was gently mocking.

"What do you mean?"

"Well, we've lost some of our sources, but we have others to look into now. Thea and I are going back to see Father. You and Drew can see Mrs. Lucy. I think it's about time we figured out what that old man left behind that was worth this." His light eyes slipped behind me. "We don't have tons of time, so…"

"I'm ready," I said, straightening.

*****

I hated lying to Liz. I wanted to be with her while we were both getting over the shock of the fire, but I knew that Thomas was right. There was no time to waste. Spring break would soon be over, and that would take Thea and Thomas away until summer, but besides that, the intruder was apparently getting much bolder. And what really frightened me was that he was willing to show violence, and that too was escalating. He obviously hadn't found what he was looking for. If he had, he wouldn't have found it necessary to take our papers, to destroy my computer, and to threaten me. We had to figure out what he wanted before he went any further.

The sun was bright, not cooperating with my glum mood, although I held fast to the little part of my heart still warm from the kiss and the promise of Drew's dark eyes. The parking lot at the retirement village was a little empty, but I could see activity behind the windows. When I swung the door open, a small belch of warm air slid through to fan my face. We signed in at the desk; I wasn't delivering today, and I hoped the ladies wouldn't be disappointed.

Drew hadn't yet met Mrs. Lucy, and I felt a slight pang of guilt. She was so happy to see us, and I hated to tell her about the fire. It had been her home first and foremost. For her, the memories were mostly sweet, and I didn't want to ruin any of that. I couldn't force myself to smile.

But Mrs. Lucy's eyes were bright when she caught sight of us. She looked at me with new interest. It was the first time that I had brought a friend with me, and Drew had a way of making an impression. He took her hand in a gentlemanly manner, and his smile was fairly enchanting.

"Mrs. Lucy, this is Drew, my…" I paused at the word, and Drew filled in.

"…boyfriend." He smiled again. "Nice to meet you."

"It's nice to see that Victoria has some new friends," Mrs. Lucy said, her smile revealing those bright white dentures.

"I came to ask a favor," I said quickly. I was slightly worried that Mrs. Lucy might reveal some of my more emotional visits.

Mrs. Lucy just looked at me.

"We are still looking into the history of the house," I said, but I was having difficulty keeping eye contact.

"Are things going alright at home?" Her voice was concerned, and I knew she had read me.

"Fine," I said quickly. "We are fine. But we wanted to learn more about the history of the house. Drew is very interested in local history," I added, throwing him a glance.

"Really?" Now he was even more attractive to the sharp old lady. "Well then, I would be happy to have you look through my things." She paused and her face screwed up in thought. "I just need to find the key for the storage area. Let me look in my room. You'll be here?" Her eyes were back on Drew.

"Yes, ma'am."

"And Victoria, you can help me look."

I had been skillfully out maneuvered and followed her out of the lobby area and down the hall. I hadn't seen her room, but it was much as I had expected. Her little apartment held the favorites from the house, the curved sofa with the rose patterned covering, the antique sewing machine with the framed photo of her and her husband on their long ago wedding day, and a small Oriental rug that had doubtlessly protected her feet from the cold wood floors.

"You are telling me everything?" Her voice was very serious.

"We've had a few accidents," I said softly. "But we are fine. And now some of my friends are helping me."

"Well, that's good. I am so relieved that you finally decided to talk to someone."

"I have, and I have some good people helping me. But, Mrs. Lucy, I want to tell you something so you won't hear it from someone else. There was a fire at the house." I continued quickly before she could speak. "It was a small fire and ruined our couch and a few other little things. But the house is going to be alright, and our insurance will help pay for repairs."

She looked white around the lips, and I felt a surge of alarm.

"Mrs. Lucy, do you want to sit down?"

"No," she looked at me sternly. "I'm fine, but are you?"

"Yes," impulsively I reached out and took her soft cool hand in mine. "We got out with plenty of time. The firemen came, and the fire was put out quickly." I looked at her. "I didn't want you to be upset, but I knew that someone else might come along and tell you, and I wanted you to hear it from me."

"Thank you," she said softly.

When we returned, Drew was surrounded by a group of older women, standing taller than them all, but leaning down to catch their words.

"Are you ready?" I couldn't help but grin.

"Sure, okay," he smiled. "It was nice to meet you," he said to the group. "And you," he added, turning to Mrs. Lucy.

"You will take care of Victoria, won't you?" she asked.

"Of course," he responded.

*****

The storage area was typical of the building, brightly lit, fresh concrete floor swept clean, each door individually locked. Mrs. Lucy's was one of the first. We used the key, pushed the door open, and I felt a surge of dismay. The tiny space was packed. When she had said that they had given much of her belongings to the Historical Society, I had assumed that that meant that the items she had kept would be limited and fairly important. Instead, it seemed that their move had been a hasty one. The boxes were packed and taped with sloppy strips, stacked in between older pieces of furniture that had apparently not been good enough to keep upstairs.

"And where are we supposed to start?"

I looked at him grimly. "Maybe with some of the older things?"

"Good idea," he agreed. "Probably most of the old man's things had been packed away a long time ago and just stored in here as they were left."

"So we can start in the front, moving things forward after we have looked at them. We have just enough room in here to shift everything."

"As long as we're not buried alive," he said, but he was smiling. He was actually enjoying himself.

"You like this?" I asked, incredulous.

"I like being with you, so I like this."

"Sweet talker," I muttered, but I knew that my cheeks were a little red.

He dropped a quick kiss on my cheek and started toward the first stack of boxes. "Alright, now get to work, slacker."

It took us almost two hours to set out the three oldest boxes. They were predictably buried in the farthest corner of the little storage area, doubtless the first load to have been dropped off.

"You want these out in the hallway?" Drew asked, nudging one of the boxes with his foot.

"I guess that's where it would be easiest to see," I said. "You take some, and I'll get some. We can go through them out there. The light is better too."

He dragged out two of the boxes, and I followed with the last. My back was aching, so I slid down to sit on the cold concrete. "We can start with this one." I pried the lid open, glad that the old tape had lost its adhesive, and the box was easily opened.

The box was brimming with old papers, brittle and yellowed, that turned my fingers a dusty grey. There were old receipts, typed letters in fading ink, bits of envelopes, and notes about household affairs. If the papers were from the old household, they weren't the old man's. These were house records, documents that told of the day to day lives of the inhabitants of the house.

The second box held more promise. There were loose stacks of photos, from black and white prints to formal portraits on crumbling cardboard backing. A heavy photo album with traditional photo corners anchoring a pathetic few pictures lay at the bottom. Most of the pictures had come loose, but I turned the page with caution. And there it was. The photo Mrs. Lucy had told me about. The photo of the family, stiffly posed in front of a much newer version of my house, the trees spindly saplings in the background. The mother was stiff and solemn, the father like a statue painted in grays, and the girl in front, doubtless Mrs. Lucy's ancestor, looked as though she wanted to cry. And maybe she did.

After removing the book, I reached in the box for some of the loose pictures. There were two that caught my eye, one of a serious little boy, forced to sit and pose for the picture in his mother's lap when the look in his eyes suggested that he would have rather been running wild in the grass. The other was the whole family, this time a true studio portrait, the mother seated in a chair, her two children at her side, her husband on the other side, and an older man, white haired with a rather unkempt beard and light eyes, standing behind her chair. Was this her father? I guessed it was, and from the photo, he was well on his way to losing his sanity.

"Nice family," Drew said dryly. "I love these old photos. Why didn't anyone smile?"

"I heard that it took so long to take the picture that the people were told not to smile. It would be too exhausting."

"Hmm," he said softly. "Well, let's check out the last one."

He pulled open the box top, and a puff of dust rose in the florescent light. He started pulling out stacks, but these were different. These were handwritten notes, a trio of leather bound books, a few more pictures, and a metal box.

"Well check this out!" Drew had opened one of the journals and was looking at the writing.

"What?" I asked, leaning over close.

"Looks like journals, but no name on them. They are all in the first person, but I can't find any dates either."

"Can you read anything?"

He was squinting, nose close to the paper. "In this one he refers to Paris. Some French words, maybe cities? We'll have to look this up. But it does show that they belonged to a traveler." He flipped through several more pages. "Here's something in Spanish. Crap, I can't remember any of the Spanish I learned in high school. Just when I might have needed it." He sighed, flipping carefully through the book as I pulled out some of the delicate papers and started examining them. "Hey," he said, his voice low.

"What?" I looked up. He was holding out a pencil sketch, the lines faded but still visible.

"Look at this? Doesn't this look like…"

"The cross." I leaned closer. "It looks like the cross from the picture of St. Francisca. The one that she kept. The one that was buried with the pirate."

"The one that the old man found? Or stole?"

*****

I had to return home to see Liz. But home wasn't that house anymore, it was a little room somewhere closer to Louisville proper, thin carpet that was so new it smelled like the store, and white painted walls that allowed every breath from the neighbors to filter through into our space. It wasn't the greatest space in the world, but it's what insurance would pay for, so we had to be satisfied. There were advantages to the hotel however. It was much closer to Liz's place of business and closer to her friends. It also gave me more freedom to be pursuing my outside interests. While Liz was busy moving things into the adjoining rooms, going through our smoke stained belongings, and trying to set up housekeeping, I was calling Thea.

"So what's the news?" she asked, her voice pitched low.

"I think we're finally getting somewhere." I kept my voice low as well. The hotel suite, as it was called, only boasted one bedroom, and I had given it up to Liz. She was shut up in there, for my privacy as much as anything else, but I knew she might be able to hear me. I quickly gave Thea a description of the photos and the journals that we had taken from the basement storage. "Mrs. Lucy was fine about us using them for some research, and I told her we would take them to the historical society when we were done. She doesn't really want any of the things down there, but especially not the ones from before her time living in the house."

"I'm going to be in town in the morning to run some errands for my mom. Are you going to be home? Would you mind if I stopped by to see the things that you found? I can tell you about what we came across, but it doesn't sound quite so interesting."

I readily agreed to the visit. I wasn't working in the morning. I had told Blythe that I needed some time off, and although she had tried to get me to take the week, I had asked for only a few days. Keeping busy was good for my mind, even if it was wearing my body out.

Liz and I ate a very quiet dinner that we had made from a loaf of white bread, a block of cheese, and a can of tomato soup. She was watching me across the table, and had that pinched and sad look again. I decided it was time to make her feel a little better, so I told her about Drew's statement earlier in the day.

"He said he loves you? Really! That's great." She stopped, aware of her words. "It is, isn't it? You like him too, right?"

"Of course I like him, and it is a really good thing." I tried not to look too starry eyed. "He's a really good guy, good for me, and he really cares about me. I can tell."

"Then I'm glad," Liz declared. "Ah, and so relieved." She sat back, putting her spoon back in her empty bowl. "You've been so weird lately. So secretive, so tired. You haven't told me where you were going or what you were doing. And then with the fire..." she let the words drift off.

"I'm fine. It's all an adjustment, but the house will be fine, and in a small town like this one, I imagine the guy who did it will be pretty easy to catch up with. Have they said anything about that?" I wasn't successful at sounding casual.

She shook her head and stood to begin clearing the table. "No, nothing. I'm not sure how quickly they would call me even if they knew. They might have to keep it something of a secret until everything is settled." She pushed a lock of blond hair out of her face. "I'm not really familiar with what they do after a fire, but they said that they would call me when the place was done, the inspection and all. And they said they even had some names of people they would recommend for repairs."

"Sounds good," I agreed, and started washing some of the dishes under steaming water. "So we just wait. How long do we have these rooms?" "It's rented by the week, but I don't think we'll need it long. We can probably go back home soon and even live there while they finish the repairs."

I nodded. The house would be sitting empty for several nights then, vulnerable to anyone who might want to get in and go snooping. Damn, but not if I could help it!

*****

Thea brought egg muffins from a fast food restaurant. Not as good as Blythe's, but better than anything that we had in our meager store of groceries. She had huge Styrofoam cups of coffee, hot and sweet. I smiled gratefully and gestured her to the rented couch that came with the tiny rented rooms.

"The place looks nice," Thea said and tried to look sincere.

"It's a little," I tried to think of a word for it, "cheaply made."

She raised her eyebrows.

"It's uncomfortable and crappy, but it's temporary, so we're okay."

"And your house?"

"We'll get word today hopefully. Then we need to figure out how to get everything back to livable." I sighed and stretched out my legs, studying my chipped toe nail polish. "More work and more fixing, but at least nothing important got burned up."

"Just wrecked," she said grimly. "You are so lucky that you woke up in time. You never said. What made you wake up? Was it Monty?"

"I'm not sure," I said slowly. I hadn't told anyone why I really had awakened. It hadn't been my dog, or the noise, or the smoke. It had been my father. My dead father.

"Tori?"

I looked at her, her soft eyes, her curly hair framing a gentle face. "It was my dad."

"Your dad." She kept her voice soft too.

"I haven't told Liz. With everything else that has gone on, if she found out any of this she would have me back in therapy before I could turn around. But it's true. Dad woke me up. I heard him say my name. He was there in my room, just like he used to do when he was waking me for school. He was talking to me, telling me to get my sister."

"Oh, Tori."

"I am not crazy." My voice was firm, but a little higher pitched than I would have liked. "You know I'm not. You've seen things too. Don't deny it!"

"I'm not," she said quickly. "And I'm going to tell you something that I haven't told anyone, and I mean anyone." She licked her lips in a nervous gesture, and tucked her legs up under her. "I've seen a ghost too."

"One of the ones from the stories?" I asked.

"No, I saw Daniel."

I blinked, my mouth opening with an automatic question, but I closed it again and let her speak.

"It was when the truth was coming out, and everything was hitting the fan. I was at home, but Thomas wasn't with me. He had headed back home too. He wanted to spend some time with his family. But while Thomas was there, Savannah came to visit in the cemetery. And there was nothing normal about that night. I didn't see her come; I just found her out among the stones. And the wind was weird, the sky and the pressure, I don't know, I just knew something was different. I knew that it wasn't her, or not all of her. Tori, the wind was blowing, the trees twisting, the air was different, like the world was depressurizing! I was so terrified. And she was talking to me, talking just crazy. She knew me. She knew who I was, but the way she was screaming, it was like someone who had lost their mind.

So I called Thomas to tell him to come to her, or ask him what I should do. But he was at home, too far away. And she was too. I think he was wondering about my sanity. He walked in her room and saw her lying on her bed, asleep. But he could hear her ranting over the phone. I had my cell phone out there, and it wasn't like some ghost voice. It was really real, and so was she. She was crazy with grief and blamed herself in some way for the accident. And then, while I was talking to him on the phone, and her standing in this wind storm in the cemetery, my phone died."

She blinked and took a deep breath. "So I was alone out there, afraid for her, and, to be honest, afraid of her. And then he came. I knew it wasn't Thomas. I would have known Thomas, even without seeing him. But it looked like him." She sighed. "I'm not explaining it well. They are twins, I mean, they were identical, but not so that you couldn't tell them apart. And as soon as he showed up, I knew it was Daniel. And she knew it too. He just talked, gently, you know, letting her know he was alright and none of it had been her fault. There was nothing that she could have done to change what happened." Thea took a deep breath. "And then it was over, and they were gone. But I never told Thomas about seeing Daniel." She rubbed a slender hand over her face, and I could see she was trembling. "I will tell him someday. But not now."

"I don't know what to say," I murmured. "But you seem so close to Thomas. Why not tell him? It's not like he wouldn't believe you."

She sighed softly. "I have a lot of hang ups, and it's taking me some time to get over all of this." She brushed a stray curl back. "It's not always a bed of roses to have your dad the funeral director in a little town where everyone knows everyone else. And I didn't make anything easier on myself. I started doing the sculpture I'm so proud of using funeral flowers. Imagine how well that went over with the conservative folks. They knew my mom was artistic -- she teaches art -- and that was acceptable. And my dad's job was kind of a necessary evil. But I mixed them." She was frowning, her eyes unfocused as they gazed at the memories playing in her head. "The kids loved to tease me about Dad, but when I started messing with the flowers, a whole new set of nicknames came up. Kids will be kids, and sometimes they can be pretty brutal."

"I'm sorry," I said, picturing the young Thea, or Dot as they called her then. Wild hair, old house tucked next to the graveyard, a handful of fading flowers meant for the grave, she would have been the perfect victim.

"Don't feel sorry for me about that. It was a long time ago, and I am getting over it. But the idea that we have ghosts now..."

We were silent for a long moment. I couldn't say why I was surprised. It wasn't a far leap to go from what we already believed to a full blown afterlife experience.

Thea spoke softly. "Tori, my dad has been in the death business, working at the funeral home, for a long time. But our religion always made me think of death as a temporary thing, like boarding some celestial bus. But this thing with Thomas had really stretched my faith, and really all I believed in. But that night, the night when I saw Daniel, I also saw life after death. It may not have been Heaven with chubby angels and halos, but it was proof that we do go on." She waited a moment. "I firmly believe that it was your dad that saved you. Just because he's not here for us to see doesn't mean he's not here."

I nodded silently, and she handed me a tissue. I had managed not to cry for such a very long time. But this time I decided it was okay.

*****

So this is where you felt it?" Thomas stood, a quiet figure painted in silvers and golds. His strange topaz eyes were looking in my direction, but I wondered if he were really seeing me.

"This was where it was the worst. I felt like something was here, almost haunting this space."

"And now?" He was looking at me, focused.

"I don't feel anything now." My eyes scanned the sunlight scene. "I don't feel anything good or bad. It just feels…" I tried to find a word, but failed. "It feels normal."

"Even over here?" Drew was standing by the well, and even the sight of him, standing so close to that open stone mouth, made me shiver with the memory.

"I don't feel anything," I stepped a little closer to him, "but I can't say I love to be here. Or that I like to see anyone else this close."

Thea nodded. "Okay, so what was the point of this little experiment?" She was looking at Thomas, but I knew she was including both of the guys in the statement.

Drew shrugged. "We just wanted to see if it was a one-time thing, a night thing, I don't know, something that only happens when you're alone." His eyes were on mine again.

"But I wasn't alone." I argued. "I had Anna with me, and trust me, she felt something too." I frowned. I hadn't spoken to Anna much since the fire, and I hated that I had gotten so immersed in this mystery that I had forgotten her.

"Okay, well, while it's light out, we can at least look around some." Thomas leaned over and peered into the mouth of the well. He plucked at the wire mesh with his fingers, tugging lightly. "This is a little loose. They should probably look into that. Wouldn't want any kids to fall into it."

I drew slowly closer. But all I could feel was the spring sunshine on my face, the gentle breeze. Birds fluttered and tweeted in the distance, giving their own melody to the afternoon. I stood opposite Thomas, looking at his pale hair blocking his face as he leaned over the well.

"It's not even that deep anymore. And there's no water to speak of. It might be damp down there, but it's not holding much. Probably tried to fill in some when it stopped being in use." Thomas looked up at me. "But don't lean on this too hard in case it won't hold weight."

I nodded and put my hands gently on the top of the grating, feeling the cold metal against my fingers. I spread out my palms, like some ancient blessing, and stood very still. Nothing. Just the spring weather, the slight sounds of my friends shuffling around me, the occasional engine purr from up the road. I pulled my hands back, startled when a tug at my wrist stilled my hand, but then released. Then, like a slow motion film, I saw my mother's charm bracelet, one of the bigger charms caught in the wire. With my movement, the clasp had released, and before I could drop my hands, the bracelet snaked through the wire grid and fell, a glittering arc, into the darkness.

"No!" I yelped, my hands slamming against the wire.

"What was it?" Thomas was the only one close enough to see the cause of my reaction, but Drew moved quickly to my side.

"My bracelet," I felt tears in my eyes as the enormity of the situation soaked in. "My mother's bracelet. I was wearing it. I didn't want to leave it in the house because I was afraid that something would happen to it! Now this." I grabbed the grating with my fingers and began yanking it, pulling hard with all my strength.

"Wait!" Drew's hands were at my shoulder, and

Thomas leaned close and put his hand on the grating.

"It's loose anyway," Thomas said his voice soft and reasonable. "We'll get tools from the shed at Thea's house and pry this up. Then we can reach in with something. There isn't much water; it shouldn't be that hard to get to."

I flattened my hands against the metal again and peered into the darkness. "But I can't see it. I can't see anything."

"We'll need a flashlight." Thomas turned to Thea. "Let's go to your house and get some tools. We'll get the thing open and check to see if we can get the bracelet. Then we can talk to your dad about maybe fixing it."

I knew that Thea's dad was once the caretaker of the property. This was good. I forced myself to relax. Thea's dad would have tools to help us open it, and maybe he would help us find the bracelet if we weren't able to get it on our own. I had met him a few times, and despite the fact that he had once been the director of the funeral home, a really creepy choice of occupation in my opinion, he seemed to be pretty cool.

"We'll be back in a sec," Thea said over her shoulder, already moving quickly across the grounds, calm like her dad.

Drew pulled me back from the side of the well and put his arms around me, resting his cheek on my hair. "The good thing is that we can fish it back out," he said softly. "It just might take a minute. And you're feeling okay about the place now, so that's good too."

I nodded, but said nothing. I just stood still in his arms, flickers of pictures in my mind, my mom's smile, her laugh, the way her eyes lit up when she teased, the way she tugged my hair playfully when making a point.

"We got it!" Thea's voice was particularly loud across the quiet space. She was moving at a fast walk, but Thomas was faster with longer legs. He motioned Drew to join him, laying out the tools on the new grass.

With a crow bar in hand, Thomas started working on some of the heavy wires. Drew joined him with a large screwdriver, and with the help of old and crumbling mortar, the metal was separated from the base. They moved in tandem, stepping around the sides of the well, prying and pressing, the metal singing in protest.

"Okay, it's loose. You grab that side," Drew commanded, and he and Thomas took their places on opposite sides. The metal didn't look heavy, but I could see their muscles straining with the weight. Together, they walked it a few feet away from the well and laid it in the newly greening grass.

I approached the well with trepidation. I had thought before that the presence seemed to be in there, but this time, nothing still. I breathed a sigh of relief and looked down into the darkness.

"Here's a flashlight," Thea said, handing me a long Maglite. I directed the beam toward the mouth of the well and started to pan it around the inside. The stone was indeed mostly dry, with thick mud at the bottom, dark and moist, but not thin enough that anything would sink beneath the surface. Time had dried out the underground water source, it seemed.

"There!" Thea was smiling, excited. "You can see it there. It's caught, I think. Not all the way down."

"So how do we get it?" I looked at the shine of gold against the dark stone.

"We can just climb down." Drew glanced at me.

"Really? I mean, no! That's crazy." I backed away from the well, shaking my head.

"I have rappelled for years," Drew said, shrugging. "This isn't that much different."

"I have a ladder," Thea said slowly.

"We don't know what the floor is like. We don't know if it would work." I was unconsciously running my hand through my hair and had to stop myself.

"It's a hook ladder. The kind that you use to get down out of two story windows. It was a fire safety thing that my dad got years ago. It's not long, but it should reach far enough, and it can hook over the side."

"Worth a try," Drew said, and Thea started heading back home before I could say no.

*****

Twenty minutes later we were watching Drew step carefully down the ladder. The top was bent around the lip of the well, the rungs snaking off into the darkness.

"Is it secure?" I asked worriedly.

"It's fine from up here." I wished I could sound as calm as Thomas.

"I feel okay. This is easy compared to some of the things that I've done in the past." Drew's voice was strangely hollow in the tight space of the well. We could see him moving slowly, hands holding the rungs as his feet scuffed at the sides of the well. "Hold on. I think I see it. Here. Turn the flashlight to the left." He paused and took another step down. "No, my left. There. Hold still. Gold, right Tori?"

He was joking but I couldn't resist. "Yes," I said too loudly. "Can you reach it?"

"Yeah, it's hooked on something." He paused, the ladder swaying slightly. "It's hung up on something, but I can't tell what."

We could barely see the pale blur of his fingers. "It's tangled with some cloth. A rag or something." He cursed softly.

"You need something to cut with?" Thomas asked.

"No, not yet." He was very quiet. "Ah, it came loose." He was silent for a long moment. "There's something in this rag." Then we heard him again. "What the…?"

I waited, but couldn't hold myself quiet. "You have it?"

Silence for the longest most painful moment.

"The bracelet is in my pocket," he responded, but his voice was odd. "Thomas, move the light just one more inch." I could see the beam shift.

"Drew?" My voice was soft.

"Oh, God." His voice was a soft prayer.

"Drew? What's wrong?" Thomas voice was different now.

"I think it's bones. I think I found bones." His voice was still low and the sound made me shiver. "I'm coming up." When his face topped the wall of the well, I saw that his complexion had lost all color. His eyes were glittery dark holes, shocked.

Thomas reached down, helping Drew from the darkness. We managed to guide him to the bench where he collapsed, still pale. Between his long fingers, I could see a rough cloth bag. He slowly set the grimy bag on the bench, releasing with it two tiny bones that had been caught in the rough cloth.

"They look like…" Thea whispered, then her voice faded to nothing.

"Fingers," Thomas murmured. "They are finger bones."

"They're too small," I protested through a tight throat.

"Not for a child's hand," Drew said, his voice hollow. "I think I saw more down there. Other bones. Damn. Look in the bag."

Thomas picked up the fragile cloth, damp and crumbling. The handful of objects fell out. A feather, a couple of grimy marbles, some tiny beads, a bit of fluff that might have once been material, and a small leather bag. Thomas plucked up the smaller bag while I gently took a marble, unconsciously shining the glass with my shirt tail.

It was blue, the brilliant cobalt blue of old glass, a perfect child's fascination.

"Oh," Thea's voice had me lifting my eyes, first to her face and then to the direction of her gaze. Drew had opened the leather bag and spilled the contents into his palm. It was a cross, old and dull gold inlaid with blood red garnets. And it was familiar.

"We need to call someone," I said, my voice shaking.

"I'll call my dad. He can look at the bones and see if they are..." She couldn't finish, but we all knew what she meant. The missing cross, the missing boy, both found in the dark well. It was the clash of stories, the missing link. The sad end, the sad truth of what had happened in my home so many years ago.

For the second time in a week, the early responders arrived, but this time their mission wasn't nearly so well explained. Thea and Thomas drew the first group off to the side to explain what we had found in the well. Together they joined Drew in silence on the bench and solemnly looked at the bones.

Thea's father stood at a distance, his face pale and tight. He had his own beliefs about the fragments we had found but wasn't sharing with us. Instead, he had immediately called in the emergency personnel that could get to the site.

The area was cordoned off until they could determine if a crime had really been committed, and we were forced back to the porch of Thea's house. The flashing lights had been extinguished, but there were a fair number of people in the adjoining homes that were out as well, standing on front stoops or craning necks to see what the uproar was about. Crime was big news, and, unfortunately, tragedy was bigger.

Drew sat on the steps, and I dropped next to him. I had just told my sister that I was going to be late. It took some time to explain my presence. Why had I been in the cemetery? Why had I been leaning over the well? What were we doing there in the first place? Why had we decided to go in after the bracelet? She hadn't asked why I wanted the bracelet back, she well knew the answer to that one, but the rest seemed to frustrate her.

"What did your sister say?"

"There wasn't much she could say. She just said she hoped I would get back before it was too late and to call her on my way." I leaned against him, feeling the heat of him through my thin shirt. "She's trying not to act like she's parenting me. I'm too old for that. But it's hard for her to not know where I am or what I'm doing all the time." I curled my fingers around the bracelet. "And I feel the same way. I find myself checking on her to make sure I know where she is at all times too."

"She's your family. That's what family does." Drew put his arm around me and snuggled me closer.

"It's him, isn't it?" I asked softly. "It's that poor little boy who disappeared. He somehow ended up with his grandfather's cross and fell in the well."

"Might be," he said softly.

"It is." I looked out at the figures of the men beside the well. "They're going to find the rest of his skeleton. But we found the most important parts. He had it all with him. All of his valuables. I doubt he had any idea where the cross came from. He probably picked it up because he thought it was pretty. But his grandfather knew."

"You think the grandfather could do what we do? Thomas, Savannah, and me?"

"Yes," I licked my lips and leaned back to look into his eyes, so dark and serious. "I think that the grandfather figured that out before he ever came here. He became a recluse, buried himself in this little town instead of traveling like he had. I think there was a reason. I think he knew he had found a miracle, and he didn't want anyone else to know what he had, what he could do. But then the little guy took it. And the grandfather died, and no one could find out what had happened to the cross or the boy."

"Except Daniel. He knew something, and he brought us here. He was looking for the cross. He knew about it, the legend maybe, and maybe even what it was capable of, or that it was a lost relic of a saint. But he knew what he was looking for. And he must have found it. Not actually laid his hands on it, but found out where it was last seen."

"But why you all? Why now? If that cross has been in the well for all of those years, within close distance of the whole town's population, why aren't there people right and left blinking in and out of existence? It wasn't proximity that made you do what you can do."

"I just don't know," Drew looked back out into the graveyard. "All I know is that we came here with Daniel the first time, and whatever he found out from that visit made him more determined; he wanted to come back. And of the group that came, Daniel, Thomas, Savannah, and me, well, we all can do it. We can all bilocate, and we have witnesses."

"So you think that Daniel could do it too?"

"I'm guessing he could. I don't know. It wasn't anything I can recall him mentioning. Seems like I would remember that conversation. But I have to think that he had a very good reason to come back here that day, the day he died." He rubbed his hand absently over his forehead. "I wish I could remember."

"And neither you nor Thomas remembers the accident or how it happened, and Savannah wasn't even there."

"Yeah, just one more thing that we can't explain."

Thea stood at the gate, and I could see her turn, looking toward us as the figure of her father grew closer and clearer. Drew and I stood, fingers twined, and descended the steps. I knew what we would hear, but I didn't want to know. I had seen that child's face, seen the way he strained to free himself, to escape the constraints of the tight clothes and formal posture in that old photograph. I had seen his youth, his earnest eyes, and it made me ache to think that it had all ended for him so early. Too damn young.

*****

Savannah was absolutely nothing like I had pictured her, and I was disappointed in my own short sightedness. She was tall, with golden blond hair that fell in a sunlit wash down her back. Her eyes were not the strange gold of her brother's, but a changeable color that might have been green and might have been blue, depending on the weather. She looked as though a stiff breeze would knock her into the next day, but her mouth had a strangely stubborn set to it that I recognized from my own reflection.

She had come down for the funeral.

I stood, uncomfortable in the hated funeral attire that had been my uniform for my parents' ceremonies, and watched as Thomas leaned his bright head down to listen to his sister. There was no denying the resemblance. But as much as Thomas stood calm and still, his sister seemed to vibrate with some inner frantic activity. She was beautiful in the way that a portrait might draw your eyes, but she was broken, and I felt that understanding as well. We were broken. And God help her, she was glowing.

The funeral for the little boy was well attended. It seemed fitting that the remnants of so many families that had governed here when he was alive were there to see him finally brought to his grave. The preacher from the Baptist church where his family had attended so many years ago was there, and Father Joe from St Benedict's stood in solemn black to co-officiate. The men met on Tuesday's for dinner every other week, and had been friends for many years, so it was right that they were there together.

Drew came late, looking uncomfortable in a borrowed suit that was too short in the sleeves. His hair was tamed with difficulty, and his jaw freshly shaven. I wondered where he had gotten ready, and where he had acquired the suit. He looked almost as miserable as I felt, and he came up beside me to take my hand.

Liz was there as well, although I told her not to come. She was there for me, and even though she didn't know why, it touched me all the same.

To the wailing hymn of "Amazing Grace," played long and slow on the bagpipes, the little body was buried next to his parents. I didn't cry. I couldn't, but Thea's eyes were suspiciously damp, and Thomas was staring off, hands fisted in his pockets. I knew that in one of those pockets was the cross. It was the only thing that we had withheld from the authorities. We had no intention of keeping it but had no idea what to do with it either. Thomas had elected to carry it on his person, all the time, every day, until the mystery was solved. We had agreed, but I could see my own fear mirrored in Thea's eyes. Surely now he knew, that evil shadow. And that was what was the most frightening. He was still out there, determined to get his hands on the cross, we were sure. And we were also sure that he wasn't ready to give up.

After the funeral was over, we went with unsaid words over to the site of the well. The mesh top had been replaced with something much stronger and more secure, and it was being considered whether or not the well should be filled in.

We sat in our black finery on the heavy concrete benches in the watery sunlight. It had rained earlier in the morning, and the ground felt a little soft under my short heels. I kicked them off for a moment and tucked my feet up under me, trying for a little comfort. Savannah accompanied us, her face averted. It was a strange moment for me. For the first time in a while, I was on the outside looking in. Savannah was family. She had been there in the beginning, had been with Thomas, Drew, and Daniel on that first fateful trip. So in some ways, their history was much deeper than anything I had with the group. But yet, she knew nothing about the truth. They had gone out of their way to keep her in the dark, treating her like a wounded soul, waiting for her to heal before they told her the truth. I just hoped that they weren't waiting too long.

I shifted uncomfortably, my thoughts flitting to the future. It was Saturday, and Thomas and Thea would be returning to Lexington for the last six weeks of school early on Sunday. Savannah would be heading home in the morning as well. With final exams and term papers, none of them would be coming back in town for the remainder of the school year, and I was feeling a faint pressure. Without them, it would just be Drew and me trying to protect ourselves, the house, and my sister from the unknown threat.

And what of Drew? When Thomas left with the cross, there was a chance that the threat would follow him to Lexington, and I would no longer be the focus of the danger. And what then? Would Drew stay here with me? Or follow Thomas and Thea to the university? It seemed like a crossroads for all of us.

"Tori, are you ready to head back?" Liz sounded tired, too tired, and her face looked thin and pale. I felt a stab of guilt for what I was putting her through. I hadn't thought. I hadn't realized that my own investigations would be keeping me from helping her. And that's what I needed to do now. I needed to help her finish with the arrangements to get our house back in shape, to let us go home.

"Sure," I said, slipping my shoes back on and standing in the soft grass. "I'm ready."

"Okay," she turned, flashing a quick polite smile to my friends.

"I'll talk to you all in the morning," I said softly.

*****

Savannah was on the porch when I pulled up. Her long blond hair was pulled back in a severe bun on the back of her head, accentuating her angular face, and the air of frailty that seemed to cling to her.

"Tori," she greeted, and waved.

"Hey! Is everyone up?"

"Yeah, they are finishing up breakfast. We already packed." She fell silent, her eyes sliding past me to the graveyard beyond.

"Strange neighbors," I said softly.

"You could say that."

I could hear the footsteps inside but didn't want to move from the porch. It felt strange to leave Savannah alone out here.

"Is your house going to be okay?" Savannah's voice jolted me from my thoughts. "Thomas told me about the fire. I hated to hear that. You just moved in."

"It will be fine. We have some estimates for repairs, and insurance will cover some of it. It's just the timing that really, well, it was bad. But at least no one was hurt."

"Do you know what caused it?"

Ouch. It was a good question, and one that I didn't want to explain to her. I went with the explanation that we had proposed to the fire department. "We didn't see any-one. It was just the window breaking and the flames. We think that people might have thought that the house had been left empty and mistakenly pulled a prank." I shrugged. It wasn't a great excuse, but I hadn't any other ideas, and the thought that the fire was set intentionally, well, I just didn't want to share that idea with someone as seemingly fragile as Savannah.

Footsteps sounded on the old wooden floor just inside the house. "Do you know what happened to my tee shirt?" Thomas asked, bursting through the front door.

"Why would I?" Savannah's response sounded typical for a sibling.

Thomas rolled his eyes. "Didn't you borrow it last night?"

Savannah huffed out a sigh and turned back to go in the house. "I'll look for it," she snapped, "but I thought I gave it back to you." She left the screen door slam behind her, but I could tell that some of her temper was just for show.

"How's it going with you?" Thomas' voice had gone from playful to serious.

"Fine." I looked into the darkness of the front hall. "I'm doing fine. I'll be fine. We'll be getting the house ready this week and hopefully move home by the weekend."

"You look upset." His brows were drawn over those odd eyes.

"I'm okay. Really." I pushed my hair away from my face. "Yesterday was just a little too much. Too emotional."

"I'm sorry for that," he said, his expression tight. "I know you and your sister are going through a lot. We really haven't helped. But I'll take some of the pressure off. I have the cross. It won't leave my possession for a minute."

"I know that. And I'm not worried, not about me anyway. Really. I just, well, I hope this doesn't make him go after you and Thea."

"We are going to take that risk. He's already shown that he can go after you. We'll be surrounded by people all the time in Lexington. Less chance for him to catch us alone." He paced the porch. "We'll watch after each other and Drew,"

"And Drew what?" Drew strolled past the line of bushes shielding the porch and climbed the step with easy strides.

"And Drew will mind the homestead." Thomas smiled a welcome, looking relieved to see his friend.

"Look, about that." I couldn't believe I was going to say it, and my heart felt like a heavy lead weight in my chest. "As much as I would like to have him around here, I think Drew should go to Lexington with you and Thea. I don't think that we're going to be getting any more late night visits. He knows what he was looking for has been found, and it wasn't even in our house. The mystery has been solved to some extent. I think that his next plan will definitely be to go after you, you and the cross."

"You can't be serious?" Drew's voice was rough and disbelieving. "What makes you think that I, well, that I would let you stay here by yourself?"

"I'm not by myself," I argued. I wanted to stop protesting. I wanted to agree wholeheartedly that he should stay. Selfishly, I wanted to know that Drew was there, my protector, my savior, part of my heart. But I couldn't let my friends be in danger just because I didn't want to be away from Drew. "I will have Liz. And I have the rest of the community around here. I have Blythe. And all my new friends."

"Thea and I will be okay in Lexington, and it won't be for long. Just keep us updated, and we'll watch our backs." Thomas looked like he wanted to reassure me, but at the same time, I had the feeling that there was something that he wasn't telling me.

"I can keep you updated, and Drew can help watch your backs," I said, crossing my arms over my chest, defiant.

"Tori, I'd like to talk to you for a second," Drew interrupted. His voice was a little loud. "Alone." He took my hand and began walking without giving me time to protest.

He tugged me around to the back of the house where a picturesque old gazebo stood under the shade of mature trees. He climbed the steps with long strides and I had to rush to keep up with him.

"What!" I demanded, dropping onto one of the benches that lined the walls of the gazebo.

"Tori, what are you doing? What are you thinking? Suddenly, you're like superwoman, going to save your sister and everyone else while I go off and leave you to it? Did you really think that I would go for that? First of all, you and I know the cross is gone, but we have no idea what He thinks. And we are just assuming that He was after the cross in the first place. What if that's not it? Or that's not all? We know ourselves that it wasn't just the cross that made things happen to us, and if He is like us, then there is more to his problem than just finding the cross."

I knew it all made sense, but I didn't want Drew to feel like he had to stay, and I said as much to him.

"You know, you can really be dense sometimes." He was leaning close, his dark hair framing his narrow face, his dark, dark eyes settled on me. "Even if I knew for sure that He was out of town, following some lead or another, I wouldn't leave you. Even if this were all over and I stayed in one place all the time -- no more night time wanderings -- I wouldn't leave you. I guess that's just what I'm trying to say. I won't leave you. Not for anything. Not even for you."

So I followed my heart and not my brain and kissed him, feeling the tears well in my eyes, letting them trickle down my cheeks, unchecked. I didn't have a happily ever after. It wasn't that. But I was loved, and I would never be alone.

Note to my readers:

The first of my trilogy, Grave Reminders, was started several years ago. At the time, brain injury was something that I had only dealt with in a professional capacity and early in my career. Most of my patients that I had seen with brain injuries were several months to years post onset, and therefore, their stories of early survival were not familiar to me.

Much more recently, my family was directly impacted by a car accident and subsequent brain injury. The accident reflected the one in my book a little too closely for my comfort, but the recovery was not at all what I had written about.

The recovery from brain injury and coma is not the gentle awakening that I depicted in my book. Coming out of a coma is gradual, frightening, and takes a very long time. The professionals that deal with the patient are of vital importance, and full of knowledge that we, as nonprofessionals in that field, know little about.

Fortunately, my family member is well on the way to recovery, but it is not without difficulty and emotion. My undying gratitude and respect go out to the medical staff at the University of Louisville Hospital where my family member began recovery from a coma, and to Frazier Rehabilitation where the journey was continued.

The truth that I have found is that brain injury is a journey, and the human mind is a mystery. There are miracles in the world, and I have had the privilege to observe one personally.

For further information on brain injury, consult: Brain Injury Association of America at http://www.biausa.org/

Acknowledgment:

I would again like to thank my wonderful publisher and fellow author, Tony Acree; my editor, Julie Gabis; and all the authors at Hydra Publications for their encouragement and suggestions.

I would also like to thank all my friends for supporting my writing, giving me good advice, and putting up with my crazy imagination.

Thanks also to all those who have read my books. It's all for the joy of the story!

About the author:

Rachael Rawlings is a full time mother, wife, writer, pet owner, and Speech Language Pathologist. Her main goal is to show readers a good time, make them think a little, and make them wonder and marvel about things that are all around us.

She lives with her husband, James, a professional architect; her three children, Faith, Nicholas, and Chase; and two dogs. She is also owned by two parrots who continually surprise her in their sheer intelligence (a new definition of bird brained). She grew up and lives in the small town of Crestwood, Kentucky.

She thrives on good coffee, chocolate, and great friends and family. To learn more about Rachael's work and her upcoming releases, visit her on her website: http://rachaelrawlings.wix.com/rachael-rawlings